REVOLUTION Nº. 9

ALSO BY NEIL McMAHON

To the Bone
Twice Dying
Blood Double

REVOLUTION NO. 9

A NOVEL

NEIL McMAHON

HarperCollinsPublishers

HarperCollins books may be purchased for educational, business, or sales promotional use. For information, please write: Special Markets Department, HarperCollins Publishers Inc., 10 East 53rd Street, New York, NY 10022.

FIRST EDITION

Designed by Elliott Beard

Printed on acid-free paper

Library of Congress Cataloging-in-Publication Data
McMahon, Neil.
Revolution no. 9: a novel / Neil McMahon.
p. cm.
ISBN 0-06-052918-0 (acid-free paper)
1. Revolutionaries—Fiction. 2. Kidnapping—Fiction. 3. Cults—Fiction. I. Title: Revolution no. nine. II. Title: Revolution number nine. III. Title.
PS3568.H545R48 2005
813'.54—dc22 2004054211

05 06 07 08 09 ❖/RRD 10 9 8 7 6 5 4 3 2 1

In memory of my father, Daniel Patrick McMahon,
who spent forty-three Chicago winters working outside,
providing water for the citizens.

Acknowledgments

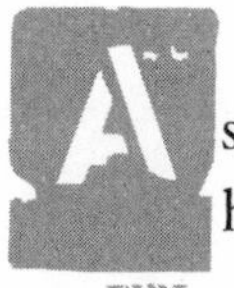s always, this book owes a great debt to many people who helped in its making. To name a few:

Chuck and Lois Anderson, Frank and LaRue Bender, Dan Conaway, Lisa Grubka, Mike Koepf, Drs. Dan and Barbara McMahon, Kim McMahon, Jill Schwartzman, and Jennifer Rudolph Walsh.

Let them eat cake.

MARIE ANTOINETTE

Part 1

Prologue

The man who called himself Freeboot crouched in the darkness outside the main security station at Sapphire Mountain Estates, a gated community forty miles north of Atlanta, Georgia. It was 2:11 A.M. He had been hiding for almost twelve hours—first in the back of a delivery truck, then after dark, when the groundskeepers and golfers chasing stray balls were gone, sneaking through the shrubbery to here.

Getting into and around a place like this was not hard. Getting back out again was a different thing.

The sky was blue-black and starry, the air frosty. His *maquis* partner, Taxman, had warned him about the November cold, even in the deep South. Taxman had done a lot of training in the Georgia woods, during jump school at Fort Benning. *Travel light, freeze at night,* went the riff. But Freeboot hardly felt the cold. In the California mountain hideaway where he spent most of his time, he went barefoot except when it got so bad that frostbite might slow him down. Tonight, he only wore boots to keep from leaving footprints.

At 2:17 A.M., the Estates' security patrol car returned from a routine cruise through the streets. The car, like the rest of security here, was no Mickey Mouse setup. Freeboot could see the barrel of an assault shotgun above the dashboard.

The driver, a uniformed guard armed with a large caliber semi-automatic pistol, parked under the sodium lights and walked to the station, a concrete building that looked like an above-ground bunker. Like the barrier fence, and anything else that might remind Sapphire Mountain Estates residents that there was a hostile world out there, it was placed out of view of the luxury houses.

The guard was young, Hispanic-looking, and buff, with a tight-fitting tailored uniform. He seemed alert if not wary, on the cocky side. Like a pimp, Freeboot thought. No—more like a whore, peddling his ass to the kind of people who lived in places like this.

Necks, Freeboot called them. They owned it all now, but the heads were going to start rolling—bigtime.

When the guard got to the building's heavy steel door, he passed his magnetic badge through a scanner, then pressed his palm against a glass plate. A few seconds later, the door's electronic bolt opened with a solid *thunk.*

He stepped inside. The door closed behind him.

Getting into that building, for Freeboot, was Phase One of this operation.

Security guards were usually untrained and sloppy—even easy to bribe. But these guards were a cut above. The residents of Sapphire Mountain Estates paid for the best, and they got it. A low-end house here cost 2.5 million dollars. The compound was surrounded by an inertia sensor fence that could pick up, literally, a mouse crawling through. The only entry point was a kiosk manned by another armed guard and backed up by a video camera that scanned each incoming vehicle's make and license plate, not allowing it to pass unless it agreed with computerized data on an authorized list. A third guard kept watch inside the main station, where individual perimeter and trap alarms from every house were wired in on dedicated phone lines. The system was as secure as anything outside of top-secret military installations. There had never been a whisper of trouble here.

In just five minutes that was going to change.

Freeboot checked his watch, then pressed the beeper on his two-way belt radio—once, for alert, then five times slowly. Immediately, it beeped in return—the signal that Taxman was in place, just outside the entry kiosk.

Freeboot flexed his surgically gloved hands to limber his fingers, and screwed a stainless-steel sound suppressor onto the barrel of his HK MP5/10 submachine gun. It was set to fire a thirty-round clip of 10-mm ammunition on full auto. It was also equipped with a high-intensity Tac light, to illuminate and temporarily blind anyone who stood in its path. Along with the gas mask and PVS-14 night-vision goggles in his pack, the Tac light would come into action during Phase Two.

With three minutes left to go, Freeboot reached into a pocket of his black fatigues and took out a can of Copenhagen. Instead of chew it was filled with a finely ground white powder. He dipped in the tip of his survival knife and raised a good-sized mound to each nostril, inhaling sharply. The harsh wild rush of methamphetamine burned up behind his eyes and swelled through his brain. The stars took on a crystalline glitter, and the chilly breeze cut into his flesh with a delicious edge.

He was ready. He pulled his ski mask down over his face, slipped the HK's sling over his shoulder, and eased his wiry body into final position—in the building's shadows, five meters from the door. A backlit man stepping through would be a perfect target, standing in what was known as a vertical coffin.

Two minutes and twenty-four seconds later, his radio beeped twice, fast. He picked up the baseball-sized rock at his feet and sidearmed it into the security fence. It hit with a whispering rattle, the same kind of disturbance as a raccoon or deer brushing against it would make, and that was what the guards would think it was. But they were required to go out and check.

A minute passed, then another. The guards were in no hurry about this kind of thing. False alarms caused by animals happened all the time.

He flexed his fingers again, waiting.

There: the *thunk* of the iron bolt. The guard appeared a second later, saying something laughingly over his shoulder to his partner inside the room. Freeboot kept waiting, so that the guard would block the door open as he fell.

When he turned and took another step forward, Freeboot opened fire, starting at the knees and sweeping up, left hand flat over the HK's muzzle to keep it from jumping. The silenced staccato rounds were hardly louder than a kid would make sputtering through his lips. The guard slammed back against the door and slid to the ground, his eyes still open.

Freeboot sprinted past him into the building. The other guard swiveled in his office chair. His face just had time to register terror before a second burst from the HK tore into his chest. He let out a sobbing groan and slumped into a huddle.

Freeboot gripped the back of his chair and heaved it forward, dumping him onto the floor. This man was older, heavy-set, with a clipped brindle mustache. He wore a wedding ring on a thick finger. Freeboot flipped the HK's selector switch to single shot and fired an insurance round into his ear canal, angling it slightly upward. He stepped to the first guard and dragged him inside, pausing to pull off his cap and unsnap the keyring from his belt. There was no need to fire another round into this one.

For ten more seconds, Freeboot waited, getting control over his breath, listening for beeps on his radio that might signal trouble. None came. Which meant that Taxman had now killed the guard at the Estates' entry kiosk, and that the local police hadn't been alerted. If that had happened, the third member of their team, monitoring a police scanner in the getaway car, would have picked up the call and sent them a warning.

From here on, there was no need to try the risky task of disabling any alarm systems. No one was watching the watchers, and no one was left alive to respond to the alarms when they went off.

He beeped his belt radio three times—*all clear here, ready to move on.*

The answering three beeps came from Taxman. He was ready, too. He had earned his name because he collected what was owed.

Freeboot closed the door behind him and trotted to the patrol car, pulling the guard's cap onto his head. Driving deliberately, he headed for the entry station to pick up Taxman. It was 2:25 A.M. Phase One had gone down without a hitch.

The home of Mr. and Mrs. David C. Bodewell was a long, low hacienda-style complex that took up most of an acre. An intruder could waste precious time trying to find his way around inside, but Freeboot and Taxman had memorized the layout. The blueprints had been easy to get.

The place bristled with silent perimeter and trap alarms, and there was one more major wrinkle in this operation: a live-in bodyguard with an attack-trained Rottweiler. The dog was not much of a worry. The bodyguard would require more care. A quiet annunciator in his attached ground-floor apartment would alert him as soon as an alarm was triggered. Like the other guards, he would first think it was caused by an animal, but very quickly, he would know this was a break-in. If he was loyal, he would move to protect his employers. Or he might hide, try to ambush the attackers, or get outside and go for help.

Taking on a personally guarded house added considerable risk. Which was precisely why they'd chosen it.

He swiveled to the gaunt figure of Taxman, crouched beside him on the street. Freeboot nodded. Taxman nodded back.

They sprinted toward the house.

Taxman circled it, placing four high-powered quad-band cell phone jammers at strategic corners. Freeboot ran straight to the rear, where the underground phone and power lines rose up through conduits into metal service boxes. These were locked with padlocks. He blasted the phone-box lock with freon from a spray can, freezing it instantly and turning the metal as brittle as glass. It snapped with a blow from a hammer. He yanked the box open and ripped through the low-voltage phone line with his knife.

No one was going to be calling out now.

The power was next—another quickly snapped lock, the master breaker pushed to OFF, and the few dim lights that showed through the windows went out.

Freeboot ran on around the house's corner to the bodyguard's apartment. Taxman had already lined the door with det cord, stuffed tightly against the stops, then sprayed with sound-deadening foam insulation. Both men stepped to the sides and pulled on their gas masks and night goggles. Taxman pressed the detonator.

The door blew into the house with a barely heard *whump*, and hung sagging from the top hinge.

Freeboot lobbed in a grenade of CS gas, throwing it as hard as he could. It exploded with a searing burst that should blind the bodyguard at least for a few seconds.

They went in one at a time, low and fast, leaping to opposite sides. Nearby, a large dog was barking in deep, ferocious challenge. Freeboot scanned the room swiftly. Furniture and objects showed luminescent green through the goggles.

But there was no human figure.

Then he saw something move, a flicker of light on the other side of the room's interior door. Just as he recognized it as a man's arm extending toward him, a gunshot smashed into the wall behind his head.

He dropped prone to the floor. More shots blasted past him. Blinded or not, the bodyguard was aiming damned close.

Freeboot fired a burst in return, but there was no time to tell if he had hit—now the dog was charging, a thick snarling shape that appeared in the goggles to be burning with ghostly fire. Taxman met it with a swooshing spray of hydrocyanic acid. The dog yelped, a high-pitched sound that turned to a near scream as the acid burned its eyes and throat. It pitched forward, paws flailing at its face, sliding and thrashing on the hardwood floor.

The bodyguard was gone.

"You *fucker*," Freeboot hissed. The man was better than they had figured. Now he was loose in the house, and there was the risk that neighbors had heard his unsilenced gunshots.

Freeboot and clamped his hand on the HK's squeeze-activated Tac-light, flooding the far side of the room with an instant of brilliant light.

There was blood spattered on the wall where the bodyguard had crouched.

"I'll get him," Freeboot told Taxman in a harsh whisper. "You take care of business."

They shoved through the interior door and separated, Taxman running to the master bedroom suite. Freeboot followed the blood trail, stalking cautiously, weapon ready. The splashes were almost continuous. The bodyguard was badly hit, but a desperate man was all the more dangerous. Freeboot moved through a large laundry room, then into a shotgun hallway. The door at the end was closed. Blood was pooled on the floor in front of it.

From deep inside the house he heard a muted *puh-puh, puh-puh, puh-puh*—Taxman firing businesslike two-round bursts.

He had found Mr. and Mrs. Bodewell.

Freeboot charged down the hall, dropping to the ground at the last second like a baseball player sliding into home, and driving both boots into the door below the knob. It burst open. He just had time to see the bodyguard's flaming-green outline as more gunshots smashed into the wall above him.

Lying on his back, aiming between his own spread feet, Freeboot fired a long burst in return.

He heard a shriek of rage and pain that could have come from an animal.

The man lay still. Freeboot stayed flattened for ten more seconds, then got to his knees.

A bullet slammed into his armored gut like a cannonball, spinning him back against the hallway wall. His hands flew loose from his weapon, but it was still on its sling, and the barrel swung around to slap him hard across the face.

He growled with fury and clawed for control of his gun. His finger found the trigger. This time, he took an extra second to sight at his target.

The bodyguard was holding his pistol in both hands. It was wavering, like it was too heavy to hold. He fired one more round past Freeboot's head, before Freeboot emptied his clip.

The pistol dropped from the bodyguard's hands.

Freeboot stood slowly, shaking. He snapped a fresh clip into the HK, then stepped to the guard and delivered the insurance round to his head. His gut ached from the bullet that had almost taken him out. He welcomed the pain, letting it fuel the anger that he turned now on himself. That had been a mistake, his mistake, and a bad one. It could have fucked up *everything*. From now on, he was going to take men like this more seriously.

He strode back to the door where they had come in, past the Rottweiler lying on its side with tongue hanging out and forelimbs stretched, as if it was running in its death dream. Too bad about that. It was a good dog, dying while doing its job. It couldn't have known what kind of people it was protecting.

Taxman was waiting at the outside door, with a long, thin duffel bag slung over his shoulder. Inside it were the trophies that were going to put the cap on this mission: a set of golf clubs.

It was 2:34 A.M. Phase Two had taken just over three minutes. Now came the third and final phase—getting out.

They loped around the house once more, collecting the phone jammers, then drove the security car to the entry kiosk. Several hundred yards outside it, two Yamaha Y2F dirt bikes—quiet, light, and fast—were hidden in the woods. These would carry them three miles to a road that didn't lead directly to the Sapphire Mountain Estates entrance, where their getaway car was waiting—a luxury Mercedes sedan driven by their third partner, Shrinkwrap, dressed as a wealthy middle-aged woman. If police did happen to be in the area, they wouldn't dream that there was any connection with the attack.

Freeboot and Taxman would ride in the trunk to a rented storage unit in Atlanta. There they would switch vehicles and clothes, and head separately for home—clean-cut, respectable business people, invisible among millions of others like them. The stolen Mercedes would be picked up and chopped for parts. Their bikes, guns, and gear would be safely hidden or destroyed. Any video cameras that had taped the assault would show only two men dressed in black from scalp to toe.

Freeboot kicked his bike to life, toed it up into first gear, and popped the clutch, spinning the rear wheel and raising the front one, surging forward in a long, fierce leap of triumph. They had brought it off, the toughest and wildest operation yet. Within hours, this would be headline news, its implications plain:

The only way the necks were going to stay safe was to build maximum-security prisons.

And live in them.

BLOODBATH LINKED TO "CALAMITY JANE"

By Harold B. Lorenz

The Atlanta Journal-Constitution

Published on: 11/21/03

Atlanta—A multiple homicide that shocked the nation two days ago has taken a bizarre new twist.

Early this morning, police broke up a fight in a homeless camp near Atlanta's Peachtree and Pine area, where a man was using a golf club as a weapon.

It has since been confirmed that the club was one of a rare collection stolen from the house of Eurolon CEO David C. Bodewell. Bodewell, his wife, Paula, and four security guards were murdered last Tuesday in what appeared to be a carefully planned raid on the exclusive community of Sapphire Mountain Estates, north of Atlanta.

The golf club was identified as a "Calamity Jane" putter—one of only a half-dozen that were handmade for golf legend Bobby Jones in the 1920s. A search of the homeless area turned up several more clubs from Bodewell's collection. Apparently, they had been tossed in a Dumpster.

"We can't speculate at this time on why the golf clubs were taken, or how they ended up where they did," Atlanta police spokesman Charles Richardson said. Richardson also declined to comment on a possible motive for the murders. But another source, speaking on condition of anonymity, said that nothing else of value appeared to have been taken from the house.

The community's residents, shaken by the murders, expressed deep concern at this new development. "You're telling me they killed six people for some golf clubs, then threw them away?" said an outraged neighbor, who also asked not to be identified. "That's crazy."

Police gave assurances that the investigation was being pursued with every available resource.

One

Carroll Monks was planning a trip to Ireland. His grandfather had grown up near Kilrush, on the west coast, before emigrating to the States. Monks had seen a photo of the place—a stone hovel in a barren field, miles from the nearest tiny village.

But Monks himself had never set foot on Irish soil. Why that was so was a puzzle even to him. The only answer he could give was that his life for the past thirty-odd years seemed to have been one long struggle to stay on top of whatever he was doing, while stumbling toward the next goal—college, medical school, five years in the navy, getting established in practice. Then marriage, children, divorce, and the thousands of vicissitudes that went with all that. Most of the traveling he had done had either been out of necessity, or vacations that were aimed at pleasing his children.

But the lapse was still inexcusable, and he was going to rectify it, come next March. He was not in search of his roots—he intended to make that clear to everybody he met. Mainly, he hoped to drink in some good pubs, walk on deserted beaches, and listen to a lot of rain, while he was warm and dry inside.

He was warm and dry right now, inside his own living room. It was early December, getting toward dusk, and the northern California winter was starting to settle in. A fire crackled in his woodstove, with cats sleeping in front of it, waiting for him to break out the slab of fresh salmon that they knew was in the refrigerator, ready to broil on a charcoal grill. Meanwhile, to get himself in shape for the journey, Monks had put aside the vodka that was his usual preference and taken up an apprenticeship with John Power whiskey, a working-class Irish malt with a good rough edge. He liked to sip it neat, slowly, sampling various stouts as chasers. The effect was like nectar and ambrosia combined.

He had been reading up on Irish history and had a pile of maps and guidebooks that he consulted while plotting his course. His main focus was a leisurely trip up the west coast, through Galway to Donegal, staying as close as he could to the ocean. He had no fixed schedule. In early spring, lodging should be easy to find. He would be traveling alone. Ideally, he would have a female companion along, but there was no one on the radar just now. He was starting to wonder if there ever would be again.

Monks decided to pour one more short splash of whiskey before starting the charcoal for the salmon. He was getting to his feet when a knock came at the front door.

This surprised him. His house was a good hundred yards off a little-traveled county road, surrounded by redwoods, all but hidden from view. He would have heard a car coming up his gravel drive. So the caller was on foot—but there were no near neighbors, and no one in the habit of dropping by.

He stepped to a window that gave a view of the deck outside the front door. His surprise deepened. A young woman was standing there. The evening darkness was closing in, but he was quite sure she wasn't anyone he knew. She was looking around, in a way that suggested she might be nervous at approaching a stranger's house at dusk.

Monks walked to the door and opened it.

She was in her early twenties, tall and full-figured; not really pretty but attractive, with olive skin and strong Mediterranean features. Her black hair was pinned with a clasp and worn long down her back. She was dressed as if for business, in tailored slacks and a silk blouse. She smiled but that looked nervous, too.

"I saw your lights," she said, with a slight stammer. "I got a flat tire, down on the road."

Monks's heart sank a little. Changing a tire, in the dark, on a vehicle he didn't know anything about, was not an enjoyable prospect.

"I'll come take a look," he said.

She murmured thanks.

He was wearing jeans, a flannel shirt, and well-worn Red Wing work boots—clothes that would do. He got a powerful Mag flashlight out of the front closet and put on a wool-lined Carhartt jacket. Then, seeing that she had crossed her forearms and was rubbing her upper arms with her palms, he said, "You're welcome to stay here and warm up while I go check it out."

She shook her head. "That's okay."

"You want a coat?"

"That's okay," she said again. "I've got one down there. I didn't think it was this cold."

Monks switched on the flashlight, illuminating their path down the gravel drive toward the county road. The woods were still. A few brave tree frogs emitted hopeful croaks in the chilly damp air, trying to strike up the usual evening chorus, but apparently most of their comrades were bedded down in amphibean comfort, exercising selective deafness.

"I can't promise I can do this," Monks warned. "Is there somebody around here who could come pick you up?"

"No."

She didn't live nearby, then, and wasn't visiting someone who did. He wondered what she was doing on a narrow, out-of-the-way road that ran from noplace to noplace else. Probably she was just lost.

"Do you know where the jack and spare are?" he asked.

"No."

"Do you have an owner's manual?"

"I'm not sure."

His lips twisted wryly. There was nothing like traveling prepared. But he reminded himself that at her age he had been pretty feckless, too.

"We might have to call a tow truck," he said.

She nodded, still clasping herself.

Monks thought about trying to keep up small talk, but it seemed clear that she wanted to get this done and get out of here. He could hardly blame her. He probably seemed harmless, but he was still a strange man that she was alone with, in a lonely place. And given the age gap, she was doubtless bored to tears, just on general principles.

"By the way, my name's Carroll," he said.

"Marguerite. Hi."

He left it at that.

When they reached the road, the canopy of foliage overhead parted, revealing a streak of sky. But clouds had thickened into a solid cover during the afternoon, obscuring the little daylight that was left.

"It's down that way," Marguerite said, pointing to the right. They walked in that direction, Monks searching with the flashlight's beam until it glimmered off the chrome bumper of a vehicle that was pulled into a turnout.

He almost groaned. It was one of those huge, bloated SUVs, a Yukon or Expedition or something on that order, and brand new. He had unconsciously pictured her driving something small and sassy. But this monster, as his friend Emil Zukich was fond of saying, was as heavy as a dead preacher. That was going to make it tricky and maybe dangerous to jack up, working off the soft and uneven dirt surface of the turnout—assuming he could even figure out how to operate the jack and find the proper lifting point. For all he knew, the system might be computer-operated. He had a heavy-duty bumper jack in his Bronco, but he wasn't at all sure that bumpers on the newer vehicles were designed to handle that kind of weight.

"How about taking a look in the glove box," he told her. "If there's an owner's manual, that might be where it is."

She walked to the front passenger door. Monks flashed the light beam on the tires. The two that he could see, on the driver's side, looked fine. The flat must be on the other side, although the SUV didn't look like it was listing.

He started to walk around it. The flashlight's traveling beam caught something pale and round inside—a face. Monks was surprised again. He had assumed that she was alone.

Then he realized that she had disappeared.

A second later, what his eyes had told him caught up to his brain. He flicked the flashlight beam back to the face inside the SUV. It was a young man's, pale and tense, staring at him.

Monks stared back, not believing what he thought he saw:

His son, Glenn, gone from Monks's life for almost five years.

Glenn reached to the window and rapped on it sharply with his knuckles.

Something hard and blunt rammed into Monks's lower back, forcing an *unhhh* of breath from him and shoving him forward a step.

"Turn off the light and drop it," a man's voice said behind him.

Monks did. A second man stepped into view on the left. He was big, squarely built and cleancut, wearing a business suit complete with necktie. But he was aiming the kind of short-barreled shotgun used by SWAT teams—a 12-gauge with a five-round magazine, capable of cutting a human being in half.

"Walk into the woods," the voice behind him ordered.

Monks did that, too, for ten or fifteen yards, until he was hidden from the road. He couldn't see what was prodding him along, but he had no doubt that it was the barrel of another gun. The thought of running flitted through his mind, but the way the men were positioned, he could not possibly escape their fire.

"Lay down on your belly. Hands behind you."

He got facedown in the scratchy redwood duff. The musty scent of damp earth filled his lungs.

The big man strode forward and put the shotgun barrel to the side of Monks's face, just in front of his left ear. The other man knelt on his back and pulled his wrists roughly together. Monks felt restraints tighten around them, and heard the ratcheting clicks of handcuffs. It started to filter in that they probably would not bother to cuff him if they intended to kill him—at least, right then and there. But the fact that they had let him see faces was not a good sign.

"Taxman! Car!" Marguerite's voice hissed from the road. Monks felt the man who was kneeling on his back jerk in response. Then he felt cold steel laid against his cheek—a knife blade. It turned so that the edge rested lightly against his flesh. Monks could just see that it was a survival knife with a blade at least six inches long, serrated along the back edge to leave ragged, hard-to-close wounds. The other man stepped behind a tree, gun barrel pointing upright, ready to fire.

Monks could hear the approaching vehicle now, coming southward on the county road, driving at a modest speed. It slowed into the nearest curve, then accelerated again. If it stopped to check out the distressed vehicle, the assailants might flee. Or they might gun down the occupants and cut Monks' throat.

He lay absolutely still, not breathing, trying to gauge the car's speed and position. It slowed as it passed the SUV.

But it kept going, the whoosh of its tires growing fainter, until the night was quiet again.

The knife was lifted away from his face. The one called Taxman bound his ankles together with several wraps of duct tape, then kept taping up to his knees, swathing his legs like a mummy's. He jerked Monks up into a kneeling position, and wrapped his upper body from shoulders to waist, pinioning his arms. Then the two men together rolled Monks into a sleeping bag and zipped it shut. They picked him up as if they were carrying a stretcher, and loaded him into the SUV's rear compartment.

Taxman bent close to Monks. It was the first glimpse of him that Monks had gotten. He was also well dressed, his hair short and blond, giving him the look of a prematurely balding accountant. But his lean face was etched with intensity. His age was hard to guess—

somewhere between thirty and forty. His breath smelled of mints, but Monks caught a hint of a harsh smell that he recognized from the ER—methamphetamine.

"Tell me you'll stay quiet, I won't gag you," he said. This time, the twang of Texas or the South came through clearly.

Monks nodded.

They quickly threw more sleeping bags over him, covering his face, then piled other stuff on and around him. They closed the rear door and locked it. Other doors opened and closed, and the engine started. Gasoline sloshed in the tank underneath him as the SUV lurched across the rutted turnout to the paved road.

He knew that they were heading northeast. In another twenty-five or thirty minutes, he felt the vehicle go through a series of stops and turns, then accelerate to a steady high speed. They had turned onto Highway 101—north, he guessed, although he couldn't be sure of that.

Right this second, he was almost certainly surrounded by other vehicles driving alongside, literally close enough to touch. But they might as well have been on Mars.

The ride smoothed out, with the quiet drone of the drive train beneath his ear and the faint reek of exhaust and gas in his nostrils. Monks lay still, cramped and uncomfortable. By now, anger was rising in him to join his fear, although there was still plenty of that. Outwardly, these people looked like a church group—maybe fundamentalists of some stamp. But they operated with military precision. And that brief look into the eyes of the one called Taxman had chilled Monks more than the guns.

He knew he'd made enemies over the years, dangerous and violent ones. The possibility that he or his family might become victims of sadistic revenge was never far from his mind.

But what tore at him more than anything else was the young man he had seen inside the van: his son. Who apparently had identified Monks by rapping on the window—a Judas kiss.

What the hell was *Glenn* doing in on this?

Two

When the SUV finally stopped for good, Monks guessed that they had been driving for close to six hours. It was sometime around midnight, and the only thing he was sure of was that they were in the middle of nowhere. The first two to three hours had been on freeway, uninterrupted, strengthening his sense that they were heading north, probably on Highway 101. Then came another hour and a half of increasingly slower, curvier roads. The rest was gravel or dirt, rutted and rough. His body had taken a beating. He had started to lose circulation, particularly in his tightly cuffed hands. His wrists were chafed from twisting, trying to keep his fingers from going numb. His bladder was ready to burst.

He had spent a lot of time during those hours grappling with his disbelief at what was happening, and racking his brain for an explanation. He had strained to listen over the vehicle's noise, but could not hear any conversation. If his captors had been talking, they had done it very quietly.

But Glenn kept coming more clearly into focus in his mind as the center of whatever this was about.

Monks and his son had had a lot of trouble with each other, starting when Glenn was still very young, and getting worse as he reached his teens. Glenn had finally dropped out of high school and left home at seventeen; he had last been heard of living on the streets of Seattle, panhandling, doing drugs and God knew what else. His IQ had been measured in the 160s. He was a natural math whiz and able to do anything with computers. But he was also diagnosed as moderately antisocial, psychology's euphemism for sociopathic—not overtly violent himself but seeing others as pawns to be used for his own purposes.

The other side of the story had to do with Monks himself, who had done a poor job of controlling his own impatience with the insolence of youth. It hadn't helped that his anger had often been fueled by alcohol.

Still, it was hard to believe that Glenn had a strong enough thirst for vengeance to harm him. It seemed more likely that he had gotten in with criminal companions, and they had cooked up an extortion scheme—treating Monks roughly to show that they meant business, betting that he would cough up money and stay quiet about it rather than prosecute his own son. He admitted that they were probably right.

The vehicle's doors opened and closed as the passengers got out. The same two men came around to the rear and lifted Monks out, laying him on the ground. The sky was thick with faintly luminescent fog, allowing him to see a little in spite of the darkness. The men had changed clothes at some point, into the uniform of the backwoods: logger boots, jeans, and wool shirts. Monks glimpsed a couple of patches of light—windows in a nearby building—before the thin-faced one named Taxman knelt on his back, pressing his face into the earth.

"Hammerhead," Taxman said commandingly. "Go tell Freeboot we're back." The bigger man trotted away, carrying his shotgun like a toy in one hand.

Monks felt Taxman's knife slicing the duct tape free. It just grazed his skin, moving with smooth precision.

Then a woman's voice cut the air.

"Where've you been, pet? I thought you were just going to be gone a couple of hours."

This was not Marguerite, the young woman who had come to his door, Monks was sure. The voice was older, sharper, its tone sweetly cool—the tone of a woman who suspects that she has been deceived.

Taxman stopped his knife work and turned toward her. But it was a younger man, standing farther away, who answered:

"On a mission." He inflated the word *mission* with importance, but his voice had a nervous, blustery edge.

Monks recognized it, deep in his bones, a voice that he had heard make its first newborn squall—Glenn's.

Monks quietly turned his head toward the talkers. He could just make out the figure of a small slender woman, walking closer with folded arms. Glenn was standing beside the SUV, fidgeting.

"So, you lied to me?" she said, still with that dangerous sweetness.

Taxman answered this time. "Stay cool, Shrinkwrap. It was Freeboot's call." His voice was quiet, but hard-edged and authoritative.

"Really? Something too important for me to know about?"

Taxman hesitated, then said, "Freeboot decided to get a doctor. So we got one. Coil's old man."

"What?" Her voice rose sharply in disbelief. "You brought his *father* here?"

Then she seemed to realize that there was someone lying on the ground. She took three or four quick steps toward Monks and bent forward to stare at him, arms held away from her body in a posture of shock.

"Oh, my God," she breathed. She whirled and spoke furiously to Glenn. "Why didn't you tell me, you little shit? I could have stopped it."

"Hey, you can work it out with Freeboot, okay?" Glenn retorted, his own voice heated and sullen.

"Are you insane? This is serious trouble. You think people aren't going to be looking for this guy?"

"It's all going to be cool."

"What makes you so sure?"

"Because," Glenn said, "he owes me, bigtime."

An instant of crystalline stillness followed in Monks's mind, an interlude when all sound and motion seemed to stop completely, even the beating of his heart.

A dining room littered with broken dishes and food on the floor, from another of Glenn's endless tantrums. Monks, trembling with anger, left hand clenching the taunting boy's collar, right hand raised to slap him. Gail, Glenn's mother, clinging to Monks's arm and screaming at him to stop.

He pushed the memory back into the ugly shadows where it lurked, along with too many others. But it went a long way toward explaining this. By Glenn's lights, Monks had it coming.

Glenn started walking away. The woman called Shrinkwrap said, "Wait a minute, pet, we're not done talking," and strode after him. Monks heard their voices for another half minute—hers, harsh and controlling; his, defiant. Then they faded with distance.

She had called him "pet" twice. Monks had not been able to see her clearly, but he was sure that she was in her thirties, and maybe older. Glenn was twenty-two.

Taxman was busy with his knife again. He finished slicing through the tape, and finally unlocked the handcuffs. Monks rolled onto his back and rubbed his sore wrists, grimacing at the hot shooting pain of returning circulation.

"Empty your pockets," Taxman said. Monks could see now that he was built like a ferret, his body as thin as his face. With his light, close-cropped hair, his head was a pale orb, giving him a spectral presence.

Monks rose stiffly to his knees and dropped his possessions on the ground: wallet, keys, Kershaw folding knife, and a few coins.

"Your watch, too."

Monks unstrapped it and added it to the other items. It was a sturdy Casio diver's watch, which he liked because it remained unscathed by punishment and occasional dousings of body fluids in the ER. It had a small compass on the wristband, an affectation in most circumstances, but useful if you took a wrong turn on a back road.

He tried to get a glimpse of the compass to orient himself, but there wasn't enough light.

"You want to take a piss, go ahead," Taxman said.

Monks managed to stand up, staggering as the stinging prickles shot down his legs. Marguerite was still standing beside the SUV. She seemed anxious, as if she were waiting for something. He hesitated, expecting her to at least turn away as he unbuttoned his fly, but she paid no attention to him. Apparently, those kinds of social graces were not an issue here. He turned his own back and urinated copiously.

He could see now that he was in a clearing the size of a football field, with the dim shapes of several buildings scattered around. One, made of logs, had the lit windows that he had seen earlier. The others were dark. The air was significantly colder than at his own place, and heavy with the scent of conifers. He could just make out the trees' tall shapes around the clearing. The fresh wind rustled their branches and blew against his face, bringing the smell of woodsmoke.

What it all added up to was that they were somewhere deep in the mountains of north-central California. There were thousands of square miles of alpine forest up here, most of it far from any town or even a paved road.

Monks buttoned up and turned back. The possibility had also occurred to him that a member of this band was sick or hurt, maybe even wounded in the course of committing a crime, and they didn't want to risk going to a hospital. It still seemed extreme to kidnap a physician; there were easier ways to get medical care while staying anonymous. But maybe using Glenn as a buffer figured in there, too.

"If somebody needs a doctor, why don't you take me to them," he said.

Taxman ignored him, instead watching a figure that was trotting closer, out of the darkness. It was the big man, Hammerhead.

"Freeboot wants you to wait in the lodge," he said to Marguerite. "He's giving a training session."

She recoiled in shock. "That *fuck*." The word came out in a harsh expulsion of breath.

"He wasn't expecting us back so soon," Hammerhead said. He sounded unhappy, apologetic, as if trying to mollify her.

"Why should I care?" she said. "He has the right to do what he wants." She tossed her hair, defiant now, then stalked toward the building with the lit windows.

"Marguerite," Hammerhead said, taking a quick step after her.

But Taxman interrupted with his hard-edged drawl. "You done good tonight, HH. Don't fuck it up."

Hammerhead, Monks thought. Taxman. Shrinkwrap. And Glenn, it seemed, was called Coil.

Hammerhead turned back, with his heavy jaw clamped tight. The name fit, Monks had to agree. His head was large, square, and seemed to bulge slightly at the temples, an effect that was accentuated by jug ears.

"He said for us to come on," Hammerhead said.

Taxman looked at Monks and pointed with his knife to one of the unlit buildings fifty yards away.

The two men flanked Monks as they walked to it.

This structure was small, about half the size of a one-car garage, and made of peeled logs that were weathered with age. There were no windows, only a door of heavy planks. The smell of woodsmoke was strong here, and Monks could see a thin plume rising from a stovepipe in the roof.

Taxman motioned Monks to wait. Hammerhead pulled the door open.

A cloud of warm damp air spilled out, carrying the pungent scent of heated cedar. At the room's center rear, a huge old iron stove blazed, with dancing flames showing through cracks in the casting. A metal bucket of water and a dipper sat on the floor in front of it. Crude three-tiered benches had been built against the walls. Monks realized that it was a sauna.

There were two people in it. One was a woman sitting sideways on a bottom bench, nude, leaning back against the wall. She was young, perhaps twenty, and quite pretty, her hair touseled and damp from steam. Her feet were up on the bench, her knees at her shoulders and apart. Her head was turned to one side, her eyes closed. Her right hand was poised between her thighs, wrist arched delicately, fingers touching her vulva.

The other was a man of about thirty-five, sitting against the opposite wall, watching her intently. He was naked, too, and also an impressive sight—tightly muscled, with corded forearms and knotty veined biceps. His skin, glistening with steam and sweat, seemed to glow in the firelight like molten bronze. He had a thick dark stubble of beard and hair.

Monks's instant impression was of the blacksmith god Vulcan, taking time away from his forge to sport with a nymph.

So this was Freeboot. Deeply involved in a training session.

Freeboot's head turned sharply toward the open door. The woman turned more slowly, her eyes opening and fingers pausing.

Hammerhead said, "Whenever you're ready."

Freeboot nodded. Hammerhead closed the door.

The woman came out alone a minute later. She moved as if she was in a dream, groping for a robe that hung from a peg on the log wall, slipping it on, then fading off toward another nearby building. If she was aware of the three men watching her, she gave no sign of it. The aroma of cedar lingered in her wake like perfume.

Taxman opened the door again and nodded to Monks.

Monks stepped inside, expecting the guards to follow. But the door closed behind him. The air was sweltering. Immediately, he felt the flush of blood rising to his skin, and started to sweat.

Freeboot was still sitting on the bench. His body was relaxed, but his eyes stared at Monks with hypnotic intensity. Monks noted again his superb musculature. He was not tall, nor thick like a weight lifter, but he looked like he was strung together with cables. It came home to Monks that the guards hadn't come in because there was no need for them. Trying to attack this man would be like taking on a cougar. His arms and upper body sported large dark blotches, which Monks at first thought were birthmarks. Now he realized that they were tattoos that apparently had been filled in solid.

"Sorry we had to bring you here like that, man," Freeboot said.

"Nobody *had* to do anything to me."

"I can understand that you're pissed off."

"If Glenn had just asked me to come here, I would have."

"It's not that simple," Freeboot said. "We don't know if we can trust you."

Monks's mouth opened in outrage. This was the second time he had heard that what had happened to him was, essentially, his fault.

"If *you* can trust *me*?" he said.

"We'd like to treat you right. It's up to you."

Freeboot stood in a quick fluid motion, vibrant with strength and grace. He lifted the full dipper out of the bucket, and flicked the water onto the blazing stove. Steam poured off the iron with an explosive hiss. Monks threw his forearm across his face to shield himself from the blistering heat. A few seconds later, another hiss sounded, and a wave of even hotter steam wrapped around him, clawing its way inside his clothes. The hiss came a third time. Monks backed into the sauna's corner and spun away from the stove, head buried in both arms, barely able to breathe the scorching air.

Over the next seconds the heat subsided, though not much, like a menacing presence that had taken a step back but was liable to attack again. Monks wiped his streaming eyes on his sleeve and turned around.

Freeboot was standing in front of the stove, looking entirely at ease, smiling slightly.

"Lose your clothes and hang for a while," he said. "Sweat out the bad vibes."

"Just tell me what you want," Monks managed to say, half-choking on the words.

Freeboot kept watching him steadily for a long fifteen seconds. Then he strode past Monks, pushed open the door, and stood aside.

Monks stumbled out into the fresh cool night and crouched, hands on his thighs, working on getting his breath back. Another explosion of steam sounded inside the sauna, this one louder and longer than any of the others, as if Freeboot had emptied the rest of the bucket onto the stove.

Half a minute later, the sauna door swung open. Freeboot stood framed in the firelight, damp and shining, like a burnished statue.

"All right," he said. "Let's get down to business."

He stepped out, took jeans and a shirt from pegs on the wall, and, still wet, pulled them on.

"Coil—your kid, we call him Coil 'cause he's wound so tight," Freeboot said, "he tells me you're a medieval scholar."

Monks had started feeling sharper. The shock of sudden heat and then coolness had helped.

"I'm not a scholar of anything," he said.

"But you know about the Free Companies, right?"

"I don't understand what that has to do with me being here."

Freeboot's gaze hardened into a stare. "I'm trying to get around to that, if you'll give me a chance."

Monks hesitated, unwilling to enter into a genial discussion. But to be overly stubborn would be childish and could backfire.

"Yes," he said. The Free Companies were bands of brigands, loosely organized into private armies, that scourged Europe during the Middle Ages, preying on the undefended populace.

"You think that could happen these days? Here, in the States?"

"I've never thought about it," Monks said.

"Well, do think about it, man. There's twenty million people out there who got nothing. Outlaws, or just one step away. And *zillions* of guns."

Freeboot nodded for emphasis, apparently satisifed that he had made his point. Then, barefoot, he started across the clearing with a rangy feral stride.

Monks and the guards followed, this time to the large cabin with lit windows that they called the lodge. He guessed that it was close to a hundred years old. Its logs were almost three feet thick, the kind of old-growth Doug fir you hardly ever saw anymore. They had settled with age, and the chinking was gone in spots, but the structure and metal roof looked intact.

When the door opened, Monks had the sense of looking into a tableau from hundreds of years ago, the kind on display in museums. A fire crackled in the big stone hearth, lighting the room. The air was thick with the smell of generations of roasted meat. There was a long table of rough-hewn wood, strewn with liquor and beer bottles.

The two women in the room were also frozen, tableau-style, in their poses, but their clothing put them into modern times. Marguerite had changed into tight low-cut jeans and a skimpy blouse, the outfit that seemed to be a uniform for young women these days. Her long black hair and Mediterranean face gave her a look that could have graced a Renaissance portrait, if you ignored the exposed midriff and pierced navel. She looked forlorn, adding to the sense of a lady pining for a lover. Monks recalled her obvious upset at hearing that Freeboot was giving "training."

He recognized the other woman as Shrinkwrap. She was in her late thirties, small and thin, with an aura of no-nonsense intelligence. Like everyone else, she was wearing blue jeans and had a red bandanna tied as a hippie-style headband, but her shoulder-length hair was professionally cut and well cared for. She didn't seem happy, either, with a hostile gaze that was fixed on Monks.

There was no sign of Glenn.

Freeboot crossed the room to stand beside Marguerite, his hand sliding down, with automatic familiarity, to caress her rump. She lowered her eyes, with the deferential air of a consort in the presence of her lord. He was not much taller than Marguerite, under six feet, and with his taut body hidden by clothes, he looked less fearsome than he had when he was glowing in the sauna. But his eyes still commanded.

"We've got somebody who's sick," Freeboot said to Monks. "You willing to help?"

So: that *was* it.

"It depends," Monks said warily.

"On what?"

"On a lot of things. I'd have to look them over and see if I *can* help, for starters."

"What I'm *asking* you is, are you willing?"

Monks hesitated, then said, "I'll give you my opinion on the best course to take."

"Let's quit the word-game bullshit, man. You took the Hippocratic oath, right?"

Monks's mouth opened in astonishment that Freeboot both knew the term and what it entailed. And he was right. Monks had had a vague notion of using his skills as a bargaining chip. But the truth was, there was no way he could *not* treat someone in need, insane though the circumstances might be.

"I'll do what I can," he said. "Have you got any medical supplies?"

"Tell us what you want. We'll get it." Freeboot seemed confident of this, and Monks decided not to point out that obtaining things like prescription medicines might not be easy or even possible.

Freeboot walked to a doorway that opened off the cabin's main room. There was no door, only a heavy wool blanket hanging in the opening.

"In here," he said. He pulled the blanket aside and waited for Monks to go first.

Monks did, cautiously, fearing the sight of a wound that had gone untended for days.

This room was very dim, the only light coming from a single kerosene lamp turned down low. The rustic impression was enhanced by an old-fashioned enamel pitcher and basin on a dresser. There was a jumble of clothes on the floor, and two beds, with someone asleep in one of them. As his eyes adjusted, he could make out a bare arm and long fair hair splayed over the pillow. He stepped closer, assuming that this was the patient.

"Not her," Freeboot said. "Him."

He pointed at the other bed, and Monks realized suddenly that there was someone in that one, too, scrunched back into the corner, almost hidden in the shadows.

He felt his scalp bristle when it hit him that he was looking at a little boy, about four years old, staring back with hollow eyes in his small, pale face.

Three

Monks felt the surge of adrenaline that he usually only got when something really bad came through the ER doors. He knew already that this child was very sick. His first, worst fear was meningitis.

"Hi," Monks said, managing to smile. "What's your name?"

The little boy did not answer. His hair seemed colorless, his eyes sunken and dull, and his cheeks were too thin—the terrifying look of old age in a face that was just forming.

"He can talk pretty good when he wants to," Freeboot said from the doorway. "His name's Mandrake. The root of mystical power."

Monks grimaced. For adults to take on absurd names was one thing; to burden a child with one was another. He was vaguely aware that the mandrake root had occult significance. He wondered if Freeboot knew that Mandrake had also been a comic-strip magician of a few decades before.

"He's your son?" Monks said.

Freeboot nodded, then stepped to the other bed and shook the shoulder of the person sleeping in it. The shake was not gentle.

"This is his mom," Freeboot said.

The woman stirred, then slowly sat up. She was in her mid-twenties, sallow and blowsy. With her messy lank hair, she had the look of a flower child gone to seed.

"I brought a doctor, like you broads wanted," Freeboot said to her with clear sarcasm, even contempt. "You can watch him do his doctor thing."

So—it seemed that Monks owed his presence here to the women. "I need more light," he said.

Marguerite turned up the kerosene lantern and brought it to the bedside. Monks leaned closer over the boy, moving slowly so as not to frighten him.

"How you doing, Mandrake?" Monks said, and sat beside him on the bed. "Not feeling too good, huh? I'm a doctor. I'm going to try to make you feel better."

He smoothed the boy's hair back, feeling his forehead. It was clammy and cool, and Monks relaxed a notch. If it were meningitis, Mandrake would have a burning fever, and be dead within a few hours.

There were still plenty of other serious possibilities.

Monks's hand went to his mouth and eased it open. The lips were cracked, and the inside looked dry and cottony. His breath did not have the sweet milky smell of a normal child's at that age. It was sharp and oddly fruity.

The first diagnostic tick registed in his brain—acetone. Ketoacidosis?

"Can you tell me what's hurting you, Mandrake?" he said. "Your head? Tummy?"

Mandrake did not respond.

But his mother suddenly said, "Hi," in a cracked, sleepy voice.

Monks waited, thinking she was going to tell him something. But she only watched him with vague eyes, then looked around the room as if trying to remember where she was. Such a heavy sleep—especially in a mother with a sick child—suggested sedation.

"He's had tummy aches," Marguerite said. "He's been throwing up."

"Every kid has tummy aches and throws up," Freeboot muttered. He stomped around with a few agitated steps, then subsided.

"Anything else?" Monks asked.

"He's pissing the bed again," Freeboot said. "After we broke him of it a year ago."

"Drinking lots of water?"

"Yeah."

"How long has this been going on?"

"He started acting weird a couple of weeks ago," Marguerite said.

"Acting weird how?"

"Just weird," she said defensively. "He *looked* sick. Didn't want to go out and play."

Freeboot snorted in derision. "He's just scared of the bad weather."

Monks lowered the covers from Mandrake's chin down to his waist and lifted up his pajama top. His fingers felt the padded waistband of a diaper.

"I'm just going to touch your tummy for a second, Mandrake," he said. "It won't hurt, I promise." Monks gently massaged the abdomen, feeling for lumps or abnormalities, and continuing his covert check for signs of abuse. So far, there hadn't been anything obvious. At least it did not seem that the child had been actively harmed.

Mandrake only continued to watch Monks apathetically. Most kids that age would have squirmed, cried, had to be restrained by a parent or a nurse. Such passivity would have been a dangerous enough sign in an adult. In a child, it was chilling.

Monks gently pinched a fold of skin between his thumb and forefinger. The skin felt thin, without turgor, its usual rubbery quality. When he released it, it didn't snap back flat, but subsided only gradually, like a slowly collapsing tent.

Along with the smell of acetone, that was the second solid bit of diagnostic information.

"Has he been eating?" Monks asked.

"Like a little pig," Freeboot said, with an air of triumph. "Now you tell me, would he be doing that if he was really sick?"

Monks's jaw tightened, his anger moving another notch toward the red zone. It was hard to imagine that anyone could ignore the fact of a child eating desperately, but shrinking to skin and bones. And yet, Monks had seen similar neglect many times.

He pulled the pajama top back down and tucked Mandrake in again.

"Okay, Mandrake," he said. "I'm going to talk to your dad. I'll be back to visit you again in a little while."

Monks patted the boy's shoulder, stood, and motioned with his head for Freeboot to leave the room with him. It was an automatic gesture, developed over many years of being in charge at a patient's bedside. But he saw Freeboot's eyes narrow, and realized that even this tiny assertion registered as an insult to his authority.

Freeboot turned his back and pushed through the curtain, leaving Monks to follow.

"Freeboot thinks it's all in his head," the mother said, from her bed. Apparently, she was starting to grasp what was happening. "Like, you know, he *wants* to be sick."

"Freeboot's wrong," Monks said curtly.

"Do you know what it is?"

He shook his head, although in truth, he had a pretty good idea.

He stepped out through the curtain. Marguerite was lingering outside the room.

"What kind of drugs is she on?" he asked, pointing back toward the woman in bed. If she had borne or breast-fed Mandrake while using—or had contracted HIV or hepatitis—that could add an ugly complication.

"Motherlode? She's heavy into 'codes." This was slang for oxycodones—synthetic opiates.

"For a long time?"

"She always messed around with them. This last year or so, she's been pretty much out of it all the time. She just lays around." Marguerite's resentment was clear. "Freeboot won't let her sleep with Mandrake, because he says she'll roll over on him and smother him."

It was a tender sentiment for the mother of one's child.

"Who takes care of him?" Monks asked.

"Me, most of the time."

"When's the last time you saw him drink water?"

"Just a little while ago," she said. "I checked up on him as soon as we got back." Her gaze faltered, and Monks was tempted to finish the sentence aloud—*from kidnapping you at gunpoint.*

"It's very important that he keeps it up," Monks said. "At least a couple of glasses every hour. Try to give him some more now. If he won't drink, tell me immediately."

As he spoke the words, he realized, with a mix of helplessness, anger, and fear, that he was involving himself, even assuming responsibility. But right now, keeping that little boy alive was what mattered more than anything else.

Monks walked on into the lodge's main room. Freeboot was standing in its center like a presiding judge, somber, arms folded, with Shrinkwrap, Taxman, and Hammerhead as the jury.

"Mandrake needs immediate hospitalization," Monks said.

The room's attention turned to Freeboot, with gazes shifting, openly or covertly, to watch his reaction. He remained poker-faced.

"What's the matter with him?" Freeboot demanded.

"I'd need a lab report to tell you."

"Then how do you know he should go to a hospital?"

"First off, he's dehydrated to a life-threatening degree," Monks said. "That's why he's drinking so much water. His body's trying to stay up with the need. But he's passing it faster than he can take it in. The only way to replace it at that rate is by IV."

"We're not going to hook him up to any of that shit."

"Hooking him up to 'that shit' will keep him alive," Monks said. "There are other problems, too. You said he's eating a lot, but he's losing weight, right? With nausea and vomiting? A normal kid that age is a bundle of energy, but he's lying there like an old man. He needs a thorough workup by specialists, and he needs it now."

Freeboot shook his head. "Not for Mandrake."

"Why not?" Monks said. "Is it money? I can get you help. I'll pay for it myself, if it comes to that."

"We got money," Freeboot said, with clear condescension.

"What, then? Are you worried about the police? We can keep them out of it."

Freeboot shook his head again, this time impatiently—the gesture of a man wasting his breath on someone too dense to understand. Then his forehead knotted with worry, as if his own pain was showing through. Monks couldn't tell if it was genuine or purely a performance.

"I want what's *best* for him," Freeboot said. "But it's complicated. This is all about *faith*."

Monks wasn't surprised to find an element of religion woven into this. He had encountered a number of people who resisted medical care for religious reasons, and he knew of instances where it had resulted in death—too often, the death of a child.

"I'd be glad to hear about your beliefs some other time," Monks said. "But don't tell me you'd let your son be a martyr to them."

"I didn't say beliefs. I said faith. There's a difference."

"I've got plenty of respect for faith," Monks said. "But it wasn't faith that built the truck that brought me here, or the guns you're holding me with. It was reason. And so is medicine."

Freeboot's gaze turned appraising, as if to concede that Monks might be worth taking seriously, after all.

"What you see with Mandrake—it's all adding up to something in your mind, I can tell," Freeboot said. "I can think about it better if I know what it is."

Monks's many years of training had made him cautious about pronouncing a diagnosis until he was as certain as possible. But the normal rules were not operating here, and Freeboot seemed to be offering a glimmer of rationality. Monks decided not to waste the chance.

"Next time he urinates, collect it in a clean container and bring it to me," he said.

Freeboot looked surprised, even startled.

"What's that going to tell you?" he said warily.

"Maybe nothing," Monks said. "Maybe a lot."

Freeboot barked, "Marguerite!" She appeared quickly in the doorway of Mandrake's room.

"Get the kid to pee in a cup and bring it here," Freeboot commanded.

She looked surprised, too, but went back into the room without a question.

"You must be ready for some chow," Freeboot said to Monks. "How about a drink first? Vodka, right?"

"No, thanks."

Freeboot's eyes flared again with quick anger.

"You don't seem to understand, man," he said. "You're our guest."

He stalked to the rough wooden table and picked up a small bottle by the neck, upending it and taking a long swig. The liquor was clear but oily, with something thick and pinkish bobbing inside it. When he set it down, Monks glimpsed the label: Mezcal con Gusano Monte Alban. It was mescal, the real thing, and the "something" was an agave worm.

He also noticed that the fingertips of Freeboot's hands were scarred into thick lumps of callus—maybe a childhood injury from touching something hot.

A quick series of beeps sounded across the room. Monks realized that they came from the belt radio that Hammerhead wore. They seemed to have a cadence, like a code.

Hammerhead pulled the radio free and spoke into it. "Brother, this is Site Three. Over."

A man's voice spoke, backed by faint static. "Brother this is Captain America, requesting permission to enter. Over."

Hammerhead hesitated, his gaze flicking toward the bedroom, where Marguerite was still with Mandrake.

"What's your position, Captain America?" Hammerhead barked. "Over."

"I'm right outside, man." Even with the static, Captain America sounded annoyed.

Hammerhead looked questioningly at Taxman. Taxman nodded.

With obvious reluctance, Hammerhead said, "Permission granted."

The lodge door opened. Another man stepped inside. He was about thirty, tall and good-looking, with wavy blond hair and an air of assurance. He carried an AK-47 or similar-type assault rifle with a large night-vision scope.

He stepped to attention, facing Taxman, and raised the rifle to port arms, extending it forward as if he were offering it.

"Take this, brother, may it serve you well," he intoned. "Security was turned over to command of Sidewinder at oh-one-hundred hours."

Taxman acknowledged this, with a slight lifting of his chin.

Captain America relaxed, slinging the rifle over his shoulder, muzzle down, and glancing at Monks incuriously.

"So, Marguerite's back?" he asked, looking around.

"We put in a long day, man," Hammerhead said immediately, with a trace of belligerence. "She needs to rest."

Freeboot swung toward Hammerhead with the riveting gaze that Monks was starting to think of as "the stare."

"You don't talk like that to a made *maquis*, HH," Freeboot said. His tone was harsh with warning.

"*I'm* the one who was on the mission with her," Hammerhead said sullenly, but his eyes shifted away.

"You're a fucking grunt. You don't touch the brides. Maybe you'll make *maquis* someday, and maybe you won't."

Then Taxman said, "You seem to be developing a little attitude problem, HH. Guess we'll have to work on that."

Under the hard stares of both men, Hammerhead deflated into fidgeting. Captain America watched, with the air of a seasoned gunfighter irritated by an upstart punk.

"Marguerite needs to help out here another couple of minutes," Freeboot told him. "She'll be ready after that."

Captain America sauntered to the table and twisted the top off a bottle of Red Hook ale.

Monks glimpsed his fingertips. They were thick with callus, like Freeboot's.

Monks scanned the other men's hands covertly. They were the same.

That could not be accidental.

The fingerprints had been deliberately obliterated, by burning, cutting, or chemicals.

The blanket in the bedroom doorway shifted aside and Marguerite came out, holding a chipped white enamel mug. The room became still again as she carried it to Monks. He took it from her and knelt beside a lantern so that he could get a good look. The urine was pale yellow and had the same unpleasant fruity smell as the child's breath.

But with no technological means to measure the blood sugar, there was only one way, the way the old-timers had done it. He dipped his index finger into the cup, then put the finger in his mouth. He waited until the taste was gone, then did it a second time.

There was no doubt. Along with the sour taste of the urine itself, there was a cloying sweetness. It was saturated with sugar.

Monks got to his feet. All attention was focused on him.

"Diabetes mellitus," Monks said. "Judging from the other symptoms, it's very advanced. If it's not treated, it will kill him. Soon."

Freeboot erupted from his tense, staring pose in a convulsive jerk, his hands rising from his sides as if he was ready to fight.

"How the fuck can you tell that?" His voice shook with rage that seemed far out of proportion.

"It's sweet," Monks said. "His blood sugar's out of control. Go ahead, taste it. Then taste your own. You'll tell the difference." He offered Freeboot the cup.

Freeboot strode to him and yanked it away, hoisting it to his mouth as if he was going to down the urine in a single gulp. But the cup hovered at his lips, untasted, for several seconds.

Then Freeboot spun away and slung it into the fireplace. The cup clanged against the stones, the urine spraying into the flames.

"There is *nothing. Wrong.* With *my son*!" he roared.

His back remained turned to the room, and Monks had the queasy sense of having offended a primitive, egomaniacal tribal ruler, who next would whirl back and order the death of the messenger bearing bad news.

But when Freeboot turned around again, his face had become an almost mimelike mask of calmness.

"Diabetes," he said. "There's a medicine for that, right?"

"Insulin."

"All right, we'll get some, and you give it to him."

"Whoa, wait," Monks said. "First off, it's a very complicated procedure. You need a precise way to determine dosages and measure blood sugar. Second, a few shots of insulin are not going to make that kid well. He needs major treatment on several levels, and follow-up treatment for the rest of his life."

"I'm talking about right now. We get him feeling better, who knows? That which doesn't kill us makes us stronger."

Monks's outrage leaped again at the thought that a life-threatening illness might make a four-year-old child stronger.

"It *is* going to kill him!" he finally exploded. "What the hell's the matter with you?" He stepped closer to Freeboot, holding his gaze, trying to make contact with the father who had to be in there somewhere.

Freeboot seemed unperturbed. "Let me think it over."

"There's nothing to think over," Monks said. "He needs to get to a hospital, now."

"Why should I believe you?"

"What would I have to gain by lying?"

"Maybe you're trying to fuck with our heads."

"Oh, for Christ's sake." Monks turned away in disgust.

"So, we'll just try some of that insulin for a few days," Freeboot said. "If it helps, maybe I'll start listening to you."

He turned his gaze on the others, imperious now, and spoke with the clipped efficiency of having made a decision.

"Taxman, Shrinkwrap, we've got to talk. You"— he pointed at Captain America—"take your bride. Hammerhead, you stay here."

Marguerite flashed a bruised glance at Freeboot, then stepped out into the night. Captain America followed, closing the door behind them.

Hammerhead watched them with flat, unblinking eyes.

Freeboot swung to face Monks. "You go on back with Mandrake."

There was no point in arguing further. Monks did as he was told.

When he stepped into the bedroom, Motherlode was sitting on the edge of Mandrake's bed, petting him and whispering to him—finally acting like a mother, if a stoned and disheveled one. She was wearing a rumpled flannel nightgown, her breasts loose and sagging beneath it.

"Is he going to get better?" she asked Monks.

"If we get him proper treatment, he will," Monks said, making another bid for an ally.

"That's why I wanted a doctor."

That's not enough, Monks was about to say, but it was another pointless argument. Whether Freeboot had ground her down to this state or she had found her own way to it, there was no help here. On the one hand, it was hard to feel sympathy for a mother who could fall into a self-induced stupor beside her sick child. On the other, Monks pitied anyone that desperate. She seemed bewildered, more than anything—incapable of dealing with this crisis.

She stood up, opened a dresser drawer, and took out a bottle of Percocets.

"Will you take care of him now?" she asked.

Monks looked at the fearful, uncomprehending little boy, in the hands of his addict mother and berserk father.

"I'll do what I can," he said.

She murmured thanks, and with a suddenly furtive air—clutching the pills, avoiding Monks's gaze, and not looking back at Mandrake—she edged out of the room.

A moment later, the blanket in the doorway shifted aside, and Hammerhead came in. He dropped something on the floor that clanked when it hit.

Monks realized, with numb amazement, that it was a pair of handcuffs.

"Put them on," Hammerhead said.

"You can't be serious."

"You seem to have a little attitude problem. We're going to have to work on that."

Monks stared at him, looking for some sign of sarcasm—the recognition that he was parroting Taxman's words about himself, from just a few minutes earlier. But his face showed nothing except barely controlled anger. It hit Monks that this was really about Marguerite, whom he clearly was sweet on, walking off with the handsome Captain America. He was shifting the blame, projecting his rage onto a safe target. It was akin to Glenn's claim that Monks had this coming because he "owes me bigtime," and Freeboot's blaming Monks for his own maltreatment, because he couldn't be trusted.

This was a trait that Monks associated with children and with psychopaths, and a memory flashed through his mind of a court defense that he had once heard from a bank robber who had gunned down a young female teller: her death was her own fault, because she had pressed the alarm button.

"Do you have any idea of the consequences of kidnaping me?" Monks said. "In the eyes of the real world? You're looking at prison."

Hammerhead raised his shotgun a few inches and pressed the muzzle against Monks's knee.

"There's no need for that," Monks said. "I know I'm outgunned."

"Coil says you got a reputation for causing trouble. Don't try it with me."

"Okay," Monks said. "I won't try it with you."

Four

Freeboot ran like a wildman, pounding barefoot over the camp's familiar paths, then out into the forest and onto the deer trails that he knew just as well. He was hot with rage.

Monks had made a fool of him. He had *lost* it, in front of everyone.

He just couldn't get past the fear that drinking that piss would infect him with the weakness it carried.

After half a mile the trail took a sudden rise up a steep rocky crag. Freeboot drove himself to the top, leaping from foothold to foothold like a mountain goat, his hard, horny feet gripping the rocks surely and silently. Finally he slowed to a walk, circling the crag's summit with hands on hips. He was breathing hard, but not winded. His legs ached with the strain, but he was ready for more.

He took the Copenhagen can from his shirt pocket and dipped his knifepoint into the powdered crank. He blasted three sharp hits into each nostril, a dose that would have left a normal man crawling around on the ground, screaming. As the drug filled him, he stood and opened his arms wide to the night sky, feeling like he could leap up into it and fly to the fucking moon. Most nights, he spent several hours out here in the woods, prowling his turf. In clear weather he could see almost to the Pacific, across the swaying treetops of the redwood forest that rose and fell down the mountain slopes like the waves of a deep green sea. The nearest paved road was fifteen miles away, the first tiny town was three miles farther, and tonight, even the few dim lights of the camp were lost in the blanketing mist.

Everything that he was going to do—that only he *could* do—was lying there at his feet, waiting.

All right. He was feeling better now. Monks had won that round. You had to respect the motherfucker.

But it was just starting.

Freeboot shook an unfiltered Camel cigarette from a pack and lit it. An occasional smoke would not hurt a man if he flushed his lungs rigorously with clean air every day.

He took a different path back down the crag and toward camp, moving with a stride that was almost a lope, but stealthy enough not to alarm the herd of deer that bedded down nearby.

He paused at one of the hidden seismic geophones that were buried around the camp's perimeter. His favorite night game was to trip a sensor to alert a sentry, lure him into a snare, then disarm him and leave him tied to a tree for the others to find. The way he was feeling tonight, he would have hung the man upside down and thrashed him with a fir branch.

But there was business to take care of. Freeboot loped on to the bunker, a shaft cut into the rocky earth by coolie labor back in gold-rush days when this place had been a mining camp. The entrance was hidden by a shed with a false floor. He bolted shut the shed door from the inside, yanked up the wooden hatch, and dropped down the ladder into the hollowed out antechamber. The bunker was secure and soundproof, outfitted for comfort, with chairs, cots, and a propane heater that vented through a hidden flue. There were battery-operated electric lights and laptop computers, with a gas-powered generator to recharge them. The catacombs of mining tunnels that branched out held stocks of food and water, along with weapons and other covert equipment.

Bunker-wise, Hitler had nothing on Freeboot.

Taxman and Shrinkwrap were already inside, waiting. Freeboot walked directly to an IBM ThinkPad and slotted in a CD that had been delivered earlier that evening. The screen changed as the CD's contents came up.

"We've got some issues here, Freeboot," Shrinkwrap said. She was trying to sound cool, but her mouth trembled a little. He could read her emotions as clearly as he could hear the forest creatures moving through the night. She was angry, she was afraid, and, like always, she was edgy because she knew that only he possessed the *power.*

But he needed her, so he spoke lightly.

"Had to happen, Shrink," he said. "Motherlode was freaking about the kid. I could feel her getting ready to do something stupid. This will calm her down."

"You should take him someplace, man. Like I said."

That had been Shrinkwrap's idea when Mandrake started acting weird—to take him several hundred miles away to another state, and abandon him in front of a hospital. He was too young for anyone to identify, and he'd be taken care of.

"You still could," she said. "This is no place for a kid." She wasn't bad-looking, although thin as a bird, and she looked more feminine now, with a little pleading in her eyes.

Her anger was easy to deal with. This softness was not.

"Mandrake's got to get his shit together," Freeboot said uneasily. "Let it go, okay?" He pulled a bottle of the Monte Alban mescal from a shelf and drank from it, still watching the computer screen.

It was showing a news clipping from that day's *Atlanta Journal-Constitution*—a small item, the kind they stuck down at the bottom of a back page because it wasn't really news anymore.

CALAMITY JANE MURDERS STILL A MYSTERY

Atlanta—The murders of prominent businessman David Bodewell, his wife, and four employees last November 19—dubbed the "Calamity Jane murders" because Bodewell's collection of rare,

> *so-named* golf clubs was later found among the homeless in downtown Atlanta—is no closer to being solved.
>
> "There's not much to work with—no motive and no evidence," an anonymous source inside the police department has stated. "Whoever did it was either real lucky or real careful."
>
> Police are continuing to pursue the investigation aggressively. . . .

"No, it's not okay," Shrinkwrap said hotly. "There's a million fucking doctors out there. Why'd you have to pick Coil's dad?"

"Because Coil's dad won't take a chance on sending his kid to prison."

"When's he going to get that chance? Don't tell me you're going to let him *go.*"

"I want him to *think* I will. And you never know, he might come in handy down the line."

"What the fuck are you saying—'down the line'?"

"Some of the shit Coil's told me, Monks has got a crazy streak," Freeboot said, with a mocking edge. "Maybe he'll come around."

She stood up from her chair and stabbed toward his chest with a shaking finger.

"Quit fucking around, man. A dumbass trick like this could bring us down," she said.

Freeboot gave her a heavy-lidded, measuring look. Shrinkwrap was a psychologist and very smart, but her buttons were easy to push.

"Where's Coil?" he said.

"In our cabin," she said warily. She knew the gaze she was seeing.

"What's he doing?"

"Getting high, probably."

"I need him to find me some insulin."

"Hey, lighten up. He just got back from a mission."

"I'm trying to make him feel more like a *maquis*, Shrink. Let's face it, he's a mama's boy."

She flinched. She was more than fifteen years older than Glenn Monks—the latest in a long series of the bad boys she craved.

"What are you going to do, B&E a drugstore?" she said sullenly. "There's no place within a hundred miles of here open this time of night."

"Don't you think maybe I know that?" Freeboot swigged from the mescal bottle again, still watching her.

She lowered her gaze, defeated.

"Have him hack the local pharmacy records and find somebody around here who buys that stuff," Freeboot told her. "Old people, or a woman living alone. Then call down to Base and tell Callus to go get it. Mask and gun, scare the shit out of them. Take everything they got, needles, the works. Give them a couple hundred bucks and tell them if they keep quiet, he won't be back. They call the sheriffs, he will. And I want everybody moving with the fucking speed of light, starting *now*."

Freeboot watched her thin blue-jeaned ass hurry up the ladder. He drank again from the bottle, a long burning pull, then leaned over the computer's keyboard and brought up a master file.

"Where you think Hammerhead's at?" he asked Taxman. Hammerhead wasn't hell for brains, but he was fierce and loyal.

"He did okay tonight," Taxman said.

"I've been working him up, about Marguerite and Captain America."

"He's right on the edge, for sure."

"You want him in on this next one?"

"Let's have a scalp hunt tomorrow night, give him a chance to get savage," Taxman said. "If he makes it, I'll take him along."

He spoke with his usual quiet drawl. Somebody who didn't know better might mistake it for timidness. Taxman was ex–Special Forces, who'd left the army in disgust after the Gulf War because there wasn't enough close-range killing. Now he got his fill of it, leading the almost thirty *maquis* that he had trained so far. The most experienced ones were out there in the world, unknown to anyone but each other—drifting, quietly stirring up anger in homeless camps and ghettos, and waiting to be summoned for their next mission.

Freeboot turned back to the computer screen and scrolled. A collage of newspaper headlines appeared, dated several weeks apart over the past months.

SEDONIA STUNNED BY KILLINGS

GROSSE POINTE POLICE TIGHTLIPPED

DOUBLE MURDER IN DARIEN

There were eleven sub-files from the past two years, made up of clippings about the killing of rich citizens in different parts of the country. The outrage tended to start as long front-page reports, only to shrink and disappear as police admitted their frustration.

The "Calamity Jane" file was the latest one. Freeboot transferred the clipping from the disc to the master folder. He had an online search done daily for news about any of the murders, and he read it all carefully. It was important to stay on top of developments.

"I think it's time for us to let The Man know what he's dealing with," Freeboot said. There hadn't been any reason for police to link the killings yet, at least officially. The *maquis* had played it safe at first, choosing low-security targets while they perfected their operations.

Taxman nodded. "Let's jack it up a notch." He knew a lot of ways to get under people's skins. Dumping the golf clubs at the homeless camp had been his idea.

"What you got in mind?"

"Pull up Emlinger on the screen."

Freeboot scrolled farther down the master file, to an alphabetical list of names. There were several hundred of them, mostly men but a few women. Each name was followed by a short description.

He paused at an entry that began:

Emlinger, Robert James, b 1951.
Res 1155 Laurel Lane, Atherton, CA.

Pres/CEO of several companies since 1985. Restructuring/outsourcing specialist w history of diverting assets to execs in bankruptcies/laying off employees wo benefits.

Atherton was a several-hour drive south of here. The FBI knew that serial killers tended to start close to home, then branch out geographically. Freeboot had been careful to do it the other way around.

He double-clicked on Emlinger's name, bringing up a longer file. It included photographs of Emlinger and his family; a plan of their spacious house and grounds, including the security system; city and area maps; and a detailed analysis of their personal habits and daily routines. Emlinger looked like a generic corporate executive, with gold-rimmed glasses and perfect teeth, brimming with confidence in his own net worth. Mrs. Emlinger was a Stepford-type trophy wife, almost twenty years younger than her husband, and very good-looking.

"She's got a thing about jade jewelry, antique Chinese stuff," Taxman said, tapping her photo with his finger. "He bought her a collection of it for a wedding present—used to belong to the Princess of Monaco, or some such shit. If *that* ends up in a Dumpster, they're gonna read the mail."

He stepped to a dinner plate where several lines of white powdered meth were laid out. The tiny crystals glittered like broken glass.

Freeboot took a closer look at the computer photo of Mrs. Emlinger. She was a green-eyed blonde. No doubt jade looked good on her.

"I like the way you think, young man," Freeboot said. "You got a future with this company."

"I'm going to name you Circe, baby," Freeboot told the girl who had been in the sauna with him earlier. They were naked, lying face to face, in the afterglow of energetic sex. "You know who she was?"

She shook her head shyly. Her eyes were big liquid pools of adoration, pupils dilated from the finger hash that came from picking sinsemilla buds.

"A witch. She turned dudes into animals. And you turn me into a wild beast. A *swine*."

He lunged face first into her breasts, growling and nuzzling her with his bristly beard. She squirmed, cooing with delight like a child.

They were in the structure that Freeboot had named the Garden. From the outside, it was a log building, like all the others here—a crude bathhouse, with a big stone basin for the hot springs that flowed from the ground at a perfect 112 degrees. But inside, he had transformed it, stocking it with things that he hadn't even known existed until he was able to buy them. Then he learned about them fast.

The rough log walls were hung with old tapestries from Europe. Thick Persian rugs carpeted the plank floor. A two-thousand-year-old Greek statuette sat on top of a Chippendale console. The central piece was the Louis XV king-sized bed that Freeboot and Circe were lying on. Part of a wall had to be chainsawed out to get that in. The moisture and warmth from the hot springs maintained a jungle of exotic potted plants. There was every kind of liquor and every kind of dope. Freeboot wanted the feeling in here to be overpowering—*lush*. But above all, the Garden was for sex. The brides were a reward for the *maquis* who performed their missions well, and a tormenting lure to recruits.

It was Freeboot's own version of the garden of delights of the Old Man of the Mountain, chief of the original assassins. That old dude was slick. He had drugged young men with hashish and brought them into a place that had every delight they could imagine—women, wine, more drugs. He promised them that if they died for him, this would be their heaven for eternity.

The world had changed since those days. Not many people were going to settle for pie-in-the-sky anymore. But the basics still worked. Freeboot, and Shrinkwrap with her psychological savvy, carefully handpicked the young people they drew in. All of them were aimless and hungry. The men wanted power; the women, love;

and they all wanted to feel superior. It was perfect raw material for shaping into devotion, and the two of them knew just how to do it—break down the personality, then rebuild it with increasing status and privileges as they got more bonded, until finally they believed that they were godlike—while totally obedient to Freeboot. During the process, Taxman trained the men up into skilled assassins. The women didn't need much physical training. Most of what was required of them came naturally.

"Now, we're going to do with our souls what we just did with our bodies," he murmured to Circe. He played gently with the damp strands of hair that curled down her neck, stroking her hypnotically, coaxing her to relax against him. "I want you to open up like you never have before. Make yourself bare, and let me in."

"I don't know how." Her voice was muffled, a little frightened.

"I'll show you. Just don't fight me."

Freeboot had learned a long time ago, using LSD, that he could separate a part of his mind from the rest—like a tentacle, like a snake—and send it into other minds. The younger and more stoned they were, the easier it was. It was like opening the door to somebody's living room and seeing them sitting on the couch watching TV, so wrapped up in it, they'd forgotten where they were. There were several screens, broadcasting the different channels of thoughts, memories, feelings, everything that went on in their heads.

Feelings were the most important. They were what ruled. Freeboot could *see* them, beaming out from that TV set—fear, hate, love, doubt, all the pressures that built up in people's lives, mixing together to push them into what they did and said.

And he knew how to push those feelings. He didn't know *how* he knew, he just did. He shone his energy, his power, on the ones he wanted—love for the women, aggression for the men, jacking up fear in a *maquis* who was getting cocky or devotion in a bride who was restless.

When he went back out that door and closed it again, they didn't know what had happened, didn't even know that he'd been in there.

But that energy he pumped in was *him.* As those feelings got stronger, Freeboot was the hidden essence of them, like oxygen in air. Every breath they took contained him.

When he finished with Circe, she was trembling a little.

"That was good," he said. "You're going to be a sweet bride. But one thing you got to understand—some of the other girls are going to be jealous of you. You have to keep yourself above that."

"Okay," she breathed.

"Good girl." He petted her once more, then stood. "I've got to step out a while. Go ahead and toke up some more of that hash. I'll be back."

He pulled on his jeans, then took a money clip from his pocket and laid five one-hundred-dollar bills beside her on the bed.

"When you get back to town, buy yourself something pretty," he said. Devotion might be a matter of the spirit, but it rolled more smoothly on wheels well greased with things that could be touched.

Circe got up, too, and slid luxuriantly into the stone bath. Lying back, with the clear water rippling over her young body, she was a luscious sight.

"Freeboot?" she said. Her face was childlike with seriousness. "Can you make me stop dreaming about flunking out of high school?"

He grinned. "Don't worry, baby. Pretty soon you won't even remember it."

Five

Monks's shackles were locked around his ankles, with an eighteen-inch chain connecting them, like a slave would have worn. The chain was locked again to a cable bolted to the floor, giving him just enough slack to move around the room. He'd had to take off his boots to put them on. They weren't tight enough to hurt, but they weighed. He wondered where you would find something like that these days. A specialty shop. Or maybe on e-Bay.

There was no window he could see out of to watch the sky, no way to tell the time, but he guessed that it was around three A.M. by now. He and Mandrake had been alone for the past couple of hours. He had thought about trying to escape, but the shackles cut off any hope, and it was clear that the camp was being guarded. Ludicrous as this bunch might seem—adopting the term *maquis*, for Christ's sake, the sterling French resistance fighters of World War Two—they were at least organized. Captain America had been on duty, then had been relieved by someone called Sidewinder, announcing this in a ritualistic fashion: *Take this, brother, may it serve you well.* Whatever that meant.

Monks sat again on Mandrake's bed with a cup of water, as he'd been doing every half hour or so. The bed's other occupant was the only stuffed animal that the little boy seemed to have, a fat, four-foot-long lime-green snake with a happy grin. The small pile of books on the dresser had a few old children's standards—Hans Christian Andersen's fairy tales, Dr. Seuss—but was mainly made up of more modern works, like copies of *Heavy Metal* magazine and *Angry Blonde*, the rap lyrics of Eminem.

Monks cupped the back of Mandrake's neck with one hand, then poured a slow trickle of water into his mouth.

"Come on, buddy," Monks said. "You need this. Attaboy." Mandrake sputtered, but swallowed. Monks kept the water coming until his head twisted aside.

"This must be a pretty neat place to live, huh?" Monks said. "Up here in the forest? I bet there's deer that come around." His hands drifted gently over Mandrake's body as he spoke, absorbing information about his condition. The boy's eyes had opened a little while he was drinking the water, but then closed again.

"You know, what those deer really like is bread," Monks said. "That's a good way to make friends with them. You want to try feeding them tomorrow?"

No response. Monks reached under the covers and felt the diaper. It was wet. There was a box of Huggies beside the bed, another bizarre touch in this rustic scene. He pulled off the wet one, tossed it into a slops bucket, and got two fresh ones, using one to dry Mandrake and putting the other on him. It took Monks a moment to figure out the self-adhesive strapping arrangement. Back in the days when his own kids were in diapers, his wife had mostly used the washable kind.

His mouth twisted. He had been trying not to think about Glenn.

He covered Mandrake up and walked across the room to a crude wooden chair. The cable dragged behind him on the floor.

Monks had been dredging up everything that he could find in his memory about diabetes. It was a condition he encountered frequently in the ER, but usually as a complication or a contributing factor to the presenting ailment. He had diagnosed it enough times in children to recognize it tonight. And he seen plenty of people come into the ER deathly ill from it—usually because they hadn't taken their insulin, or had ignored dietary rules. He knew that it was easy for diabetics to get very sick very fast, and much harder for them to pull back out.

But extended treatment of diabetes lay in the realm of specialists—internists, endocrinologists, and pediatricians. Even under ideal conditions, in a hospital setting, he wouldn't have considered himself qualified, let alone in a situation like this. And without the all-important lab workups to measure blood sugar and electrolytes, he felt as helpless as a soldier going naked into battle.

He was sure that he was looking at juvenile-onset diabetes, technically known as "Type 1," or "insulin-dependent" diabetes mellitus—usually called IDDM. Patients who did not get insulin died.

And there were other complications. Mandrake's dehydration was advanced. He was drinking as much water as he could, but the sugar in his urine was carrying out even more than he could take in. Soon he wouldn't be able to drink enough to keep up. That would bring on a coma and, eventually, death.

He was also losing potassium, which had its own spectrum of ugly side effects, including paralysis and respiratory failure. That, too, could be fatal.

Then there was a rarer nightmare, but perhaps the worst of all, and one seen most often in kids—cerebral edema. The brain swelled, compressing the brain stem, and causing death within a few hours. It was treatable if caught in time, but that required sophisticated equipment.

Monks had no accurate way to measure how close Mandrake was to a crisis, either. But his gut told him that even if he had insulin, even if he could deal with all those factors and stabilize the boy's condition, it would only be for a matter of days. And something as simple as a cold or an infection could quickly destroy the precarious balance.

He was staring at Mandrake in the room's dim light when he heard the lodge's door open, then footsteps cross the main room. The old wooden floor telegraphed the sounds, a series of creaks and hollow thumps.

Monks moved quietly to the bedroom doorway and peered through the hanging blanket. The newcomer was Marguerite, apparently done with Captain America. She was kneeling at the fireplace, setting a metal cook pan on the glowing coals.

She stood, shoved her hands into the back pockets of her jeans, and paced, her head bowed as if in concentration. After half a minute, she went to the table and poured a glass of wine. She drank it down in a few fierce swallows, then poured another.

It seemed that she was troubled.

Monks went back to his chair. A few minutes later, he heard her footsteps approach the bedroom. She stepped into the doorway, carrying a tray with a covered plate and a mug. But she did not come in. It occurred to Monks that she was staying beyond the radius of his fetter, as if he were a vicious dog.

"I warmed you up some food," she said.

He hadn't eaten since lunch, and the savory smell of roasted meat started his belly growling. But he was not yet ready to succumb. It added to the mean edge he was harboring toward his captors.

"You don't feel strange about serving dinner to somebody who's chained to the floor?" he said.

"Look, this wasn't my idea." She kept her head half turned away, as if to hide behind the long hair that covered the side of her face.

"That's what the Nazi camp guards claimed after World War Two. Watch a movie called *Night and Fog* sometime."

"You don't understand, man," she said, dropping back into the defensive mode that he had seen earlier.

"I'm afraid I don't."

"Freeboot's not like other people."

"I understand *that.*"

"I mean—he doesn't go by the same rules."

Monks thought about pointing out that people who made up their own rules tended to be called "felons," but he decided to back off—not out of compassion, but in the hopes that he might be able to win her confidence and use it to his advantage.

"You're the only one here who seems to give a damn about him," he said, nodding toward Mandrake.

"It's not that they don't care. It's just that everybody's . . . wrapped up in other stuff."

"So I've gathered," Monks said.

Monks got the water cup and sat on the bed, coaxing Mandrake to drink. Marguerite hesitated a little longer, then walked in and set the tray on the table.

"If you want to crash, I can take over that," she said.

"I'm all right for now."

She went to the doorway, but lingered, one hand resting against the jamb.

"I couldn't believe what you did back there," she said. "Tasting pee."

"Practicing medicine's not always pretty."

"It freaked Freeboot out totally," she said. "It was like you read his mind. He's terrified of diabetes. He had an uncle who went blind. The doctors didn't help *him* any."

Monks registered the information. That probably figured into why Freeboot had reacted so strongly.

"Sometimes there's nothing that can be done," Monks said.

It took him another minute to get an adequate amount of water into the little boy. Marguerite was quiet, and he thought she had gone, but when he stood up, she was outside the doorway, watching. She beckoned to him with a timid wave.

"Could that happen to Mandrake?" she asked quietly. "Going blind?"

"I wouldn't worry about it," Monks said. "Unless he gets to a hospital, he's not going to live anywhere near that long."

Twenty minutes later, the blanket was pulled roughly aside again. Monks was surprised—he hadn't heard footsteps approach this time. Freeboot strode into the room with a small duffel bag full of stuff, which he dumped on the table. He was still barefoot.

"Here's your insulin," he said triumphantly.

Monks was surprised by this, too. After the couple of hours of driving on back roads, he had assumed that the nearest town big enough for an all-night pharmacy would be a long round trip.

He got up from his chair to look. There were two bottles of insulin, both manufactured by Eli Lilly. One was Humulin RU-100—regular insulin, 100-units-per-milliliter strength. The other was longer-acting Humulin NPH. There were also a handheld glucose meter and strips for measuring blood sugar, disposable lancets for drawing the blood drops—and packets of Monoject 1-cc syringes, available only by prescription.

The explanation came clear fast. The plastic caps that sealed fresh insulin bottles were missing. The bottles and packets all had been opened and were partially empty.

"You got this from a diabetic patient?" Monks said.

"Somebody we know. Don't sweat, we paid for it."

"I'm not worried about that. This medicine is that person's lifeline. They need it."

"*We* need it, man. She can get more."

Monks hesitated: push had come to shove. Now was the last moment when he could simply refuse to cooperate. It might call Freeboot's bluff—force him to take Mandrake in for treatment.

If not, Mandrake was as good as dead.

Reluctantly, Monks hefted the two bottles, one in each hand, as if that could help him gauge the dosage. In the ER, when someone came in critically ill with IDDM, the insulin was administered intravenously, with the blood sugar constantly monitored. There was always the grave danger of the insulin driving the sugar level *too* low, which could bring on hypoglycemia, convulsions, and brain damage.

He knew the appropriate dosages and procedures for those situations, and in the ER he carried a personal digital assistant for calculations and information that wasn't at his fingertips. But here, it was going to be a very dicey affair.

Freeboot was watching him intently. "You got a problem?"

"This isn't straightforward, like an antibiotic," Monks said. "There's a lot of factors involved. How about finding me some rubbing alcohol."

Freeboot's eyes narrowed, and Monks realized again that even such a mild demand was an affront to that huge ego. But he had plenty to worry about without having to pussyfoot around.

"We don't keep anything like that around here," Freeboot said.

"Vodka, then."

Freeboot stalked to the door. "Marguerite!" he barked into the other room. "Bring me a bottle of vodka."

Monks went through the flow chart in his head once more. An adult patient would typically take both kinds of insulin together, morning and evening—perhaps ten units of the regular, to help metabolize meals, and twenty units of the NPH long-term, for general stabilization. But the NPH was of no use to someone in crisis, and ten units of the RU-100 would be way too much. Mandrake weighed no more than fifty pounds, and, sick as he was, the risk of overlowering his blood sugar outweighed the possible benefit of a high dose.

Monks decided on three units, injected subcutaneously rather than intravenously. If there was no adverse response, he would repeat it in two hours, then start lengthening the interval.

The vodka arrived, handed silently through the doorway by Marguerite. The smell of marijuana smoke wafted in with her. The vodka was Stolichnaya. Apparently Freeboot wasn't roughing it when it came to liquor.

Monks didn't bother to ask for cotton swabs. He wadded up a few tissues, soaked them with vodka, then sat on the bed again. Mandrake still seemed to be asleep, and didn't stir when Monks pricked his finger with a lancet.

Monks squeezed a drop of blood onto one of the strips and fed it into the meter. The LED readout showed 326 milligrams per deciliter—severe to dangerous. Normal was 80 to 120.

Mandrake's eyes fluttered as Monks eased him onto his back.

Monks rubbed his shoulders and started talking, trying to soothe him.

"What about fishing?" Monks said. "You ever go fishing? I bet there's some monster trout up in these streams."

Mandrake's eyes drifted shut. His diaper was wet again. Monks unfastened it, then peeled the wrapper off one of the pre-calibrated syringes and drew three units of the RU-100 into it.

"Maybe *that's* what we ought to do tomorrow," he said, swabbing Mandrake's abdomen with fresh vodka-soaked tissues. "We'll dig up some big fat worms and catch a trout for your mom to cook. How's that?"

He pinched up a roll of unresisting flesh and made a quick stab with the needle, slowly depressing the plunger as he kept talking. The shot was subcutaneous, not penetrating into muscle, but still a sting. Mandrake did not react at all.

Monks withdrew the needle and swabbed the spot again, then eased the diaper free. He tossed it in the bucket and got a couple of fresh ones.

"I'm starting to take you seriously," Freeboot said, watching him dry the little boy.

"That warms my heart," Monks said curtly.

This time Freeboot didn't seem offended. He leaned back against a wall and took a flat round can from his pocket—Copenhagen chewing tobacco, Monks observed, the kind favored by cowboys. But instead of taking a chew, Freeboot dipped in the point of his knife, and brought it out mounded with white powder. He inhaled it with a quick, harsh snorting sound.

He dipped the knife in again and offered it to Monks.

"Biker crank," Freeboot said. "Keep you going."

Monks shook his head.

"You a law-and-order guy?"

"If I was judgmental about what I saw in the ER, I'd have shot myself in the head a long time ago," Monks said.

Freeboot lifted the knife to his nose and inhaled again, then wiped the back of his hand under his nostrils and put the can away.

"I've got a couple of questions," he said.

"I'm not much for polite conversation when I'm chained up."

Freeboot ignored this barb, too. "About what's going on with the kid. I want you to help me believe you, man."

Monks reminded himself that stubbornness wasn't going to do either Mandrake or him any good.

"I'll tell you what I can," he said.

"It gets passed on by bad genes, right? The diabetes?"

"My understanding is that there's some genetic predisposition, but it's not cut and dried. Diabetic parents can have nondiabetic kids, and vice versa."

"But it isn't something you catch, like AIDS or hepatitis?"

Monks noted that Freeboot had chosen as examples two diseases that were prevalent in prisons. Like his tattoos, it suggested a familiarity with that milieu.

"No," Monks said, "it's genetic, but so are thousands of other things that might or might not ever show up. Something triggers them, and there are probably thousands of triggers, too."

"Say, the parents don't have it, but the kid does. Is there any way to tell if one of the parents passed it on?"

Monks paused in his diapering and glanced at Freeboot, remembering what Marguerite had said about Freeboot's diabetic—and ultimately blind—uncle.

"I don't know what the state of the art is," Monks said. "That's not my field. But I'd definitely suggest talking to a specialist if you're planning to have more kids."

He realized that he was speaking as if this was a normal consultation with a concerned parent. Enough was enough.

"I need my wristwatch back," Monks said. "Timing's going to be critical from here."

Freeboot shook a cigarette from a pack—an unfiltered Camel, an odd choice for a man who so obviously kept himself in superb physical condition—and then took out matches, but didn't light up.

"What do you think you're seeing here?" Freeboot said. "A bunch of batshit bush hippies, right?"

"I've already told you," Monks said impatiently. "I see a little boy who's badly in need of help. The rest, I don't care about."

"How many people you think are ever born who leave a real mark on history?"

"What the hell has that got to do with it?"

"You think *you* will?"

The question was so absurd, Monks was almost amused. "My tombstone's going to read: 'Occupant.' "

The nuance did not seem to register on Freeboot. He pointed at Monks with his first two fingers, the cigarette held between them.

"To be that kind of leader, you got to have *virtu.* It's something you're either born with or you're not. Like diabetes."

Monks blinked. He didn't know much about Machiavelli, but he recognized the term *virtu.* It wasn't "virtue" in its usual sense; rather, it was the power to govern effectively, requiring a combination of cunning and ruthlessness.

"What I'm saying is, if you got it, you get yourself through the hard shit," Freeboot said. "If you don't . . ."

Monks waited, expecting some platitudinous followup, like: *the hard shit's gonna get you.*

But Freeboot merely shrugged. Then he pushed off the wall with his shoulder and padded out into the main room.

Monks wasn't quite sure what that exchange had been about. But he knew he been told that he wasn't as smart as he thought.

"Go find Taxman and get Monks's watch," he heard Freeboot say to Marguerite. "Then stay here and help him."

"So you can get back to training?" she retorted, with a biting tone that was clear even though it came from the other end of the lodge.

Monks moved quietly to the blanket and peered out. Freeboot

was advancing toward her with precise, noiseless footsteps, backing her into a corner. He did not touch her, but she wilted under his stare.

"I have had enough bullshit tonight," Freeboot said. His voice was low with menace. "Don't *you* fucking start in."

She edged away sideways, her back still pressed against the wall, then turned and hurried out.

A few minutes later, Monks heard Marguerite's quiet footsteps approach again. She handed him his watch, eyes averted.

"I'll be in the next room, if you need anything," she said.

"Find me something with sugar in it. Orange juice is okay, Gatorade's better. Plain sugar mixed with water will do if you don't have anything else." If Mandrake's blood sugar level started dropping dangerously, that could help bring it back up. "And you could stoke the fire. Try to keep it constant. I don't want him going back and forth from hot to cold."

She nodded, eyes still down, and left.

When Monks put the watch on his wrist, he saw that the compass had been pried off the strap.

Two hours after giving Mandrake the shot, Monks got a fresh lancet and strip and sat next to him again. The insulin should be peaking by now. Mandrake seemed slightly more alert, his eyes half open, although still dull and gummy with apathy.

"This might sting just a little, buddy," Monks said. "It won't be bad, I promise."

This time the meter read 285. This was what he had hoped for—gradually bringing the blood sugar down, but not to a dangerously low point.

Things had been quiet in the next room for some time, with no more comings and goings. It had to be almost dawn.

Monks finally allowed himself to believe that Mandrake could survive an hour without attention, and admitted to the fatigue he had been holding off with growing difficulty. He was hungry, too. He decided, reluctantly, that it was time to give in.

He stored the insulin and syringes on a crude shelf, high up where Mandrake couldn't reach them. Out of long habit, he had developed caution to the point of compulsiveness.

Then he uncovered the plate of food that Marguerite had left earlier. There was a chunk of well-done roast beef and some boiled potatoes, cold by now but still looking good. The mug was full of red wine. The utensils were plastic, picnic-style. He ignored them, picking up chunks of the food with his fingers and cramming them into his mouth. He eyed the wine longingly, but decided he had better not drink it. He rinsed his hands and mouth, realizing that he was going to have to negotiate for items like a toothbrush, soap, and toilet privileges. Reluctantly, he urinated into the slops bucket. It was another thing there wasn't much choice about.

He programmed his wristwatch alarm to wake him up in fifty minutes, then took the pillows from Motherlode's empty bed, formed them into a bolster next to Mandrake, and stretched out beside the little boy. He stayed half sitting up so he wouldn't sleep too deeply, but finally let his eyes close.

The information he had absorbed so far played in his weary mind like flickering clips of tape on an old-time movie reel. His overwhelming sense was that he had landed in an Alice in Wonderland scenario of dreamlike madness—except that it was pervaded by very real violence, and the looming threat of a child's death. It was presided over by a macho speed freak who dominated his followers, made allusions to Machiavelli, and hinted at the grandiose importance that he would enjoy in the eyes of history, yet expressed a simpleton's distrust of medicine. His followers seemed to think they were on some TV show like *Survivor*, but they carried sophisticated weapons, and it looked like the men had deliberately mutilated their fingertips, presumably to avoid being identified.

On top of it all, Monks's son was deeply implicated, and if Monks ever *did* get out of here and blow the whistle, Glenn would be in serious trouble.

He worked to push it all aside and courted the half-sleep he had learned to count on over many years in the ER.

Mandrake was lying on his belly, the side of his face pressed into the pillow and his arms down close to his body, in the seal-like posture typical of sleeping children. Monks kept the back of one hand pressed lightly against him, so he would feel any restlessness that might signal an adverse reaction to the insulin. So far, Mandrake had hardly stirred, except when Monks roused him to drink. He seemed to have drifted into a semiconscious state, perhaps caught in diabetic torpor—or withdrawn into some inner hiding place, to escape from this incomprehensible nightmare.

But as Monks drifted off, he felt a little hand touch his, then creep into it, like a tiny frightened creature seeking safety.

Six

Monks awoke to the beeping of his wristwatch alarm. It read 3:00 P.M. He sat up, groggy and disoriented, uncertain of where he was. Then he remembered.

Mandrake's bedroom was dim and quiet, and the little boy was lying curled up with his stuffed snake on the other bed.

Monks had continued to monitor his condition through the early-morning hours, giving him water and broth, until Marguerite had come in, at about ten A.M. and offered again to take over. Mandrake's blood-sugar level had kept improving in the meantime, and so Monks had agreed. Rest was imperative in order to function with the clear-mindedness that the situation demanded. He had lain down on the room's other bed with a pillow over his head and slept deeply, a measure of his exhaustion.

Marguerite was not in the room now. He hoped that she had kept her promise to keep Mandrake drinking.

He became aware of a faint sound, a sibilant murmur that stopped and started. Then he realized that Mandrake was whispering to the toy snake. It was the first sign of anything like liveliness that Monks had seen in the boy. He hesitated, reluctant to interrupt. But the monitoring had to continue, and it was time for the next insulin shot.

"How you feeling, buddy?" Monks said, sitting beside him. Mandrake's eyes were open, but he didn't look up. "You getting hungry?"

To his surprise, Mandrake nodded solemnly.

"Good job," Monks said. "I'll get you something in just a minute. How about soup? That sound okay?"

Another nod.

Monks kept up a patter of talk as he went through the now familiar process of getting Mandrake to drink and checking his blood-sugar level. That had climbed a little, to 289, but that was okay—it was significantly lower than it had been to start with, but not dropping dangerously. As best as Monks could tell, the three-unit doses he had given were in the ball park. He decided to stay with them.

When he went to get a syringe, he realized with unpleasant surprise that there weren't as many left as he had thought. It had seemed that there were about twenty, but now he counted only fourteen.

Out of habit he pinched up a bit of Mandrake's flesh, in a different place this time. Insulin shots dissolved fatty tissue; if repeated, they could leave dimples. The absurdity of worrying about things cosmetic in this situation flashed across his mind.

"I'm sorry I have to sting you, Mandrake," he said. "But it's going to make you feel better, I promise." Mandrake squirmed a little in protest this time. The show of resistance pleased Monks perversely. Mandrake still hadn't cried at all for his mother. Monks had assumed at first that his lethargy was too deep, but maybe Marguerite had been filling that role. Or maybe Mandrake had already figured out, with the prescience that some children seemed to have, that he shouldn't expect much in the way of nurturing from Motherlode.

"Okay," Monks said, withdrawing the needle and swabbing the puncture with vodka. "Let's see about that soup."

He walked to the bedroom door, dragging the cable from his hobbled ankles, and looked into the main room. Someone was sitting in a chair beside the door. Monks recognized the bulky shape of Hammerhead. He had traded his shotgun for an assault rifle like Captain America's.

"Mandrake needs to eat," Monks said.

"I'll tell Marguerite." Then Hammerhead added stiffly, "My orders are to get you anything you want, as long as it's cool."

Monks decided not to get into what "cool" constituted just now.

"I'd like to see my son," he said.

"I'll pass that on."

"I could use some strong coffee. And I need to clean up. Soap, towel, toothbrush, all that."

Hammerhead took his radio from his belt and punched a series of beeps. He spoke into it with the clipped, quasi-military style that Monks had heard Hammerhead use last night.

"Brother, this is Hammerhead calling Marguerite, requesting immediate assistance at the lodge. Repeat, Marguerite to the lodge. Over."

A moment later, a woman's voice answered: "Marguerite copies. Over."

"The kid needs soup. And bring a toothbrush and that kind of shit. Over." He hooked the radio back on his belt, then walked to Monks.

"Lay down on your belly with your hands spread out," he said. Monks did. He felt a tugging at his ankles, then heard a click. "Okay, get up." Monks stood and realized that he was free of the cable. But the shackles around his ankles stayed on.

"I'll take you to the washhouse," Hammerhead said, gesturing with the rifle toward the lodge's door.

"Wait a minute. Can't I put my boots on?"

Hammerhead shook his head decisively. "Nobody gave me orders for that."

Monks hobbled outside in his socks like a convict on an old-time chain gang, Hammerhead and his rifle trailing just behind. It was the first time that he had been out of the lodge since arriving late last night—the first time he'd seen the camp in daylight. His impression of being in an earlier century was strengthened. The place consisted of a several-acre clearing with a dozen or so old log buildings and sheds, situated in a small canyon ringed with rocky crags. The vehicle that had brought him here was gone, and there were no others, nor any sign of electrical power. Steep slopes covered with fir and pine rose in all directions as far as he could see. The only man-made things in the entire vista besides the buildings were a few distant switchback logging roads that looked long disused. The single exit was a rutted dirt trail barely wide enough to drive on.

The afternoon was dark, a premature twilight, the sky heavy with blanketing clouds rolling in off the Pacific. The wind had risen and the air had a brisk, even wild, feel. Without doubt, a winter rain was going to roll in soon. Those tended to last for days, and in the mountains, they could readily turn to snow. The sun was invisible, but he guessed which way west lay from the wind, and his sense that the terrain in that direction was opening down toward the sea.

"Wait here," Hammerhead said.

Monks watched him walk to meet Marguerite, who was coming toward them with a folded towel in her hands. In the lonely dusk, with her long hair blowing in the wind, she looked like a tragic figure from an early romantic novel, a fallen woman moving toward some doomed assignation.

When Hammerhead got to her, she handed him the towel. They spoke briefly. The valence was unclear, but she turned her head aside and hurried on to the lodge.

Hammerhead came back and, in grim silence, marched Monks onward.

The washhouse looked like something at a national park campground, with separate men's and women's entrances marked by crudely carved wooden signs. Hammerhead gave Monks the towel and, to Monks's relief, let him go in alone.

The floor was concrete, with a drain in its center. There was a big porcelain laundry basin and a showerhead, both cold water only, and Monks was surprised to see a flush toilet. Presumably, the plumbing was fed by gravity flow from a spring or stream. An old Stihl calendar featuring two bare-breasted women holding chainsaws was tacked to a wall. That was the only decorative touch. The basin and toilet were gummy with stains and scum, the floor caked with the mud of tromping boots.

The towel had a toothbrush, a tube of toothpaste, and a bar of Ivory soap wrapped up inside. Monks felt like a prisoner of war who had just gotten a care package from the Red Cross. The sleep had done him a world of good. There was even a certain pleasure in simply being alone for the first time since he had gotten here.

He stripped, turned on the shower, and stepped in, baring his teeth in fierce elation at its chilling spray.

When they got back to the lodge, Monks paused outside the door and stepped close to Hammerhead, peering into his square face.

"What are you looking at?" Hammerhead demanded.

"Your left eye. That tic."

"I got a tick on my eye?" he said in alarm. One hand rose quickly to touch it, fingers searching.

"No. Tic. T-I-C. Like a twitch." Monks fluttered his own left eyelid in demonstration.

"That's bullshit. I don't have any tic."

"You probably don't even notice it. Ever get headaches?"

"No."

"Really? I don't mean killers. Just sort of low-level tension."

A pause. Then, suspiciously, "Maybe. Like, if I got a hangover."

"It might feel like a hangover," Monks agreed. "How about voices? You know, buzzing around in your brain, trying to get you to do things?"

"What the fuck you talking about, man?" Hammerhead stepped back, the rifle shifting nervously in his grip.

"Never mind," Monks said. "It's probably nothing."

Hammerhead swallowed hard. Then he swung the gun's barrel viciously toward the lodge's door.

"Get on inside."

Smiling very faintly, Monks got on inside.

Seven

A few minutes later, Monks walked again across the dusky, windy camp to talk with his son for the first time in almost five years. Hammerhead had come into the lodge to inform him dourly that Freeboot had given his okay. Monks's status seemed to be rising. He had not been cabled up again, and he was being granted visiting privileges.

The cabin that Hammerhead took him to was one of half a dozen that were scattered among the other buildings. Its small windows were caked with grime, and it shared the sense of neglect, almost squalor, that Monks had noticed around the camp in general. Most military operations were sticklers for neatness. But, it was undoubtedly a lot more fun to hustle around with radios and guns than to do anything as mundane as cleaning.

As they walked, Hammerhead glanced at him several times nervously, almost furtively, as if he wanted to ask a question, but couldn't bring it to his lips. Monks offered no encouragement.

As he raised his fist to knock on the door, he realized that someone inside was playing a guitar. The past rose up to twist his gut. Glenn had fooled around with guitars throughout his adolescence. As with his studies, he had showed plenty of ability but little discipline.

There was no response to the knock. Monks opened the door and leaned in.

Glenn was sitting cross-legged on a large pillow on the floor, bent over a steel-stringed acoustic guitar. His left hand slid easily up and down the neck, coaxing out the sweet dark strains of Skip James's great Delta blues. "Hard Time Killing Floor," Glenn's quavering voice rose to join the music.

"*If I ever get off this killin' floor, Lord, I'll never get down so low no more. Mmm-hmmh, mmm, mmm-mmm-hmmh—*"

Abruptly, Glenn slapped the strings to silence and looked up.

"I ain't got nothing to say to you, Rasp," Glenn said. "I'm only doing this because Freeboot said I have to."

Monks noted the use of his own old navy nickname, short for Rasputin, given to him because of his thick tangled eyebrows. Under other circumstances it might have been joking or even affectionate, but here it was clearly a taunt. He noted the grammar, too. Glenn had not been brought up to say "ain't got." His kinky ginger-colored hair bushed out from his head Afro style. A silvery skull-shaped earring, a punkish affectation, hung from his left ear.

"I'm not here to read you out, Glenn. I'd just like to know how you're doing."

"Call me Coil. Glenn was a middle-class white motherfucker. He's gone, man."

"All right, Coil it is. Because you're wound really tight?"

"You got it." Glenn bared his teeth in a defiant grin, and Monks's gut twisted again. Dark blotches were starting to form on Glenn's teeth and gums. Monks had seen similar ones in the ER. They were blisters that came from methamphetamine.

"You mind telling me how much of that stuff you're using?" Monks said.

"What stuff?" Glenn said innocently.

"Speed. And whatever else."

Glenn shrugged. "As much as I want. It's not hurting me."

"You know that's not true."

"*Jesus*, Rasp." Glenn slapped the guitar neck again, this time angrily. "You're in the door thirty seconds and already you're on my case."

Monks exhaled, biting off his next questions: *Have you shared needles? Had an AIDS test?*

"Okay," he said. "I'm concerned, that's all."

Glenn pulled a cigarette out of a pack and lit it. Monks saw with slight relief that it was a Marlboro 100—at least it was filtered. The cabin reeked of smoke. There was an ashtray stuffed with dead butts on the floor beside Glenn, along with a bottle of screw-cap Tokay wine. Paperback sci-fi novels, computer magazines, and what looked like adult comic books were scattered around. This seemed to be Glenn's corner, and it had the feel of a teenager's bedroom . But it was made eerie by the clear evidence that Glenn was living with a much older woman. Instead of a mountain man's hard and narrow bunk, there was a new, expensive queen-sized bed covered by a duvet. Through the open door to the small attached bathroom, crude and concrete-floored like the washhouse, Monks glimpsed a wooden clothes-drying rack hung with lingerie.

"Your mom and sister are doing well," Monks said.

"I don't want to hear about my perfect sister, okay?" Glenn sucked hard on the cigarette, managing to look disdainful. Stephanie was in her third year of medical school at UCSF. That would probably be a sore point to bring up to a high school dropout. But, then, it seemed like just about anything would be.

"You mind telling me how you hooked up with these folks?" Monks said.

"I was junked out. Shrinkwrap found me and took me home. She *cares* about people like me," Glenn added accusingly.

"Are you one of the, uh, *maquis*?"

"Nope. Those guys are the muscle. I do the complicated computer stuff."

"Such as?"

Glenn shook his head. "It's none of your fucking business, Rasp, okay?" His tone had the same sense of superiority, of being the elite guardian of secret knowledge, that Monks had sensed in Freeboot and the *maquis.*

Glenn started playing again, another blues. This one was jazzier, involving complex fingerpicking, with the sound of Robert Johnson's knife guitar.

"You've gotten good," Monks said.

Glenn nodded, continuing to play, and for a few seconds Monks sensed his son's pride in showing off for his father. Glenn had become a man, at least in his own eyes, and he handled the guitar with genuine feeling and talent.

Then his hands moved abruptly, the right slashing down across the strings with a discordant clash.

"Take this, brother, may it serve you well," he growled, in the deepest bass he could muster. They were the same words that Captain America had spoken ceremoniously when he came into the lodge last night.

"Tell me what that means," Monks said.

Instead, Glenn started chanting in a high-pitched nasal tone, playing the same strident chord over and over:

"Number *nine*, number *nine*, number *nine* . . ."

It took Monks a moment to recognize the source—an old Beatles song called "Revolution No. 9." He remembered it as being nonsensical and noisy.

Glenn kept up the chanting, rotating his head to it like a parody of a marionette controlled by a stuck record.

"Number *nine*, number *nine* . . ."

Monks stepped forward, dropped to one knee, and clamped his hand around the guitar neck. Glenn stared at him in outrage.

"Look. I can understand why you helped them bring me here," Monks said. "I'm willing to let it go, I won't press charges. But that little boy's going to die if he doesn't get help. This isn't some kind of game."

"*Game?* What the fuck do you know about it? I was living on the streets, man. My friends were dying."

"You were living on the streets by your own choice," Monks said. "You could have come home anytime you wanted. And a lot of people have seen a lot more people die than you have, including me."

Glenn wrested the guitar away from Monks and scrambled to his feet.

"Freeboot's doing something that nobody else in the fucking world can do, and I'm part of it. He needs me, man. You got that? For the first time in my life, I *matter.* And the way I live is up to *me,* and nobody else, okay?"

"You think you're smart and cool, but you don't know shit," Monks said, his own voice rising fiercely.

Then he stopped, and lowered his face into his right hand, thumb and forefinger squeezing his eyes shut. This was how it had always gone between them, and it was the signature of his *own* failure—his own immaturity, his intolerance of a kid's outbursts, when a father's love should have prevailed and made him just take the punch. It was true that Glenn had demanded unconditional love—the freedom to do whatever he pleased—and Monks was incapable of giving that.

But for a few terrible seconds, he wondered if he had ever loved Glenn at all—if Glenn had somehow sensed that from an early age, and all of his problems stemmed from it.

Maybe what Glenn had said last night was true: Monks *did* owe him bigtime.

He raised his head to face his son. "I'm sorry, Glenn," he said.

"Yeah, well, being sorry doesn't do anybody any good," Glenn said, with angry sarcasm. "Remember how you used to tell me that?"

Feeling suddenly leaden, Monks nodded. He sought for some line of conversation that might get Glenn to open up.

"This cause that you and Freeboot are involved in," Monks said. "Will you tell me about it?"

"I just did. Now get out of my place." Glenn slung the guitar down onto the pillow and pushed past Monks to the door.

"You can still come home," Monks said. "No judgment, just help. Don't forget that."

"I don't need your fucking help! Get out, man!" Glenn yanked open the door.

Revealing Shrinkwrap, who apparently had been standing outside, listening.

Glenn stared at her, looking shocked, then bolted past her, vanishing into the dusk.

"Proud of yourself?" she said to Monks.

"I could ask you the same thing."

Her lips formed a tight, mean line. "Don't bother. I've heard it plenty."

She stepped into the cabin, walking past Monks carefully, almost circling him. She looked more sure of herself than she had last night—attractive in a gaunt way. She had a fine facial bone structure with an aquiline nose. Her skin was smooth, almost translucent, and her auburn hair was thick and glossy. Along with the hard edge, there was a cool seductiveness.

"You can think whatever you want," she said. "The truth is, he'd probably be dead by now if not for me."

"Yes, he told me. You pulled him out of hell."

"Out of a serious emotional disturbance. I happen to be a psychologist."

"Oh, really? Is that where all this is coming from, about his abused childhood? You've been helping him recover memories?"

"He doesn't need help remembering an alcoholic, domineering father."

"Domineering?" Monks said wearily. "Because I used to interrupt his tantrums where he threw dishes at his mother when he didn't get his way? He was still doing it at seventeen."

"He was expressing the anger he got from you. Just like he got your addictive personality."

"Is that a clinical assessment? Or you telling him what he wants to hear, so you can keep a hold on him?"

"Ah, yes, the physician dismisses psychology as a soft science," she said sarcastically.

"I've got great respect for psychologists who don't use convenient labels to blame everything on somebody else," Monks said. "We sent him to two of them. A psychiatrist, too, in case there was a neurological problem or a chemical imbalance. The consensus was, 'Well, we can keep treating him as long as you want, but all he's going to do is play games with us. This is just the way he is.' "

"And instead of supporting him, you undermined him. Like you're doing now."

"His mother and I did everything we knew how, *Doctor.* With plenty of pain involved, believe me. I finally decided the only way I could deal with it was to call it by its real name. Try to keep the hurt from spreading too much. Glenn's very good at getting people to believe what he wants them to. Especially women. He was doing it as soon as he could talk."

"If he was such a charmer, how come he never had a good relationship with a girl?"

"Is that what he told you? There were plenty who were willing. But he'd lose interest as soon as they fell for him. He left a string of poor little broken hearts."

She put her hands on her hips, one foot pointing toward him, a pose that was tough but provocative.

"I guess he needed a grown-up," she said.

Right, Monks thought. Mother and lover in one package—and glad to let him do all the drugs he wanted.

"I have no desire to go into my son's bedroom," Monks said. "If he's happy, I'm happy for him. Like I told him, I'll leave here and never say a word about it, if Mandrake comes with me."

"That's up to Freeboot."

"Surely *you* don't believe a four-year-old can heal himself of diabetes through willpower."

Her gaze shifted away. "I'd handle the situation differently. Let's leave it at that."

"Unfortunately, I *can't* leave it at that," Monks said. "But if you've got a better idea than keeping me chained up here playing 'Dr. Quinn, Medicine Woman,' then by all means go for it."

Her head tilted with a calculating air. "He's sure right about one thing," she said. "You reek of self-righteousness."

The words hit hard, and it must have shown. Monks saw her take on the satisfied look of knowing that she had scored.

He turned away and walked to the door. "You'd better get him to do something about those blisters," he said. "He's looking at losing his teeth."

He stepped out of the cabin, feeling weak, as if he were bleeding internally. He stared off into the gloom in the direction that Glenn had run—his son, who in some ways seemed old far beyond his years, but in other ways would always be very young. There was an ugly irony in that the niche he had finally found, his pride in whatever Freeboot's cause was, involved madness and violence.

He *had* tried with Glenn, Monks assured himself. But it had never been enough. The more that Glenn had gotten, the more—and more belligerently—he had demanded, until there was nothing left for Monks to do but build a wall.

At least that was how Monks remembered it.

Hammerhead was waiting for him. They walked back toward the lodge, the shackles clanking around Monks's ankles.

"Uh, getting back to what you said before," Hammerhead said.

"What?" Monks said distractedly.

"That tic. In my eye."

Monks stared at him, then remembered..

"What about it?" he demanded.

"You said it was probably nothing. What does 'probably' mean?"

Monks shook his head. "It means you probably don't want to know."

"Yeah, I do. Tell me."

"Well—a tic like that is a classic symptom of a brain tumor. Pressing on the optic nerve."

"A brain tumor?"

"Sometimes if you catch them very early, they can be lasered out, or treated by radiation. But by the time they start interfering with your vision, they tend to be the size an egg, and they're growing fast. They're pretty tough to handle by then."

Hammerhead's square jaw moved from side to side, as if trying to work its way around the concept.

"Of course, I'm not *sure*," Monks said. "Keep tabs on the headaches and delusions. If they go away, that's good. But if you start noticing them more . . ." He grimaced. Then he added, comfortingly, "There's other things it could be, too. Maybe a minor stroke. That's no problem in itself, but it makes you more susceptible to a major one. Then you're talking the rest of your life in a wheelchair, wearing a diaper."

Hammerhead's face had taken on a stunned, flounder-like look.

"Is there, like—I mean—what should I do?"

"A hospital might be able to help," Monks said. "Or at least tell you how long you've got. But if you buy into the antimedical sentiment around here—" He shrugged. "Enjoy yourself as much as you can, is my advice."

Eight

When Monks stepped into the lodge, Freeboot was sitting at the long wooden table with a kerosene lamp before him, poring over an open book. The pose was so like medieval paintings of scholars like Aquinas and Erasmus that Monks wondered if it was deliberately staged.

Freeboot kept reading for another half minute, a pause that also seemed staged.

"I'm a self-educated man," Freeboot said. "I never had no benefits of formal schooling. But that also means I think for myself. My mind hasn't been crammed full of poison by people who want you to believe things *their* way.

"So here's how I see it. This country's gotten to be a big, spoiled, overgrown kid. Everybody figures if they got the best toys, that gives them the right to hog the sandbox."

He watched Monks intently, apparently expecting a response.

"I told you, I'm not interested in discussion while I'm chained up," Monks said.

Freeboot considered this a moment, then said, "All right." He dug into a pocket of his jeans and tossed Monks a small key.

Monks sat on the floor and unlocked the cuffs. The clicks as they released were among the most satisfying sounds he had ever heard. He stayed sitting down, rubbing his chafed ankles.

"Does this mean I'm free to go?" he said.

Freeboot smiled thinly. "I'm working on trust, like I told you. I expect the same back from you." He held his open palm out for the key. Monks tossed it back.

"Let's hope we won't need it again," Freeboot said. "You with me so far?"

"About the country being a spoiled kid?"

"That's right. What's it going to take to make it grow up?"

Monks chose his words carefully, very much aware of the shackles still lying on the floor.

"I don't know," he said. "I don't think there are simple answers to complex problems."

"Oh, the problem's real simple. The system's set up so all the money's *going* to a few rich motherfuckers who've already got a ton of it, and it's being *taken* from the masses who need it."

That was putting it simply, all right—a one-line summary of Marxist ideology with a contemporary spin, managing to combine the words *motherfuckers* and *masses.*

"And the solution?" Monks said.

"What you got to do with any kid that gets out of line. A good old-fashioned spanking."

Monks was startled. "Spank America?"

"Tough love," Freeboot agreed. He smiled again, and this time it seemed to have a leering, even sadistic edge. And yet Freeboot's brand of tough love seemed to have captivated Glenn, while Monks's own attempts had failed miserably. Was that the key—some mixture of cruelty and submission?

Freeboot abandoned the philosophic pose, leaning back in his chair and groping on the floor for a bottle of the Monte Alban mescal. He took a long swig and offered it to Monks. Monks shook his head.

"The next question is: How do you bring off something like that?" Freeboot said. "You'd need an army, right?"

Monks was still not clear on what "spanking America" entailed. He shrugged noncommittally.

"It's already out there." Freeboot waved one arm in a wide, circling gesture. "All those working people who got thrown out on the bricks, because somebody sent their jobs to slave-labor factories in China. All those kids coming up poor, the best thing they can ever expect is to put on a Burger King cap. There's three and a half million homeless people in this country right now, man, and thousands more every month. Another big factory closed down every time you pick up a newspaper. That's the real, hard-ass result of the big rip-off that's going on."

He watched Monks, his gaze challenging.

"I agree that spreading money around differently would help," Monks said.

"It's not just about money. Those people have lost their *dignity*. You give *that* back to them, they'll give you dedication."

"Dignity's a huge thing to offer."

"Meaning what? My mouth's writing a check my ass can't cash? Let me tell you something else. The necks think the people on the streets are just going to disappear somehow. They're fucking wrong. Those people are tough, and they're not stupid."

"Necks?"

"That's right. 'Cause when shit starts to happen, somebody's foot's going to be on them." Freeboot crossed his ankles up on the table, displaying his bare soles, dark with dirt and horny with callus. "They think they can hide in their gated communities and nobody can touch them. They're gonna get spanked *hard*." He drank again from the mescal bottle. It seemed that he was prepared to hold forth for quite some time.

"I'd better check on Mandrake," Monks said, turning toward the bedroom.

"Hey, I took your chains off." Freeboot said, annoyed. "You're not going to talk to me?"

Workers of the world, unite, Monks thought. *You have nothing to lose but your chains.*

He turned back. "I understand what you're telling me," he said. "But not why. What do you care what I think?"

Freeboot's face took on its heavy-lidded, hypnotic gaze.

"I got to have something to call you," Freeboot said. "Coil says 'Rasp.' Okay?"

Monks shrugged. He was particular about who used his nickname, but he was damned if he'd let Freeboot know that he was pushing a button.

"He says they called you that in Vietnam," Freeboot said. "You got a good look at guerrilla war, huh?"

"I was never in combat. Mostly I dealt with the results."

"Must have been ugly."

Monks felt a tremor of razor-keen memory: jerking awake on the hospital ship USS *Respite* in the South China Sea, sodden with sweat from the wet heat, the sour bile taste of fear already in his mouth and adrenaline starting to course through his bloodstream, at the far-off thunder of medevac helicopters ferrying their bloody burdens from Quang Tri.

"Very," he said.

"Well, there you go. All because those Vietnamese got fucked over too much for too long and they started fighting back."

Another simplistic judgment, about a war whose roots were a Gordian knot.

But the words that Glenn had been chanting came into Monks's mind: *number nine, number nine, number nine—*

Revolution Number 9.

Finally, the hints that Freeboot had been dropping clicked into focus.

"Are you talking about an uprising?" Monks said incredulously.

"I'm talking about Free Companies, like I told you. That's going to be the *real* new world order. Think *Road Warrior,* man. Roving armies doing whatever they want, armed to the teeth. They're already on the ground in Africa and South America, and all it's going to take here is somebody to light the fuse. They're everywhere, right there in *your* town."

"This isn't Africa or South America," Monks said. "We have systems of civil protection."

Freeboot snorted in derision. "There aren't enough cops to stop them or prisons to hold them. The necks can call out the miltary, but they got a problem there, too. What about all the ghetto kids coming back from places like Iraq? They spend a year in hell, then get home and find out they still get treated like dogshit. Whose side you think they're going to come down on?"

"There was a lot of talk like this in the sixties," Monks said. "Not much came of it."

"People had things too good in the sixties," said Freeboot, who could not have been born by then. "The people I'm talking about are *hungry*."

He stood up suddenly, with the quickness and balance that Monks had come to expect.

"You think I'm just bullshitting," Freeboot said. "I got something to show you later." He padded to the door and vanished into the dusk.

Monks stood where he was, trying to weigh what he had just heard. Clearly Freeboot thought of himself as a leader out to liberate an underdog element of the population—the foot on the "necks" would be his.

On the face of it, his ideas were a mishmash of superficial political theory, megalomania, and chest-thumping fantasy, all wrapped up in a bubble of schoolboy logic—the kind of self-contained shell that couldn't be penetrated without going more deeply into the issues, which, obviously, he had no patience for. Like a lot of self-proclaimed prophets, he had gleaned a few high-sounding bits of philosophy and twisted them to suit his own purposes. And like a lot of revolutionaries, he seemed to idealize violence.

To imagine that this little clutch of misfits could cause widespread unrest was absurd. But it was still disturbing. Freeboot possessed undeniable charisma—and there was *enough* truth in what he said to make it persuasive, especially to listeners who wouldn't examine it closely.

Monks even admitted to a prickle of sympathy. Without doubt, there was a lot of gross injustice out there, and maybe in some ways it was getting worse. He'd had his own run-ins with the way of thinking that saw human beings as numbers on paper, livestock, pawns to be used by an elite who considered themselves godlike, and who kept themselves carefully shielded. And yet, society's rules were the only thing that kept most people safe from the chaos and bloodshed that had been common through so much of history.

When did it become acceptable—even necessary—to cross that fragile line?

He had to agree that in some circumstances, violence was the only way for the oppressed to recover both their rights and their self-respect. There could certainly be heroism in fighting for ideals, and glory in battle itself.

But he had seen so much horrifying pain, and dignity didn't usually go along with it.

Mandrake seemed to be asleep or sunk in lethargy. Monks decided to leave him alone until it was time for the next blood-sugar check, then to wake him and try to engage him in talk or play.

He walked back out into the main room. The shackles still lay where he had left them on the floor. He stepped around them as if they were a bear trap.

Then, seeing that he was alone, he went into the kitchen. He had wondered how food was stored without electricity. The mystery was solved by the sight of a new propane refrigerator. The rest was more rustic, with the same kind of cold-water porcelain sink as the washhouse, and a huge old Monarch wood cookstove. But unlike the rest of the camp, it was clean and well kept. He suspected the hand of Marguerite.

He quickly opened drawers and cabinets, looking for knives, but the only utensils were plastic, like the ones that Marguerite had given him last night. He went through the couple of dusty, disused-looking bedrooms next, but he found nothing that might work as a weapon. It seemed clear that this was intentional—even the fireplace pokers were charred sticks of pine. There were no other exterior doors, and the few windows were crossed with half-inch reinforcing rod, like prison bars, attached from the outside.

As soon as his shackles had come off, the thought of escape had entered his mind again, as Freeboot must have known it would. But the odds were still almost nil. Without doubt, he was being watched closely. And if by some miracle he did succeed, Freeboot might take out his rage on Glenn—even on Mandrake. There were other cards to be played before any kind of desperate attempt. Freeboot was trying to impress him, and that might just open the way to a resolution.

Freeboot's book was still lying on the table. Monks leaned over and saw that it was Nietzsche's *Thus Spake Zarathustra*—the treatise in which he propounded his concept of the *Übermensch*, seized on later by the Nazis and distorted into a superior being with the right to dominate, without regard for law or humanity.

It was another almost ludicrous touch, part of Freeboot's show—and yet the volume was worn, obviously much handled, with notes written in the margins in an uneven, illegible script. Monks flipped through it, looking for a name or some other identifying mark. The only thing he found was a ripped patch inside the front cover, suggesting that a library pocket had been torn off. Probably the book had been stolen.

The coffee that he had asked for was waiting, in a small blue enamel sheepherder's coffeepot set at the edge of the fireplace to stay warm. He supposed that Marguerite had left it for him while he was at Glenn's cabin. There was food, too, this time a sandwich of packaged baloney and cheese on white bread, and a small bag of Cheetos. It was like a boxed school lunch.

He ate standing up in front of the fire, glad for the warmth seeping into his flesh. Then he went back into the kitchen and indulged himself in the luxury of brushing his teeth again. As he was finishing, he heard someone come into the lodge. He looked through the kitchen door and saw that it was Motherlode, Mandrake's mother, going into the boy's bedroom. Monks quickly rinsed up and went after her.

Her back was turned to the doorway as he stepped through. She was reaching up to the shelf where he kept the insulin.

When she turned around, she had a plastic-wrapped syringe in her hand. She stared vacantly at Monks, and then jerked in delayed surprise.

So that was where the syringes had been going.

Probably she was crushing the oxycodone pills into a liquid solution, then shooting it. Monks had heard that it was a quicker and more powerful rush than from taking them orally.

"Mandrake's going to need all of those," he said.

"Okay. I won't take any more." She moved toward the door, still holding the syringe.

"That one, too."

Her face took on a sullen, hostile look—a transformation so abrupt and complete from her earlier placidness that it was like a special effect in a movie.

"Hey, man, you don't own this place, okay?" she said. "As a matter of fact, *I* do."

"We're talking about your son."

She glanced over at the bed, where Mandrake might or might not have been awake and listening. Then she shoved the syringe into Monks's hand and pushed petulantly through the hanging blanket into the main room.

"Why don't you *stay* here?" Monks said, following her. "Play with him, read to him."

"I can't right now."

"Are you HIV positive?" Monks demanded.

She spun to face him, as if she had been shot.

"*No,*" she spat out. She hurried on outside without looking back.

Mandrake hadn't moved, but his eyes were open. Monks sat down beside him on the bed and started reading aloud from *The Runaway Bunny.*

Shrinkwrap walked toward the lodge with a small flashlight in her hand, flicking it on and off in the three-two-three code the group used to identify themselves. Dusk had turned to full night, the moon a faint smudge behind the thick clouds rolling in from the Pacific. Hammerhead was in that darkness somewhere, standing guard, watching her approach. She shone the light on her own face.

"It's me, HH," she said. "We need to talk."

His shape separated from the shadows beside the lodge, rifle in hand, barrel pointed down. Hammerhead trusted her absolutely, and she understood him far better than he understood himself. She had found him, like the others—troubled young men whose aimless aggressiveness would almost certainly have led them to prison. She counseled them as a psychologist, bullied them like a drill sergeant, and nurtured them like a mother. Once that intimacy was established, she took them to bed, deepening the bond by deliciously violating the taboo. Then she weaned them to the care of Freeboot and Taxman, who would channel their wild energy into purpose.

Although once in a while one would come along, with just the right combination of boyishness and insolence, and she would keep him for as long as it was convenient. Right now, that one was Monks's son.

"You sure we're alone?" she asked Hammerhead.

He nodded. Still, she spoke in a conspiratorial whisper.

"Freeboot sent me to tell you there's going to be a scalp hunt tonight. And a chance for you to make *maquis.*" She smiled. "So if you bring home the hair of a certain person, you'll be initiated. I think you know who I mean."

His reaction surprised her. She had expected a show of fierce elation. Making *maquis* would mean that he would finally have what he wanted most—Marguerite. And a chance to get even with Captain America in the process.

But he only licked his lips anxiously. His big face looked pale, and his eyes were troubled, even frightened. Hammerhead followed orders well but didn't think fast, and when he was faced with a decision, he tended to get nervous. But she had never seen him scared before.

She stepped closer and touched his face, concerned. "Hey, sweetie. What's going on with you?"

"Nothing," he mumbled.

"Come on, you can tell me. You know I'll stay cool."

Hammerhead looked around unhappily, as if reassuring himself that no one else was nearby.

"He said I got this thing in my eye. A tic." His finger rose and touched his face.

"Who said?"

"Him." Hammerhead jerked his head toward the lodge. "Coil's old man."

"A tic?"

"Yeah. You know." He fluttered his eyelid clumsily.

"Well, what about it?"

Hammerhead swallowed hard. "It means I'm gonna die."

Shrinkwrap stared at him, hands coming to rest on her hips. "He told you *what?*"

Nine

Monks had discovered, twenty-some years earlier, that he made a pretty good mattress whale—stretched out on a bed, rising and falling in undulating motions, with much thrashing and loud blubbering sounds. The clowning had delighted his own kids, and now, for the first time, Mandrake was sitting up and giggling.

"Okay, hop on my back," Monks said. "We're going to dive down really deep and try to find a treasure. But the only thing I'm worried about is, there might be a mermaid guarding it. You know what those are?"

Wide-eyed, Mandrake shook his head.

"They're very pretty ladies who are half fish," Monks said solemnly. "And they're usually really nice, but if they catch somebody coming after their treasure . . ."

Mandrake started to look worried. Monks feared that he had pushed too far. He was doing his best to maintain a humorous face, but he knew that as he gotten older his smile had taken on a crocodilian look.

"They'll tickle us—like *this*," he declared, and gently scrabbled his fingertips along the little boy's rib cage.

Mandrake chortled gleefully, grabbing at his hands.

"So you have to tell me if you see a mermaid, okay?" Monks said. "We can get away, but we'll have to go really fast."

"Okay," Mandrake agreed, in a very small voice.

It was the first time that he had spoken to Monks.

Three or four minutes later, whale and rider took a breather. It had been a harrowing journey. A treasure had been sighted, but just before they could seize it—there was a mermaid! They'd escaped, but not without a desperate battle, both of them being tickled to the limits of endurance.

"We'll go again, real soon," Monks promised the panting little boy. "Now you have to drink some water." Getting Mandrake active and engaged was good; tiring him out was not.

Monks got up to get the water pitcher. The blanket hanging in the doorway moved aside. Monks stared, in unpleasant shock, at the etched, intense face of Taxman. There was no telling how long he had been standing there behind the blanket.

"Freeboot wants you," Taxman said.

"Mandrake needs attention."

"It won't take long."

Monks hesitated. He had already decided that he could check the boy's blood sugar level every two hours now—it had remained stable, and Mandrake clearly was feeling better.

"Let me just get him to drink first," Monks said.

Taxman nodded and stepped back, letting the blanket fall into place again.

Monks gave Mandrake the water cup. "Think you can do this yourself now, buddy?" he said. Mandrake took it in both hands and drank thirstily.

"Good boy," Monks said. "I'll be right back. We're going to eat some more soup and rest up. Then we'll go get that treasure."

Outisde, the night sky was thick with impending rain. The erratic breeze had turned cold, and the treetops waved restlessly. When they reached the camp's perimeter, Monks realized that they weren't headed toward one of the buildings. Instead, they kept walking on a trail into the forest. Monks blundered along at first, barely able to see the path beneath his feet. Except for the wind and the rustling trees, the woods were silent, without the night birds and creatures that he was used to at his home's lower, warmer altitude. Taxman flanked him silently. Unlike the other guards, Taxman did not carry a gun. But Monks had no doubt that he was very quick with his knife.

By the time they'd gone a quarter of a mile, his eyes had adjusted. Then, another few hundred yards ahead, he saw what looked like flames. They vanished and appeared again, flickering like a will-o'-the-wisp, hidden and revealed by the trees as he wound his way through them. When he got a good look, he realized that he was seeing a bonfire in a clearing at the base of a rocky cliff. There were dark human shapes gathered around it, some crouching and some standing.

His sudden overwhelming sense was of being a captive, brought to a barbaric camp for torture and death at the hands of his enemies. Fear verging on panic clogged his throat. He stopped and turned to face Taxman, tensing to fight or run.

Taxman was gone.

Monks stood still, breathing deeply. He didn't think the figures around the fire had spotted him yet. He could slip away into the woods, move stealthily until he was out of earshot, then take off in all-out flight.

But his rational mind started to regain the upper hand. He would almost certainly be caught within minutes. This might even be a test—Freeboot pushing to see how far he could be trusted—and if he failed it, he'd end up back in chains. There didn't seem to be any reason that Freeboot would want him harmed.

Unless he had decided that Monks was no longer useful, or that Monks had offended his giant ego beyond forgiving. Then this might be Freeboot's idea of a joke—having Monks walk freely to his own execution.

He forced himself to turn back toward the fire and continue.

The men in the clearing watched him as he came in, but no one spoke. They were all dressed as if for nighttime military operations, in black fatigues and combat boots, with paint-darkened faces and web belts bristling with equipment. All wore large-caliber semiautomatic pistols in holsters and carried assault rifles. Monks counted nine men, including the thick shape of Hammerhead near the fire, standing stiffly like a Marine on guard, and farther away, the handsome profile of Captain America. He didn't think that he had seen any of the others before. Glenn wasn't there, nor was Freeboot.

They waited in silence broken only by the crackling of the fire, the rustle of shifting bodies, and the wind, rising and falling like the breath of a sinister god. A minute passed, then another and another, each lasting sixty very long seconds.

Then came a sudden disturbance, a *sense* of movement rather than sound, from the cliff above. Monks just had time to look up and see a large object plummet down. It landed in the fire with a crash, scattering an explosion of embers and sparks. He stumbled backwards, aware of the other figures doing the same, some hitting the ground and rolling, others swinging their weapons around into play.

He hit the ground, too. As the sparks settled, he strained his vision to identify what had landed in the fire. It was an animal, a big one. An acrid burning smell was starting to rise, overpowering the pleasant piney scent of woodsmoke.

"You can dress 'em up. But can you take 'em out?"

The voice was Freeboot's, coming from outside the clearing. It had a chiding, sardonic tone. "You assholes let anybody else come up on you like that, you're all going to need wigs before this night's over."

He walked into view with his barefoot, easy stride. The men lowered their weapons and shifted uneasily, like children being scolded. Monks got up off the ground. He saw that the animal was a young mule deer buck, three or four point, its antlered head twisted at a radical angle from its body courtesy of its gaping slashed throat. Freeboot's hands and torso were streaked with blood, and the right leg of his jeans was soaked with it. Apparently he had carried the buck over that shoulder while its veins emptied out, then thrown it off the cliff.

"There's just two ways you can live in this world," Freeboot announced, his voice strident now. "You take control of *it*, or it takes control of *you*. Most of those people out there"—he swept his arm in a gesture that included the rest of the world—"are like this deer. But you *few* men here, you got the chance to be above all that."

He crouched over the buck with a long survival knife, using its serrated edge to saw from the buck's throat down through its sternum, then flipping the blade to slit the belly to the genitals. The entrails slithered out in a steaming slippery mass. His hands plunged in, forcing the rib cage open, then going in again with the knife.

"Out in the jungle, the tribes got secret societies that control everything," he called out, hands working to cut something free. His voice was powerful and resonant, like a revival preacher's. "They name themselves for hunters, the strongest and fastest. Cheetahs. Leopards. They understand that life is power, and that taking life *gives* them power."

He stood, holding up the buck's heart in one hand. It was about the size of a man's fist, ruddy and glistening in the fire's glow.

"Here we think we're civilized. But it's really just another jungle, made of freeways and shopping malls. When you go out into it, you got to *have* the heart of the hunter, and *eat* the heart of the deer."

Freeboot sliced into the heart with his knife, cut off a three inch long strip, and put it in his mouth. He chewed slowly, taking his time, pointedly making eye contact with each of the men in turn. They stared back at him, mesmerized. He swallowed the raw flesh, raising his chin so that all could see his larynx move. Then he stepped to the man closest to him, Hammerhead, and offered him the bloody heart.

Hammerhead took it without hesitation, cut off another strip, and crammed it into his mouth. He passed the heart on to the next man. The smell of the buck's charring hair and flesh was getting stronger, an evil, atavistic reek of carnage.

Monks had read about the secret societies that Freeboot touted. He had also read that children being initiated were sometimes forced to eat human flesh—even of their own murdered parents. It was a dark, mystical communion, intended to bond them to the group in a way that plunged into the most savage roots of mankind.

The heart circulated to more of the black-clad warriors, each man hacking off a chunk and chewing, until it came to one that Monks hadn't seen before, a lanky young man with a big Adam's apple. He took it hesitantly, his gaze darting around.

"You got a problem, Sidewinder?" Freeboot barked.

Monks recalled that he had heard the name Sidewinder before—the sentry who had taken over for Captain America. There was something viperish about him—his tongue flicked in and out constantly to wet his lips, and his sinuous body seemed to vibrate with vaguely menacing energy.

"Can this make you sick?" he blurted out. "Eating raw meat like this?"

Monks realized, with astonishment, that Sidewinder was talking to him.

"*What?*" It was Freeboot who answered, erupting in incredulous outrage.

"I heard this dude's a doctor," Sidewinder stammered. "I just thought—you know, maybe we shouldn't be doing this, in case there's diseases or something."

"'In case there's diseases or something,'" Freeboot mimicked viciously. "Diseases are for the two-legged deer running around out there. Is that what you want to be, one of them? *Get* your ass over here."

Sidewinder jumped to obey the command, tongue flicking nervously. Freeboot wrenched the heart out of his hand and tossed it to Hammerhead.

"Strip," Freeboot commanded.

"Oh, man. *Why?*"

"You don't fucking ask me *why* when I tell you to do something, shitheel. You *do* it."

The gathered men watched tensely as Sidewinder sat on the

ground, unlaced his boots and pulled them off, then got out of his fatigues. Naked, he looked thin and pathetic, his skin made paler by his darkened face.

Freeboot kicked the carcass. "You want to be a deer? Fine. Put that on. You got balls, you can stand up and walk around. Otherwise, crawl in and lay there."

For a few more silent minutes, the group watched Sidewinder wrestle the buck out of the fire, clumsily finish cutting loose the entrails, then struggle to stand with the carcass over his shoulders like a cape. Even gutted, it would weigh well over a hundred pounds.

Finally, he staggered to his feet, the antlered head lolling on his chest and the hind legs dragging behind his own.

"You want to be a hunter again?" Freeboot said to him.

Sidewinder nodded miserably.

Freeboot took the deer's heart back from Hammerhead, hacked off a slice, and stuffed it into Sidewinder's mouth. He chewed for what seemed an interminably long time, before he managed, gagging, to swallow it.

"You stay in the woods tonight," Freeboot said. "You can have your man skin back tomorrow. Now get the fuck out of here."

Sidewinder shuffled painfully off into the dark forest, wrapped in his bloody burden. At least, Monks thought, it would keep him warm.

"I've told you about the Old Man of the Mountain and his assassins," Freeboot boomed out to the others. "Let me tell you how much his men trusted him. He could point at one of them standing guard high up on a cliff, and snap his fingers, and that man would jump off. And because of that *trust,* they could make any king in the world do whatever they wanted. But if any one man does *not* trust, it weakens all the others. That, we will not tolerate. Anybody else got a problem with trust?" He stared from face to face.

The deer's heart finished making the rounds, with no more hesitations or questions. When it came full circle, back to Freeboot, he tossed the remains into the fire.

Monks didn't know if there was danger in eating the raw flesh, but he was relieved to see it go. He had feared that he might be expected to join in.

"Everybody get behind a good hard hit of this eyeball," Freeboot said. He took out the Copenhagen can of speed that Monks had seen before, dipping in his knife blade and inhaling. The others all did the same, breaking out their private stashes, in a parody of a military smoke break.

"Now, you better run hard tonight, and you better run fast," Freeboot said. "Some of you haven't done this before, so here's how it goes. You move up a rank for every chunk of hair you bring back. You lose your own hair, you move down a rank. No guns, just knives and Mace. No drawing blood. If you get Maced, don't fight back, 'cause knives can slip. Okay, stack up your firearms."

The men came forward one at a time, laying their rifles and pistols at Freeboot's feet. Some looked self-assured, others apprehensive.

"You'll hear a gunshot in ten minutes," Freeboot said. "That's when it starts. You come back with somebody else's hair or without your own. That's when it ends."

He snapped his fingers. The men took off in crouching runs, scattering in different directions.

Abruptly, one of the figures veered like a football running back sidestepping a blocker, and lunged straight at Monks. He barely had time to raise his forearms, covering his torso like a boxer, before Hammerhead's shoulder slammed into him. It knocked him sprawling, skidding on his tailbone.

Hammerhead charged on, never even slowing down.

Monks struggled to his feet, trying to get his breath back. Freeboot was watching him. It was the first time he had seemed aware that Monks was there.

"You're a noncombatant, Rasp," Freeboot said matter-of-factly. "But I'd get on back to camp, if I was you. Somebody's likely to make a mistake."

Monks started back along the trail at a fast walk. He had only gone about ten yards when he heard a voice hiss from the trees:

"There *are* no noncombatants."

He spun around, searching the darkness with his gaze. The words had come from only a few feet away. But the speaker was invisible.

He headed toward camp again, this time at a jog.

The voice could have been a man's, high-pitched or disguised, but he was almost sure it was Shrinkwrap's.

Ten

Monks had just gotten inside the lodge when he heard a faint, faraway gunshot—the signal for a group of cranked-up young militants armed with knives and Mace to start hunting each other's hair.

He leaned back against the wall, resting. The urge to keep running had been with him all the way. But his fear of getting caught and arousing Freeboot's wrath outweighed his fear of staying on.

One thing was clear by now—Freeboot's brand of trust had teeth.

Then there was Hammerhead. Monks had become the target of his anger, for reasons that didn't much matter. What did matter was that the thin membrane of safety that Monks had started to feel had been shredded by Hammerhead's shoulder—especially as Freeboot had watched it happen, and not said a word.

"He said you were going to bring him more soup," someone said quietly.

Monks jerked toward the voice. Marguerite was standing in the doorway to the kitchen. He realized that the *he* referred to Mandrake. She must have gone in to check on him.

"I'm heating it up," she said. "I could fix you something, too."

"I'd appreciate that."

"It'll have to be another sandwich. They cook down at another place and bring it up, but right now there's not much."

"Anything but venison," Monks said.

She looked puzzled, but then drifted back into the kitchen. Monks followed her, again smelling marijuana. A saucepan of broth for Mandrake was heating on top of the wood cookstove. She gave the pan a stir, then went to the refrigerator, taking out cold cuts and bread. There was a big supply of those; apparently, sandwiches were a staple here.

"It seems like you do all the work around this place," Monks said.

"I don't mind. It's better than doing nothing."

"That's a pretty name. Marguerite."

She did not seem displeased. "It's not my real one."

Monks was surprised. It was the only name he'd heard here that seemed normal.

"What is?"

She glanced at him warily. "I can't tell you."

"Sorry, I didn't mean to pry. Why Marguerite, if you don't mind my asking?"

"There's this old story, *Faust*? He sells his soul to the devil?"

Monks nodded encouragingly.

"Marguerite is, like, the woman who saves him at the end," she said.

So—along with Freeboot's vision of himself as part Spartacus and part *Übermensch*, there was a dash of Faust, who had dared to go beyond all limits.

"Is that how you see yourself, saving Freeboot?" Monks asked. "Faust made Marguerite put up with a lot of trouble along the way."

"Hey, man, I didn't pick it. Freeboot did." This time her voice had an edge.

"Don't get me wrong, I meant that as a compliment," Monks said quickly. "In the story, Marguerite is very bighearted, very loyal."

She ignored him, using a plastic knife to lather mayonnaise on a slice of white bread, then adding baloney and cheese. It was looking like lunch all over again.

But then she said, "He gives everybody a new name. It's, like, getting rid of who you used to be and becoming a new person."

"And all the names have a special meaning?"

"Kind of. He sees deep inside you, to who you really are."

Monks made a quick mental tally of the names that he had heard. Some, like Hammerhead and Sidewinder, seemed to suggest that Freeboot hadn't found much to work with in the way of deep character qualities. Coil, unsettling though Monks found it, did touch on Glenn's intrinsic restlessness; and Shrinkwrap probably referred to her being a psychologist. Some of the others were more obscure.

"What about Captain America?" Monks said, watching to see if mentioning Marguerite's lover seemed to strike a nerve.

She tossed her hair dismissively. "He's good-looking, cool. There's this old movie Freeboot likes, *Easy Rider*? It came from there."

Monks called up a vague memory of the movie. The Peter Fonda character, that was it.

"I couldn't help noticing that you and he seem, ah, close," Monks said.

She shrugged. "He's a *maquis*. I'm a bride."

"I don't understand what that means."

"Ask Freeboot, okay?" she said, sounding edgy again. It seemed that this was sensitive turf. She put the sandwich on a plate and pushed it toward him. "There's chips, and wine if you want it."

"Thanks," Monks said, moving a little closer to her as he picked up the plate. He was trying to zero in on the unhappiness he sensed in her—trying to gauge whether he could coax her into helping him. He decided to probe another sore spot that he had sensed.

"Motherlode told me she owned this place," he said. "Is that true?"

"She inherited it."

"Really?"

"Along with a trust fund the size of California. Her grandfather was a big logging guy." Marguerite took a bowl from a cupboard and started pouring the warm broth into it.

"So she's kind of the princess, and you're the help?"

Marguerite didn't answer, and her hair hid his view of her face. But her hands stopped moving.

"What *does* being a bride mean?" Monks said. "You sleep with anybody Freeboot tells you to? While he breaks in new brides?"

She left the room quickly, not speaking, clutching the bowl of soup in both hands.

Monks ate in front of the fireplace again, leaving her alone to feed Mandrake.

A few minutes later she came out of the bedroom and walked to the main door, still without looking at Monks. But when she reached it, she turned to him. Her eyes seemed defiant and perhaps fearful.

"I'm here because I want to be," she said. "We all are."

"Not Mandrake," Monks said.

She hurried outside, slamming the door behind her.

And not me, he thought.

Freeboot waited beside the bonfire in the forest, silent, listening, attuned to the night. Occasionally, he dipped his knife blade into the canister of meth and inhaled it.

Twenty-four hours from now, Mr. and Mrs. Robert J. Emlinger of Atherton, California, would join the list of assassination targets that were baffling police around the country.

The only question was, which one of the men out stalking each other in the forest right now was going to earn the privilege of putting them on that list.

The answer came when a hulking figure lunged out of the tree line, running toward the fire like a charging bull. It was Hammerhead, the first man back—panting, face ruddy and shining with sweat, eyes glittering with crazed elation. His knife was clenched in his right fist. He thrust his left fist forward for Freeboot to see.

It held a thick swatch of Captain America's wavy blond hair.

Freeboot smiled.

He stepped to a niche in the rocky cliff and took out a silver goblet. It was filled with a special cocktail that he had invented: red wine saturated with finely powdered hashish and laced with XTC.

He walked back to the fire and handed the goblet to Hammerhead.

"Take this, brother, may it serve you well," Freeboot said.

Eleven

"You are no longer an ordinary human being, you understand that?" Freeboot hissed into Hammerhead's ear. "The rules don't apply to you no more. The human deer will cower before you. You will walk among them and be their master, yet none will know you. You are the best of the best, the top of the elite. You are on the edge of *immortality*."

They strode along the dark foggy path toward the camp, Freeboot gripping the young man by the back of his belt to steer him. Hammerhead was lurching, his head weaving, wild-eyed, from side to side at the rush of perceptions flooding through his brain. Freeboot had been walking him around in the forest for half an hour, giving the drugs time to take hold, gauging his level of response. By now, Hammerhead was in a world that was hallucinatory, dreamlike, intensely heightened. His mind was wide open and defenseless. Freeboot was high, too, just enough to tune in to that but still stay firmly in control.

"You got one final task to complete," Freeboot said. "You do it right, you make *maquis*. Now let me show you the reward I give to them I trust. It's called 'the way of heaven.' "

They reached the bathhouse that Freeboot called the Garden. He led Hammerhead around to the back, to a locked door that only he had the key to. It opened into a dark room. Hammerhead stumbled inside, groping blindly. Freeboot closed the door behind them, then stepped up to a wooden panel in a wall and slid it open. A small window of soft light appeared. Warm air drifted in through the opening, with the fragrance of incense and marijuana.

Freeboot pulled Hammerhead close.

The room they looked into shimmered with haze from the thermal water flowing through. It was rich with plants and flowers, antique furniture, statues and tapestries. Bottles of wine and liquor on a burnished copper bar seemed to glow with their own light.

But the centerpiece was Marguerite, rising from the big stone bath when the panel opened, as Freeboot had instructed her to. She was full-bodied, firmly muscled, with generous breast and hips. Her long black hair streamed wet down her back. Her taut olive skin was beaded with moisture.

She acted unaware of the watching men. Moving without hurry, she sat on the bathtub's rim and sensuously started rubbing a fine sheen of oil onto her breasts.

Hammerhead's staring eyes looked like golf balls—Freeboot could feel his mind, sense his astonishment at what he was seeing. The precious goal, so long the object of desire, was almost within reach.

"She's going to be yours any time you want her," Freeboot whispered to him. "She'll do whatever you tell her, she's got to. And not just her. Any bride you want, any*thing* you want. You see? That's the way of heaven."

Freeboot reached over to a shelf and took down another prepared goblet. Hammerhead drained it, not leaving the window. He was still staring at Marguerite when his knees buckled. He landed on them heavily, then crashed to the floor.

This time, the red wine was spiked with GHB. It would knock him out for twenty or thirty minutes. Then he would regain a dreamlike consciousness, but not be able to move.

Next stop on the journey was a way that heaven was not.

* * *

Half an hour later, Freeboot sat in the underground command bunker, drinking mescal and watching a monitor from a hidden infrared camera that was focused on Hammerhead's face. Hammerhead was in another of the camp's old mine shafts, stripped naked and sprawled back against a rocky wall seeping with cold damp. The blackness in there was absolute.

His eyelids starting to flicker. After a couple of minutes, they stayed open. He would be aware of his surroundings now—conscious of the cold, the dark, the sharp rocks biting into his flesh—but too leaden to do anything more than twitch.

Freeboot helped himself to another sharp hit of speed. He wanted to give Hammerhead's discomfort time to solidify into fear—the nightmare of being paralyzed in a dungeon—while the luscious vision of Marguerite, impossibly far away now, tortured his memory.

When Freeboot was good and ready, he started into the dark tunnel, moving as silently as a creature of the night. The meth surged in his brain, adding its power to the LSD and tequila. He carried an arm-long brand of pitchy pine, its knotty end soaked in gasoline. He advanced until he could hear Hammerhead's rough breathing. Then he clicked his cigarette lighter. The torch burst into flame, lighting the cavern's walls with a sinister flickering glow.

Hammerhead's wide eyes stared helplessly at the advancing fire.

"I can give you heaven," Freeboot called out in a harsh, echoing voice. "But I can destroy you, too. Have a taste of hell, brother! You can't move, but you can feel, ohhh, *yes.*"

He crouched and thrust the flaming torch close to Hammerhead's bare chest. Hammerhead's eyes bulged and his body jerked. A thin choked cry forced its way out from his slobbering lips.

Freeboot pulled the torch back.

"Except it's not just a little taste like that," he roared. "It's a fire that's a million times hotter, burning from inside your bones. And it lasts *forever.*"

He leaned forward, staring into Hammerhead's eyes from twelve inches away. The young man's rioting emotions lay bare before him—terror, pain, rage, confusion.

But more powerful than all the rest put together was the urge to please his master. It was always like this. Freeboot wanted to laugh, but he kept his face stony.

"You belong to me, body and soul," he said, murmuring now, working his way further into Hammerhead's mind. "I am *in* you. If you ever disobey me, if you ever turn rat, there ain't no place you can ever hide. I will find you, and I will bring you to this."

He held the torch to Hammerhead's chest again, closer and longer. This burn would blister his skin, not enough to impair him, but painful as hell. He wanted Hammerhead to know that this had not been just a dream.

"Now I will give you release," Freeboot said, and stood. Hammerhead had managed to roll his face to the side, panting in agony.

Freeboot took a third goblet of wine from its place. This time it was laced with chloral hydrate—an old-fashioned Mickey Finn—and Valium. It would knock Hammerhead out within seconds, and keep him down for a few hours.

When he woke up, he would be on his way to the home of Mr. and Mrs. Robert Emlinger.

Freeboot gripped Hammerhead's chin, tipped back his head, and sloshed the wine into his mouth, holding it open while he choked it down.

"Sleep," Freeboot said. "When you wake up, you're going to find out the reason you were born."

Twelve

A sharp *pop* brought Monks out of the half-sleep that he had drifted into, hunched in the chair in Mandrake's bedroom. He sat up, startled and confused. He was sure that the sound had come from somewhere in the lodge. But he hadn't heard anyone come inside.

Then he smelled the harsh reek of something burning. He quickly identified it as chemical, a fuel, and he realized what must have happened: the glass chimney of a kerosene lamp had burst, as they sometimes did from their own heat. If the kerosene leaked, the log building could go up in flames fast.

He heaved himself out of the chair and strode through the hanging blanket. The fire in the hearth had gotten low and the main room was almost dark. His gaze searched for the burning lamp, not finding it. It might be in the kitchen. He started that way.

A hissing, blinding spray exploded into his face, cutting across his eyeballs like broken glass, searing his nostrils and thoat. He stumbled, clawing at his eyes.

Something smashed into the back of his right knee. He collapsed, hands flailing for the floor to break his fall. The spray blasted his eyes again. He rolled, face buried in his arms, clogged lungs choking as he tried to suck in air.

A boot pressed down hard on the back of his neck. A hand gripped a fistful of his hair, twisting it painfully. Cold metal brushed his ear.

Monks realized dimly, in disbelief, that his hair was being sawn off.

His muscles tensed instinctively to thrash his arms and legs, and shake off this horror that crouched on top of him. But a voice spoke in his mind, with eerie clarity—*If you get Maced, don't fight back, 'cause knives can slip.*

He forced himself to lie still.

The hands left his head, then the boot released his neck. His burning eyes were still squeezed shut, but his throat was starting to open with agonizing slowness, allowing in a tiny trickle of rancid chemical-infused air. He remained motionless, concentrating on breathing, terrified that another burst of the spray would shut it off for good.

Instead, the attacker kicked him in the gut. His precious bit of breath exploded out of him in a wrenching wheeze. He doubled up fetally, knees tight against his chest and head hidden in his arms, braced for the stomping that would kill him.

But the boot only touched him one more time, tapping him contemptuously on the ear—a mocking suggestion of what it could do if it wanted to.

Then the room was still.

Monks lay as he was for another minute, until his lungs were taking in enough to function without being forced. Then he tugged his shirt loose and pressed the cloth against his eyes, clenching his teeth in pain as he fluttered them open. Mace and pepper sprays were designed not to do permanent damage, but he wanted to rinse without delay. He got up to his knees, swaying, trying to orient himself.

His blurred gaze swept past Mandrake's bedroom, then swung back.

The little boy was standing in the doorway, clutching the hanging blanket like a binky, holding it against his cheek, his thumb in his mouth.

Monks bit off a curse, got to his feet, and staggered to the kitchen.

The broken shards of a lamp chimney were in the sink. It had burst, all right—the attacker had broken it to lure him out.

He turned on the water tap and crouched, gripping the sink's lip and positioning his head under the cold clear stream. He turned from side to side so the water would course into his eyes, flushing them clear. Ideally, you were supposed to do this for several minutes, but he didn't have several minutes. He dried his face on his shirttail as he hurried to Mandrake's room. His fingers touched the spot behind his left ear where a clump of his hair was gone.

Mandrake was back in bed, scrunched into the corner as he had been when Monks first saw him. He was clutching his stuffed snake in front of him like a shield. His eyes looked like Greek olives.

Monks sat down beside him, moving slowly, managing to smile.

"Wow," he said. "You know what happened out there? I went to get a drink of water, and that mermaid was hiding! She tickled me so hard I thought I was going to explode."

Mandrake's face stayed blank. His eyes stared directly at Monks, but they were shielded, his mind withdrawn. Clearly, he knew that what he had seen was not a game, and he had gone back into that limbo of the only safety he could find.

Monks tucked him in and got ready to check his blood sugar. There was no telling how the shock might affect him.

Monks was trembling, his fear giving way to fury, not just for himself, but for Mandrake. But he was helpless, without even a guess at who the attacker was. The Mace had blasted his eyes before he had gotten a glimpse, and he had never laid a hand on him—or her—so as to be able to guess at size or weight. It could have been anybody.

Including Glenn.

Thirteen

The home of Mr. and Mrs. Robert Emlinger was built like an old-fashioned mansion, with a curving staircase that led up out of the huge, high-ceilinged living room to a balustraded walkway around the second story.

Taxman followed Hammerhead silently up the steps, watching him for signs of weakness. This was where it started to get real. Hammerhead was wired with meth and adrenaline, jumpy and scared, but that was all right. Next mission, he would be expected to function professionally.

Tonight, he only had to do one thing: get blooded.

This place was an easy target, the kind that Taxman always picked to break in a first-time *maquis*. There was no bodyguard or dog, and the microwave alarm system was vulnerable to a DTMF phone that read the tones of its entry code. Atherton was one of California's richest communities, an enclave of ivy-walled houses on city-block-sized lots, set far back from the streets and sheltered by high thick hedges and black iron gates across the driveways. The residents were used to feeling secure. Taxman and Hammerhead had gotten inside as quietly as fog. There was no need for night goggles, and they carried Glock .40-caliber semiautomatic pistols instead of the bulkier HK submachine guns.

It was 3:47 A.M.

Cold December moonlight filtered into the master bedroom through a pair of many-paned French doors, outlining the man and woman sleeping in bed. Taxman could smell the faint trace of the perfume that Mrs. Emlinger had worn that day.

Hammerhead stepped hesitantly up to the bed and jacked a round into the Glock's chamber.

The sharp click-*click* brought Emlinger suddenly upright. He stared wild-eyed at the two men. Hammerhead aimed at him but did not shoot.

Emlinger threw off his covers and lunged out of bed. Hammerhead stood there, paralyzed.

From the doorway, Taxman fired three quick rounds past him. Emlinger staggered, throwing his hands above his head like a Hollywood gunfighter, before crashing against a bureau and falling heavily to the floor.

Taxman stepped into the room. He had been ready for the freeze-up. No amount of training could prepare someone for killing a human being the first time. He gave Hammerhead a hard shove with the heel of his hand and jerked his head toward Mrs. Emlinger. She was sitting up now, pressed back against the headboard, clutching the covers to shield herself.

"Stop," she gasped, holding out a hand to fend them off. Her body and her voice both trembled. "Take whatever you want."

Hammerhead raised his pistol again, with a two-handed combat grip.

"No, my God," she pleaded. "I'll do anything." Abruptly she dropped the covers. The moonlight illuminated her fair skin and shapely breasts.

Hammerhead still did not shoot. Taxman could see that his hands were shaking.

He aimed his own pistol at Mrs. Emlinger. She screamed, a desperate piercing wail. Hammerhead jerked with a violent shudder, as if the sound slashed into him like a knife. Finally, his finger closed on the Glock's trigger.

The scream was cut short by the silenced *whump*. Her hands flew back against the bedboard, her head twisting to the side.

Hammerhead stood frozen again, openmouthed, staring at what he had done. Taxman gave him another hard shove.

"You ever hang up like that again, I'll kill you myself," he said harshly. "Now make sure."

Hammerhead got closer to Mrs. Emlinger, stumbling. Hands still shaking, he shot her again in the right temple, point blank. Her body jerked obscenely with the impact, then sagged, tipping to the side, as if into sleep.

"Him, too," Taxman said.

Emlinger was lying face down on the thick carpet. Hammerhead knelt over him and fired a shot into the base of his skull, just above where it joined his neck. His face bounced off the carpet.

The collection of antique jade was downstairs in the living room, on display in a large glass case. Taxman shined a mini-flashlight over the dozens of items—delicately carved lions and Buddhas, bracelets, rings, and ornaments. He knew that it was valued at more than a quarter of a million dollars, and many of the pieces were listed in art history registries.

"Pick something out for your girl," Taxman said.

Hammerhead's eyes widened. Like a child who'd been offered a piece of candy, he moved his hand over the case, trying to decide. It stopped, pointing, above a dark-green, gold-chained pendant shaped like a roaring dragon.

Taxman smashed the glass with his pistol butt and handed the pendant to Hammerhead. "Take this, brother, may it serve you well," he said. "You're *maquis* now."

He scooped the other items into his pack, then beeped on his belt radio to summon Shrinkwrap, who was waiting a few blocks away, her hair dyed gray and her face aged with makeup—a well-to-do, middle-aged lady driving a BMW 750 iL. The jade would be picked up by other *maquis* and taken to Los Angeles, where, within hours, it was going to start turning up in homeless camps, just like the Calamity Jane golf clubs.

Fourteen

Monks stepped out of the lodge in the gray light of dawn. His eyes still burned faintly from the Mace his attacker had sprayed him with, and his ribs ached where they had crashed against the floor.

He had done a lot of thinking during the long predawn hours.

The camp was deserted except for the inevitable guard skulking near the perimeter, a thin figure with an assault rifle slung over his shoulder. Monks recognized him as the unlucky Sidewinder, who had staggered away from the campfire last night wrapped in a bloody, gutted deer carcass. He looked sullen and avoided eye contact. He had been punished for asking Monks a question about the dangers of eating raw flesh, and probably he blamed Monks, the way that everyone else around here seemed to.

Monks walked to the washhouse, taking advantage of his aloneness to look around for possible routes out of here. Nothing seemed promising. The mist was so thick that the tops of the trees ringing the camp were lost in it.

Monks had enough experience in mountain hiking to know that even open terrain was likely to be treacherous. Trails petered out, branched bewilderingly, led into deadfall-choked ravines or unscalable chasms. Without a compass, in poor visibility, getting turned around was almost a given. And this terrain was anything but open. Then there were the other obstacles—starting with armed guards.

The only faint chance, he decided, would be to enlist an ally—someone who knew the turf.

And a weapon would come in mighty handy.

"The Indians thought white men were really weird," said a voice in his ear.

Monks jerked away in shock and twisted to see Freeboot, standing close enough to touch him. *Where did he come from?* Monks hadn't heard a whisper of his approach.

"For wanting to shit inside," Freeboot finished. He was watching Monks benignly, thumbs hooked in his belt. "The more I thought about it, the more sense it made. So feel free to use the woods, Rasp." Freeboot swept his hand in an expansive, offering gesture.

Then he focused on the side of Monks's head, squinting in almost comic puzzlement.

"You decide to give yourself a haircut?" Freeboot said.

"I cut myself shaving," Monks said.

Freeboot seemed amused by the comeback. In fact, Monks's stubble of beard was bristling noticeably.

"I'm going to remind you that we've got to get your son out of here," Monks said. "I'll make you a deal. Let me take him, and—"

"You won't say nothing about us, and nobody will know where he came from," Freeboot interrupted. "Shrinkwrap already told me."

"Well?"

"Sorry, dude. No can do, not right now. How are the supplies holding up?"

"It's not *about* how the supplies are holding up," Monks said. "It's about how Mandrake's holding up."

"I thought he was getting better."

"The insulin helped stabilize him, but that's not going to last."

"You gotta get a more positive attitude," Freeboot said, shaking his head.

"I'm just telling you how it is."

Freeboot's eyes flared, in his characteristic instant transition from seeming tranquility to menace.

"You don't tell *me* how it is. I tell *you.*"

Freeboot turned away suddenly, toward a wrist-thick dead branch jutting out from a pine tree, about the height of a basketball hoop. He was less than six feet tall but he leaped up, caught it with his right hand, and dangled there.

"I was a punk kid," he yelled out. "Spent a lot of my life in jail. Dope, petty theft, finally pulled five years for armed robbery. I was looking at that third strike."

He started chinning himself with the one arm. Monks counted ten before he paused again. He did not seem to be straining.

"Then I had a *epiphany,*" Freeboot bellowed. It was another term, like *virtu,* that didn't come naturally from his lips. "I don't mean like all the guys in the joint who get religion. I saw through this fucked-up society—what it did to me, and how stupid I was to let it. That's when everything changed. I started to read, man. I started to *think.*"

He switched hands in midair and did ten more chin-ups with his left arm. Finished, he dropped to the ground, still breathing easily.

"I got my head together and I got my body in shape," he said. "I got where I need to be." He folded his arms and waited, his gaze steady on Monks.

It seemed that whatever challenge existed between them in Freeboot's mind had reached the point where the line was drawn in the dirt.

"To start Revolution Number 9?" Monks said.

Freeboot nodded, looking pleased. "Right on. John Lennon saw this coming." He spoke with the air of having privileged information. "That song was a message, kicking it off. That's why he got killed. The deal about the guy being a fan is bullshit. It was the CIA that zapped him."

"I don't recall that there *was* any message in the song," Monks said.

"That's the point, man," Freeboot said mysteriously. "He who hath ears, let him hear."

So—the Bible, the Beatles, and conspiracy theories had joined the mix. It was impossible to take seriously—and yet, the more that Monks saw and heard, the scarier it got.

"I still don't get why you care what I think," Monks said.

Freeboot's face took on a sly look. "I hear you got fucked over by the system yourself."

Monks realized that Glenn must have told Freeboot about this, too—an incident from a dozen years earlier, when paramedics had killed an elderly woman by ignoring Monks's radioed orders from a hospital ER. Then, to cover themselves, they had destroyed the recorded tape of the radio conversation. Monks was eventually vindicated, but by then he had lost his job, marriage, and a lot of his friends, and he had plunged into a rage-driven alcoholic depression that he almost hadn't come out of.

Freeboot was right. He *had* been fucked over by the system.

"True enough," Monks said.

"Cost you big, huh?"

"In a lot of ways."

"So maybe you and me aren't so far apart," Freeboot said.

"Maybe," Monks said. "Except that one of us is the other's prisoner."

"That could change. Let's say I was thinking about giving you a chance to get on this bus."

A crow cawed suddenly in the forest, a harsh grating *anhhh-anhhh* that seemed to tumble in on the wind. The big black shape swooped down out of the foggy treetops a second later. It landed near the edge of the clearing, folded its wings, and hopped to investigate something on the ground, pausing to caw again and glare around, warding off competition.

Monks kept his expression careful, as if appraising the offer.

"You don't seem to think much of doctors," he said.

"Oh, they got their uses, don't get me wrong. What it comes down to is *virtu*, see?"

"No," Monks said, "I don't."

Freeboot turned away, clasping his hands behind his back. He raised his face to the cloudy sky, as if searching for an answer. The pose seemed staged, like others that Monks had seen—and yet he had the sudden sense that this was a crucial moment—that Freeboot was about to impart something weighty, and that everything that happened from here on would depend on how it played out. Monks shifted uneasily and realized that he was getting cold. The fresh wet wind was picking up, tossing the mist-shrouded treetops.

"My son is ordained to be the root of my dynasty," Freeboot said, still facing the sky. "I know Mandrake's just a kid. I'm giving him some time, with the insulin. It's like training wheels. But if you don't take the training wheels away, he's never going to learn to ride without them. He's got to prove he's got *virtu*."

"You mean Mandrake has to pull himself out of his sickness," Monks said.

"It's not his fault, I understand that. It's his mother. No way I could have known she had bad genes. But I can't be passing *my* genes down through a kid who's damaged goods, you know what I'm saying?"

A day ago, Monks would have been astounded. Now, this only filled in another piece of the puzzle. Bound up with Freeboot's concept of himself as Nietzschean superman was a facile, distorted understanding of genetics.

Then, in an instant of electric clarity, Monks grasped the real reason that Freeboot refused to take the little boy to a hospital—the reason why a man who would eat the raw heart of a deer quailed in terror at being tainted by the urine of his own son. The issues of faith, the distortion of *virtu* into a mystical healing power, the need to be sure he could trust Monks, were all a sham. The truth stemmed from Freeboot's diabetic uncle.

Freeboot was afraid that *he*, not Motherlode, had passed on the diabetes to Mandrake—afraid that medical examination would reveal this, and bring his megalomaniacal theory of his own superiority crashing down.

And he was willing to stand by and let his son die to keep that from happening.

Once again, despising himself for it, Monks kept his true feelings to himself.

"You've given me a lot to think about," he said.

"We're just talking, that's all. We got to get to know each other a lot better. Trust, right?"

Monks nodded.

Freeboot turned and started away. The interview was over. But then he paused and looked back.

"You want to take a hot bath, let me know. We got a luxury setup." He grinned. "Maybe even provide you some company, a pretty girl to wash your back—and, hey, who knows what else?"

"I'll think about that, too," Monks said.

He walked on to the washhouse and cleaned up distractedly, trying to make sense of this gambit. Freeboot could hardly be serious about his offer to join, and Monks's initial hope—that he might be able to pay extortion money for Glenn and be set free—was long gone. After all that he had seen, that would be far too great of a risk for Freeboot. More likely, this show of friendliness was a way of keeping Monks cooperative, for as long as Mandrake stayed alive.

After that . . .

When Monks walked back outside, he saw that there were now three crows on the ground, croaking and flapping their wings at each other in contention for some bit of carrion. Sidewinder, the guard, was sighting his rifle at them and jerking the barrel up in a pantomime of each gunshot's recoil.

Monks felt the first light sprays of rain against his face.

In mid-morning, Monks heard the lodge's outside door slam violently, then bootsteps in the main room, heavy enough to rattle the lamp's glass chimney. He tensed, fearing that it was one of the guards, coming to drag him off to another lesson that Freeboot had arranged.

But a man's voice called out excitedly: "Marguerite! Where are you?"

Monks heard her muffled reply from the kitchen.

"Come when you're called, girl," the man commanded.

Monks got up quietly and went to the bedroom's doorway. The unmistakable shape of Hammerhead stood in the room's center. He was holding something behind his back. His grin looked manic.

Marguerite walked slowly out of the kitchen, her own face tense and uncertain.

"I'm full *maquis* now," Hammerhead announced. "I want you in the Garden, wearing this and nothing else."

He thrust something toward her, holding it in his big hands and letting it slither through his fingers like a snake. Monks glimpsed a gold chain.

Marguerite's mouth opened, but not with the pleasure of a woman receiving a gift—more as if it *was* a snake. Her hands, instead of reaching to receive it, twisted each other nervously.

"Where'd you get that?" she breathed.

Hammerhead frowned. Clearly, this was not the reaction that he had expected.

"Never mind where I got it. You have to do what I tell you. Put it on!"

With obvious reluctance, she reached forward to accept it, and slipped it around her neck. At the end of the gold chain hung a dark green pendant, but Monks was too far away to see it clearly.

"Now come on," Hammerhead said. He grasped her wrist, pulling her toward the door.

"Wait," she said, struggling with his grip. "I have to feed Mandrake."

This was not true, but Hammerhead didn't know that, and he seemed to realize that it was something he didn't dare interfere with. He hesitated, then pulled her close and planted a wide-mouthed kiss on her, an embrace she neither resisted nor accepted.

"Hurry up," he said into her ear, in a voice thick with passion. "I've been waiting for this forever."

He let her go and strode out of the building. Marguerite lifted the pendant off over her head and gazed at it, still looking troubled, but fascinated, too.

"If you're going to be leaving, Mandrake *could* use some soup," Monks said.

She looked up at him swiftly, then spun away, clasping the pendant tight in her fist and hurrying back into the kitchen.

He returned to his chair, bemused by the exchange but too burdened by his other worries to try to make sense of it. Mandrake was still withdrawn and listless, not responding to Monks's attempts to draw him out. At first, Monks had thought it was from the shock of seeing the violent attack last night.

But Mandrake's forehead had gotten noticeably warmer during the night, and he was developing a weak but ugly cough. Mucus was forming in his nose, streaking his upper lip. Monks feared that he was coming down with a virus, or even pneumonia.

That could easily precipitate a coma. Then the end would not be far off, and there wasn't a thing in the world that Monks could do about it.

His watch read 10:14 A.M. That left just seven hours of daylight to find a way out of here.

Fifteen

By mid-afternoon, the rain was coming down in sheets, driven by lashing gusts of wind that blew the trees around like candle flames. The gloom was already indistinguishable from twilight. The camp seemed almost deserted. Sidewinder continued to skulk around, taking refuge under the eaves of a shed, apparently forbidden to go inside; and a couple of the other men had stopped into the lodge to make sandwiches. But Monks had been alone with Mandrake for the past hour. With the rain, there wasn't much incentive to wander around.

He walked to the kitchen to check out something that he had noticed on one of his trips back from the washhouse—a gap in the old rock-and-mortar foundation, where the kitchen water and drain pipes ran in. Probably the plumbing had been added some time after the lodge was built, requiring a space for a man to slither in under the floor. The water pipe was wrapped with insulation, suggesting that it was prone to freezing. Monks had done a fair amount of plumbing on his own house, and once in a while the weather got cold enough that he needed to thaw a pipe. It was a lot easier when there was access to it from both ends.

He opened the cabinet under the kitchen sink. A section of the heavy plank floor had been cut out for the pipes, then replaced with two pieces of half-inch plywood, about eighteen by twenty-four inches, joining in the middle with hemispherical cuts around the pipes.

The plywood was not nailed down.

He quickly removed the items under the sink—cleaning supplies and a bucket to catch drips from the leaky drain—and lifted the plywood sections. He could just see a gray patch of twilight through the foundation's gap, fifteen feet away. It opened out the back, on the opposite side of the lodge from Sidewinder's watch point.

It would be a tough squirm for a good-sized man. But a good-sized desperate man could make it.

He replaced the stuff under the sink, mentally going through all the factors he could bring to mind. Then he walked to the lodge's door and stepped out into the rain.

Sidewinder walked to meet him, unhappily drawn forth from his cover.

"Where you going, man?" he said.

"To visit my son," Monks said, continuing his walk toward Glenn's cabin. He had been watching it from the lodge's windows, and had seen Glenn a couple of times, hurrying to the washhouse or on some errand. But he had not seen Shrinkwrap. He was hoping that she was gone.

"I'm already fucking soaked," Sidewinder complained. "I was outside all night and I haven't slept. Freeboot's making me stay on duty, 'cause—"

"Because you asked me that question last night?" Monks interrupted. Sardonic words came to his mind—*Sorry I caused you trouble*—but he had already made enough enemies here.

Instead, he said, "I'd have worried about eating that raw meat, too. I think Freeboot overreacted."

"Yeah," Sidewinder said, seeming slightly cheered by the sympathy.

"Look, I'm not going to try anything, are you kidding?" Monks said. "You can stay where you were and watch the door. I'll only be a few minutes."

Sidewinder glanced around nervously, as if fearing that Freeboot would materialize and smite him for this slackness. Then he nodded and hurried back to his shelter. But he unslung his rifle and stood at watchful attention.

Smoke was rising from the stovepipe of Glenn's cabin, a thin plume barely visible in the rain. Monks knocked sharply on the door, and braced himself for the possibility of facing the hostile Shrinkwrap.

But it was Glenn who answered, opening the door just a few inches. He looked bleary, surprised to see his father. If he noticed Monks's missing chunk of hair, he gave no sign of it. But, then, Glenn was a good enough actor to pull that off.

"Let me in," Monks said. "It's pouring."

Glenn's face turned reluctant, and he seemed about to object, but Monks pushed the door open and stepped past him.

Immediately, Monks saw at least one reason for Glenn's hesitation. There was a woman in the room, but not Shrinkwrap. It was Motherlode, lounging on the bed, watching the screen of a laptop computer that was playing a video—a Tom and Jerry cartoon, it looked like.

She stared at Monks blank-eyed, then glanced furtively at the dresser. He followed her gaze to a syringe—one that had been pilfered from Mandrake's supply—and a bottle of Percocets. There were other items that Monks recognized as being used to render the pills injectable—a porcelain coffee cup for grinding them up and mixing them into solution, a soggy wad of tissues for straining it, and a length of surgical rubber tubing.

One syringe. Two people.

"I hurt my back," Motherlode said.

She was wearing sweatclothes, and Glenn was fully dressed; the situation did not appear to be a sexual one. Monks figured that was none of his concern anyway. He just wanted to get her out of here.

"Mandrake would really like to see you," he told her. "Now would be a good time."

Her eyes focused a little more.

"I can't—" she began.

"Try to overcome your pain," he said, with a harsh edge. He held her gaze, letting some of his anger show in his own.

Pouting, she got up and put on an anorak, not forgetting to collect her Percocets before she went reluctantly out the door.

Glenn slapped his own thigh in anger. "*Now* you come in and fuck up my party. This ain't my room at home, Rasp."

Monks stepped to a window and watched Motherlode hurry off through the rain. As he had expected, she did not go toward the lodge to visit her child.

"She's been stealing these from Mandrake," he said, showing Glenn the syringe. He set it back on the dresser. "You ever hear that it's not smart to share a needle?"

Glenn shrugged, but he looked uneasy. "I hardly ever shoot anymore."

"This must be a special occasion."

"If you're nice to her, she'll share." Glenn grinned slyly, displaying his black-spotted teeth. "Sometimes 'codes are a good way to chill out. Especially when you've been doing a lot of crank."

"That's what you're using mostly? Meth?"

"Yeah. Shrinkwrap got me off junk."

"By getting you *on* speed?"

"Sort of. Freeboot doesn't like hard dope for the people he's got to count on. It slows you down, makes you unreliable."

"He doesn't seem to mind with Motherlode."

Glenn snorted. "He doesn't care what *she* does."

The casual callousness hit Monks with a pain so deep, it went beyond sorrow. It came to him that there was no point in worrying anymore about who was to blame for all that had gone wrong between them. They were like different, hostile species.

And yet, this was still the son that he had raised. That bond that went all the way down to the DNA in their cells—deeper than the rational mind could ever hope to penetrate—would never be erased.

It was impossible to break through to Glenn and impossible to quit trying.

Monks walked over to him and gripped him tightly by the upper arm. Glenn tried to pull away, but Monks, although decades older, was larger, stronger, and not wasted by drug abuse.

"I need you to call for help," Monks said. "That kid's going to die if we don't get him out of here."

Glenn's eyes showed alarm. "No way, man."

"If you don't, his blood's going to be on your hands. Let that sink in through your tough-guy shell, Glenn. A four-year-old."

Glenn's gaze flicked around, as if he were looking to escape. "I mean—there's no lines up here, and cell phones don't work."

"Come on, you're the computer ace. There has to be some way."

"There's satellite e-mail, but Freeboot changes the password every day. He only gives it to me when he wants something."

"Is there a vehicle we could steal?"

"They keep all the cars at the security station up the road," Glenn said, squirming under Monks's grip. "There's guards, twenty-four seven."

Monks remembered with icy clarity the group of scalp-hunting *maquis* that he had seen last night—trained, violent, and well armed.

"Do you have a gun?" he said.

"Dad, you're fucking *crazy*—"

Monks shook him hard.

"No," Glenn muttered. "I don't need one for what I do. Now, would you let me go, please?"

So—this failure was absolute. Monks had not really expected Glenn to suddenly come to his senses. By Glenn's lights, he *was* making the sensible choice—staying safe. Still, Monks had harbored the faint hope of swaying him and made one last try.

"You're strung out, at risk, maybe dangerously ill," Monks said. "And mentally impaired. You've bought into whatever fanaticism

Freeboot and Shrinkwrap are preaching, but all they're going to do is take you down."

He stared hard into his son's eyes for another ten seconds, then released him. Glenn backed away, rubbing his arm and looking badly shaken. The tough-guy skin had been bruised at least a little bit.

"I can't leave here," Glenn said, with a whine in his tone.

"Of course you can."

"You don't understand, man."

Monks exhaled. "I'm going as soon as it's dark. Say, twenty minutes. Come over to the lodge if you change your mind."

"Why the fuck did you bring this on me?" Glenn burst out, in misery and anger. "Now I'm part of it."

"You don't have to tell anybody."

"I *can't* lie to Freeboot."

Monks shook his head helplessly. There was no answer to that. He clasped Glenn's shoulder, more gently this time.

"I love you, Glenn," he said. "Believe that, will you?"

He stepped out into the downpour, leaving Glenn standing there, pale and alone.

Through the deepening gloom, Monks could just make out the thin figure of Sidewinder. He threw a salute in that direction and walked on to the lodge, clamping off his surging emotions like severed blood vessels—no time to deal with that now.

The lodge was still empty. He quickly checked Mandrake over, and coaxed as much water down him as he would take. His brief improvement had slowed and maybe reversed. Monks had anguished over whether to take him along, or race for freedom in the hopes of sending back help. Trying to carry him would impede Monks severely, and might doom them both.

But while leaving Glenn behind was wrenching, leaving Mandrake would be unbearable. Glenn was an adult, capable of making his own decisions. Monks hardened his heart. This was triage.

He was under no illusions about his chances—carrying the boy on foot, without a weapon or even decent gear, they amounted to not much better than nil. The only hope he could see was to beat his pursuers to the thick, brushy timber ahead, where their night goggles would not be of much use. If he made it to the next day's light, he would try to reach a paved road.

He broke a porcelain cup into shards and used one of them to worry slits in a wool blanket, fashioning it into a serape for himself. It was far from adequate, but wool would at least keep you warm when it was wet. He fashioned another blanket into a sling that he could loop around his shoulders to carry Mandrake. He collected the remaining insulin and syringes into a pillowcase, along with some bread and cheese that he had taken from the kitchen, and stuffed that inside his shirt.

Mandrake seemed only vaguely aware of what was happening when Monks wrapped him in the blanket, pulling his legs through the slits so they would hang free like a baby's in a carrier.

"Come on, buddy," Monks whispered. "Let's go find some mermaids."

Sixteen

Monks quickly pulled up the plywood panels under the kitchen sink, then lowered Mandrake into the crawl space. He followed head first, squeezing his way painfully through the narrow cut-out. There was only about a foot of room between the cold earth and the floor joists. He managed to reach back up and pull the cabinet doors closed. Then he rolled onto his belly and wormed his way forward, pushing Mandrake ahead of him as gently as he could.

The opening in the rock foundation was barely visible now. He pushed Mandrake out and worked his way through, one arm and shoulder at a time. The sharp rock edges scraped his skin through his clothes, and the sluicing rain was already soaking his arms and legs. Finally free, he spent a few seconds on hands and knees, getting his breath. Then he scooped up the little boy and stood, arranging the sling over his shoulders.

"I was just starting to trust you," Freeboot said, behind him. "You motherfucker."

Before Monks could turn around, he heard a distinct metallic click—like a gun's safety being released. A figure stepped into view ahead of him, from around the corner of the building. It was Sidewinder, holding his assault rifle leveled.

Monks sagged.

"Put the kid down," Freeboot said. He sounded more disgusted than angry, like a teacher whose patience with an unruly student had finally run out. It was more chilling than his rage.

Monks unslung Mandrake and set him on the ground.

"Take off your blanket."

Monks pulled his homemade serape over his head and tossed it aside.

"Callus," Freeboot called commandingly.

A third figure came striding toward them from the forest. Monks recalled seeing him at the scalp hunt. Like the other *maquis*, he was clean-shaven and neat-haired, with an insurance salesman's look that contrasted jarringly with his backwoods clothes. He was one of the older men, in his thirties, and he had an air of efficiency that was almost prim—but there was a ruthlessness about it, too.

Callus also was carrying a leveled rifle, Monks thought at first. Then he realized that it was a tree branch, four or five feet long and twice as thick as a broomstick.

Something slipped around Monks's neck, yanking tight. He clutched at it, fighting to free himself from the choking pressure. But it was futile. His fingers felt leather, slippery with rain—Sidewinder's rifle sling.

Monks drove his right elbow back into Sidewinder's gut with everything he had. He got the grim satisfaction of feeling Sidewinder double up with an explosive grunt. The sling's grip loosened. Monks stomped down hard on Sidewinder's instep with his bootheel, and fought to twist around.

Off to the side, he thought he heard Freeboot laughing.

Then Callus swung his heavy stick across Monks's shins.

Monks yelled, a roar of rage and disbelief at the agony that burst through his bones and shot up into his brain. Pain was so *intimate.* There was no way to hide. It knew everything about every tiny bit of you, flared up in every one of those millions of nerve endings that you were unaware of most of the time.

"You *cock*sucker," Sidewinder sobbed into his ear. The sling tightened viciously. Through the spots starting to float across his vision, Monks saw Callus swing the stick again. This time, the impact was hard enough to chip bone. Monks clawed back at Sidewinder's face, his feet dancing crazily, trying to run of their own accord.

A third blow crashed across his shins, bringing him to the edge of blacking out. His consciousness was filled with the torture in his legs and the sound of his own choked bellowing in his ears.

The pressure around his neck let up suddenly, and the sling was released. The rifle butt slammed into his back, driving him sprawling onto the ground.

"Next time we'll use a sledgehammer," Freeboot said. "Now get back under that floor."

Monks crawled to the foundation's opening and forced himself through, moving helplessly past the wool-wrapped bundle that was Mandrake. Maybe he had been aware of what had happened, maybe not.

"He still needs his blood sugar checked every hour," Monks panted. "And the insulin shots."

Something came into view outside. There was just enough light left for him to recognize Freeboot's bare feet.

"Yeah?" Freeboot said. "I'm starting to think you've been *keeping* him sick. Trying to get me to let you go."

"If you want him to die, you're almost there," Monks said hoarsely.

The feet stayed there a few seconds longer. Then they were gone.

"*You*, fuckhead—I ought to make you get in there with him," he heard Freeboot say to Sidewinder. "You better be right on top of him, watching every second. Callus, bring the kid."

Another pair of feet appeared outside the opening, this time wearing boots.

"You stick your fucking nose out, I'll blow it off," Sidewinder said. His voice trembled with fury.

Monks curled up again and closed his eyes, trying to rub a little of the fire out of his throbbing shins. A couple of minutes later, he heard the sound of bootsteps on the kitchen floor above him, then hammering. The plywood sheets under the sink were being nailed down. There might have been a hidden camera, watching him the entire time, he thought.

Or Glenn had gone to Freeboot and alerted him that Monks was planning to run.

Gradually, the pain subsided to a bearable ache. The discomfort of being cold and wet moved in to join it. Lying in the dirt, trapped by the floor joists, he couldn't move enough to warm himself. Within half an hour he was shivering convulsively.

A warm deer carcass to crawl into would have looked pretty good about now.

Seventeen

A couple of hours later, Monks heard Sidewinder kick loudly against the lodge's wall.

"Hey! Asshole!" he yelled. "Come on out."

Monks uncurled himself stiffly and squirmed to the foundation's opening, his raw shins scraping against the hard rock-strewn dirt. He pulled himself out into the rainy gloom, fearful that he was going to get a boot or rifle butt in the face. But Sidewinder only held the leveled weapon on him.

"Freeboot says you can go back inside," he said sullenly.

Monks's eyes teared up with pleasure when he stumbled into the firelit warmth of the lodge. But when he walked into Mandrake's bedroom, he saw that the shackles with the cable attached, were lying on the floor.

"Put 'em on," Sidewinder ordered. His raingear was dripping puddles onto the floor, and his face radiated his rage and resentment.

Monks sat, pulled off his boots, and snapped the iron rings around his own ankles.

"Freeboot's got some business to take care of," Sidewinder said. "He told me to tell you the kid better be better when he gets back."

He turned on his bootheel, in pseudo-military style, and stalked out.

Mandrake was in bed, lying on his tummy. He didn't open his eyes or respond when Monks turned him over. His forehead was hot. Whatever complication was at work was advancing. Monks helplessly moistened the inside of the child's mouth. Dehydration was quickly entering into the mix—while sheets of rain pounded down on the metal roof.

Sidewinder hadn't said how long it would be until Freeboot came back, but this much was certain: the kid was not going to be better.

Monks sat down and painfully unstuck his pant legs from the crusted blood on his shins, then pulled them up to his knees. By now the lacerations were surrounded by long purple bruises, and swollen into knobs. He explored them with his fingers, grimacing fiercely. At least they weren't the kinds of wounds that were likely to get infected, and any bone chips would eventually heal themselves. It just hurt like hell.

A couple of minutes later, he heard the lodge's door open and close. Quiet footsteps hurried across the floor toward him.

Marguerite stepped hesitantly into the bedroom. She looked concerned, even frightened. Her eyes widened at the sight of his legs.

"I heard what happened," she said. "I got Freeboot to let you back in."

Wearily, Monks nodded thanks.

She stepped to the curtain, to leave, he thought. Instead, she looked around the outer room, then came back in and knelt beside his chair.

"I'll help you get away," she whispered. "I know how. You have to take me, too."

He stared at her in numb amazement. For the first time, she seemed really to be looking at him. Her dark eyes were clear, free of the spaced-out affect he had grown used to.

But wariness followed instantly. He had not forgotten that she was the one who had set him up in the first place.

"Is this another one of Freeboot's tests?" he said.

"No." She looked puzzled. "Freeboot's gone, he'll be gone all night. So will most of the others."

That jibed with what Sidewinder had said.

"How did he catch me?" Monks asked, probing to find out if there was a hidden camera that might be watching them right now.

"Coil told him."

The news came like another ugly bucket of sludge, thrown on top of all the rest. But it had the ring of truth.

"What changed your mind?" Monks said.

As she hesitated, guilt, shame, and the admission of her own stupidity passed across her eyes.

"I didn't want to believe you," she said. "That Mandrake's going to die. But I've been watching him, while you were . . . gone. He seems like he's almost dead now."

Monks kept staring hard at her, trying to believe her.

Her gaze faltered. "I understand why you don't trust me," she said.

"Bring me a gun, and I'll start."

"I can't get a gun. But Hammerhead's standing guard. He volunteered, because of me."

"And?"

"You could take his gun," she said.

"Just walk up and ask him for it?"

"I could—you know, get him thinking about something else," she said, with her eyes still lowered. "You'd have to hit him, or something."

Sure, nothing to it, Monks thought. "With what?"

"There's pipe wrenches in the toolshed." She held out her hands about three feet apart. Monks was distantly surprised that she even knew what pipe wrenches were. But that was probably as good a weapon as anything short of a firearm. A knife or garrote was too risky against a man as strong and well trained as Hammerhead.

A hard blast across the back of the head, while not exactly honorable, might do it.

"What about this?" he said, reaching down to rattle his shackles.

"There's bolt cutters, too."

"Can you get other gear? Flashlight, matches, compass? Some food, warm coats. A rucksack, to carry Mandrake."

"I'll try," she said. She reached into a pocket of her jeans and pressed something into his hand. It felt smooth and cold like a pebble. "This will jack you up." She rose and slipped out.

Monks opened his hand and looked at what she'd given him—a small glass makeup jar with a screw-on lid. It was full of finely ground white powder.

His first impulse was to throw it out. But he hesitated. Meth seemed to be the key to the violent, psychotic edge that the *maquis* had, and that might be a big help right now.

He opened the jar and and tapped some of the powder out onto the dresser top—about half the amount he had seen Freeboot use. He didn't have a knife to inhale it with, but he knew that it could be done through a narrow paper tube, and he fashioned one from a page he tore out of one of the *Heavy Metal* magazines.

He snorted hard with each nostril. It shot in like a hot sharp wire thrusting up behind his eyes and into his brain. The burn worsened instantly, becoming almost intolerable, bringing him to panic that he had done himself serious harm. But then it gradually calmed, leaving a metallic-tinged residue—and a bristling, fiercely euphoric energy.

Monks paced the small room, allowing the ache in his shins and the clank of his chains to steadily heighten his fury, like the drumbeats of a primitive tribe in a war dance—tangible reminders of his own helplessness, of the child who was slipping away from him, of his terror that this was another trap that was going to bring him only a brutal, agonized death.

Very soon, his hands were flexing in anticipation of that pipe wrench.

Eighteen

Marguerite came back twenty minutes later, carrying a big laundry basket covered with a dripping poncho. Monks pulled the poncho off. On top were neatly folded pajamas for Mandrake. But they hid a warm hooded snowsuit underneath, and a nylon rucksack big enough to carry him. Then came a large polyfil jacket with a water-resistant shell, the kind that the men wore around camp. Wrapped up in it were a folding pocket knife, a heavy-duty flashlight, matches, and a Ziploc bag stuffed with bread, cheese, cold cuts, and candy bars. There was no compass, but this was a hell of a good start on getting out of here and staying alive.

At the bottom, his groping hand touched metal. A pair of bolt cutters and a pipe wrench about thirty inches long were nestled in the laundry like snakes in a brushpile.

"Hammerhead just called in his security check-in," Marguerite whispered urgently. "We've got an hour before they'll miss him. He's waiting for me, over at the bathhouse. Give me a couple of minutes."

"Whoa, wait," Monks said. "You have to keep him outside. I need a clear shot at him."

She bit her lip nervously. Then she brightened.

"I'll tell him I want to do it in the rain."

Monks was impressed. That was thinking on your feet.

"Get up against a wall," he said. "That'll keep his back turned."

"Don't worry, he won't be thinking about anything but me." She left again, looking scared but determined.

Monks got out the bolt cutters and snipped the chains from his ankles. His feet once again were free. He put the snowsuit on Mandrake, then slit the rucksack to allow for his legs and eased him into it. This was going to be a lot easier to carry than the clumsy sling.

Then he traded the bolt cutters for the big pipe wrench, clenching his shaking hands around its steely shaft and hefting it to gauge its balance.

Everything was going to have to go right the first time.

The driving rain slashed at his face, blurring his vision as he eased out the lodge's door. He stared into the night, crouching, waiting for his eyes to adjust. The bathhouse was about forty yards away. Within half a minute, he could see two entwined figures. Hammerhead was shoving Marguerite up against the wall, his hands working at the waist of her jeans, revealing her pale skin as he pushed them down. His rifle was slung over his shoulder.

The wrench handle was getting wet and slippery. Monks wiped it under his arm and moved forward, quickly closing the forty-yard gap. The rain helped to cover the sound of his steps, and there was no doubt that Marguerite was right about Hammerhead's mind being far from anything but her just now.

Monks slowed, taking the final steps in a mincing prowl. He was close enough now to hear the big man's grunts as he worked to rid her of her jeans. He rose out of his crouch, planted his feet, and cocked the wrench like a medieval executioner with a mace. The blow might crush Hammerhead's skull, but mercy was something that Monks could not afford.

Then he realized that Marguerite had frozen in place, and was staring fearfully at him over Hammerhead's shoulder.

With ferocious speed, Hammerhead shoved away from her and started to turn, head lowering and hands rising.

Monks swung with all the strength in his arms and shoulders, but it was not the well-placed slam that he had counted on. The wrench caught the side of Hammerhead's thick skull above the right ear, glancing upward and almost flying out of Monk's grip.

Hammerhead reeled back but stayed on his feet. With a blood-chilling sound that was part roar and part snarl, he charged at Monks, coming in low with outspread arms like a linebacker.

Monks pivoted off his left foot in a boxer's slip, and brought the wrench down hard across Hammerhead's shoulders as he lumbered past. This blow drove him to his knees. Incredibly, he kept slogging forward, clawing at his rifle to unsling it.

Monks leaped after him, boots slipping in the mud. This time, he swung the wrench at Hammerhead's right upper arm. He felt the *snap* of the humerus all the way up in his teeth.

Hammerhead roared again and fell onto his side, the broken arm flopping. Monks stepped in and yanked the rifle off his shoulder, then made a quick 360-degree sweep of the camp. Nothing else visible was moving.

His fingers traveled over the rifle's breech, identifying safety and selector switch. It was similar to the AK-47's he had seen in Vietnam. The only times that he had ever fired assault rifles were a few sessions with AR-15's in basic training. Weapons expertise was not a high priority for medical officers on hospital ships. But after treating enough wounds from larger-caliber weapons like this one, he had familiarized himself with them out of some sort of superstitious dread, as if the guns themselves were the enemy.

Marguerite was still against the wall, eyes wide with shock and jeans pushed down to her hips. Her last-second panic might have saved Hammerhead's life.

"We need a place to lock him up," Monks snapped at her. "Come on, quick."

She started to move like someone coming out of a dream, pointing at a dark shed another twenty yards away, then fumbling to button her pants.

Monks stepped back to Hammerhead and pressed the muzzle against his head.

"All I need is an excuse," Monks said. "Get up and drop your gear belt."

Hammerhead got heavily to his knees, then to his feet. Clumsily, with his left hand, he unhooked his web belt and let it fall. Besides the radio, it had a survival knife and extra clips of ammunition. Monks scooped it up and slung it over his shoulder.

"Now get inside there."

Hammerhead staggered toward the shed, left hand clasping his dangling right arm. Marguerite hurried ahead, unhooking the door's hasp and swinging it open. Monks could just make out the ghostly shapes of workbenches and machinery inside.

Hammerhead stopped, his face tight with rage and pain.

"You're dead, motherfucker," he muttered, and Monks's meth-charged brain almost ordered his trembling finger to tighten that final quarter inch on the trigger.

Instead, he said, "Turn around."

Slowly, breathing hard, Hammerhead turned to face the shed.

Monks stepped up behind him, raising the rifle as he moved, and slammed the butt into the back of Hammerhead's skull. He crashed to the ground like a fallen oak and lay still.

This time, Monks had not had the slightest hesitation. In fact, it had been thrilling.

He dragged Hammerhead into the shed and slammed the door shut. Marguerite dropped in the half-inch bolt that secured the hasp. Her rich black hair was slick and shining with rain like a wet animal pelt, and her eyes shone with an unknowable range of emotions. Monks gripped her shoulders and hugged her hard.

"Let's get Mandrake," he said, and sprinted toward the lodge.

Nineteen

Monks jogged along behind Marguerite, the warm inert weight of Mandrake bobbing gently on his back, like a child who had fallen asleep in his carrier. She led them to a steep, narrow ravine a quarter of a mile from the main camp. It looked like a giant ax split in a cliff face—the kind that was usually dry, but could become cascades during storms.

"The sensors don't work when it floods," she said into his ear, half yelling to be heard over the rushing water.

He shined the flashlight on the muddy, frothing stream, looking for a place to ford. It was about ten yards wide, the depth hard to estimate. The banks were slick and steep, but there were small trees that would serve as handholds.

"What happens when we get across?" he yelled back.

"There's a trail. But we have to be careful, they've got ATVs."

"Do you know the country out there?"

"Not really. Just right around here."

Monks decided to worry about that when and if they got that far. He slung the rifle over his shoulder, easing it beside Mandrake's head.

"Hang on to my belt," he told her.

They made their slippery way down the near bank, bracing themselves against the trees. At the bottom, he took a tentative step into the stream. It tore at his boot, filling it instantly with a powerful drag that tried to pull his foot out from under him. He crouched, hands outspread in case he fell, then started across.

There was plenty of tangled deadfall underwater that tripped their feet, but gave them more handholds. At midstream, Monks realized with relief that the water was only thigh deep. They floundered the rest of the way across and pulled themselves up the far bank. In the shelter of a big fir, they dropped to the ground, soaked, panting—

But out of the camp.

Monks emptied out his sloshing boots, wishing bitterly that he'd at least had had the intuition to put on lug-soled hiking boots when he'd left his house.

He checked his watch. It was 7:28 P.M. Hammerhead would be missed when he failed to call in at 8 P.M.—maybe earlier, if he came to and his shouts attracted someone, or he managed to kick his way out of the shed. With luck, the sentries would spend some time trying to figure out which way they had gone, but that could not be counted on. Monks figured that they had half an hour at most before they would have to abandon the road and strike off into the wilderness. The going would be much rougher then.

He took the small jar of meth and the paper tube out of his jacket's zippered inside pocket and handed them to Marguerite. He was acutely aware that their head start was dwindling fast, but an energy charge was worth the extra minute. The next hours, however they turned out, were going to be brutal.

When she was finished, he took his turn. With the drug's harsh fire piercing his brain, he gave her the flashlight, unslung his rifle, and followed her at a jog. The path was overgrown with weeds, barely visible, but he could see the vestiges of tire tracks.

His sense of direction was utterly blotted out. He could have been heading toward the moon.

He slogged along at his half-run, working to keep up with the younger, quicker woman. The meth told his brain that he could lope like a wolf all night, but his body, with the days of cumulative fatigue and his clumsy boots and wet clothes and the extra weight he was carrying, was already laboring hard. His ears strained to pick up the sound of an approaching engine over the driving rain.

If the heavily armed, night-goggled *maquis* caught up with them, it would mean a firefight.

A short one.

When the half-hour was up, Monks guessed that they had gone about two miles. He was starting to get a feel for the terrain. The trail was cut into a mountainside, running at a slight downhill grade. He watched the faint luminescent tunnel that Marguerite's flashlight opened up in the blurry night, hoping for a flat stretch to one side or the other, but the going was steep, both uphill and down. His body heat from the first strenuous exertions had evened out, and he was noticing that tonight was quite a bit colder than it had been. The raindrops pelting through the flashlight's beam were taking on the thick, splayed look of turning toward snow. So far, whatever tracks they had left would be hard to follow. But in fresh snow, footprints would be unavoidable—another reason to get off the road.

He decided to head uphill. It might help throw off their pursuers, who would expect them to take the easier course. And downhill was likely to lead them to another flooded ravine like the one they had crossed getting out of camp, but potentially larger and impossible to ford. He watched the light beam intently for the next couple of minutes, and finally settled on a rockslide as a takeoff point.

He slowed to a walk, pulling in deep rasping lungfuls of wet air, and called hoarsely to Marguerite to stop.

"Turn off the light, and don't turn it on again unless I tell you," he said when he caught up to her.

But before she clicked off the beam, he caught a glimpse of her eyes. The earlier euphoria was gone. She looked scared and tense, and while it was impossible to tell in the rain, he thought she might be weeping. He realized that with all of his own concerns, he hadn't thought about the hurricane of violence and emotions that she had been going through.

He put his arm around her shoulders.

"Look, we're doing great," he said, speaking forcefully, close to her, as he would to a green ER resident or nurse losing her nerve. "You're saving this little boy's *life*, remember that. Now come on, we're going to *make* it."

He wondered if, in the instant before the light beam vanished, she saw the madness in his own eyes.

Twenty

By midnight, there were two inches of new snow on the ground and the air was thick with big wet flakes, swirling around in a near-blizzard. The going was increasingly harder and colder. They were long past trying to run—now they were just trudging soddenly and blindly in the hope of gaining distance. His feet were aching and at the point of numbness.

He tried not to think about how easy it was to get turned around in these kinds of conditions.

They had made it up the rockslide and onto a ridge, then gradually downward into what seemed to be the floor of a broad valley. The pressing claustrophobic canopy of trees had thinned, yielding to a sense of open space. It was getting to be time for Mandrake's hourly check, and Monks was looking for a sheltering tree, when he saw Marguerite's form, barely visible a few yards off to his left, stumble and fall.

He hurried to her side, expecting her to scramble back to her feet. But she lay where she was. He knelt and put his hand on her, feeling her racking shivers. Her clothes, like his, were soaked through. He pulled the flashlight from her pack and shined it on her face. Her eyes were dull and unfocused and her teeth were chattering.

Hypothermia. She needed to warm up, fast. Stopping might cost them their lead, but there was no choice.

Monks turned in a circle, staring futilely into the night for some sign of shelter. The flashlight's beam, like headlights, showed nothing but the whirling snow. He didn't dare leave her and scout on his own—he might not be able to find her again.

"Okay, honey, come on," he said, clicking the flashlight off and stuffing it in his coat pocket. "We're going to get someplace and warm up. Just a little farther."

"I can't feel my feet," she whispered.

He stood, gripping her wrists, and pulled her upright. She was not a small woman, and it took everything he had. He realized that he also was on the edge of collapse.

With his arm tight around her waist, he walked facing into the driving snow, hoping to run into cliffs at the valley's edge that would provide a lee. The shapes of trees appeared like specters, and Monks got the dizzying sense that the branches were clutching at them. They stumbled on, slipping and panting, in a nightmare fantasy where all that mattered was the next step toward a goal that they would never reach.

Then he started seeing rocks among the trees—at first stumpy granite boulders thrusting up from the valley floor, then outcroppings and piles of sharp talus. They had come to the base of a mountainside. Up close, in its shelter, the driving snow lost its force and fell as gently as on a Christmas card. Now he could see dimly for ten or fifteen yards. With the dark line of rocks to follow, he decided to take the chance of going on alone to scout for an outcropping that would get them out of the wet. He eased Marguerite back, sitting her down against the slope, then unslung Mandrake and settled him beside her.

"I'll be back in a couple of minutes," he said, then added sternly, "Don't move, you understand?"

She nodded faintly, eyes closed. It was unlikely that she would try, but she might be hallucinating by this point and stumble off toward some imagined safety.

Monks stood for a moment, breathing deeply, trying to gather whatever strength he had left. Then he walked, fifty yards, a hundred. There were dry patches under cliffs that would be better than nothing, but no real shelter. He pushed on for another hundred yards, aching to collapse, and fearing that if he went much farther he wouldn't be able to make it back.

Then he saw a break in the cliff face, a darker splotch the size of a car. He got out the flashlight. Its beam showed a cavity ten feet deep, where the cliff base sloped back in. Boulders lay tumbled to the sides like buttresses.

He set the flashlight on a rock, leaving it on so he wouldn't miss it on his return, and started back to get the others. A fierce giddy elation pierced the numb shield of his fatigue. Now they had a chance to make it through this night.

Monks trudged back to the cave with an armload of firewood, dry branches that he'd snapped off a dead tree. Crouching under the low stone roof, he dumped them on the ground and broke them into shorter lengths under his boot, then built a small circle of brick-sized rocks and filled it with pine duff.

Marguerite lay huddled up, shivering and chattering, watching him through glazed eyes. Mandrake was sprawled in his rucksack like a lifeless doll.

With stiff, shaking hands, Monks lit a match. The pine needles glowed briefly, but didn't catch. The match went out. So did the next one.

He clamped his teeth tight, concentrating, and pawed through the duff for the driest clumps.

This time, the bristles flared up and stayed lit. He fed the flame with other clumps, then with small twigs, and finally layered bigger sticks onto the rocks in a grid, making sure there was plenty of air flow.

When the fire had built to a crackling blaze that gave off real warmth, he knee-walked to Marguerite, unlaced her boots, and pulled them off.

"Get undressed," he said.

She started working dully at the zipper of her jacket.

Monks lifted Mandrake out of the pack. The rain had soaked through the back of his snowsuit. That would be another blow to his resistance. Monks pulled the wet clothes off and rubbed him down quickly with his pajamas.

Marguerite had managed to get out of her jacket and was struggling to pull her sweatshirt over her head. Monks freed her from it, then unbuttoned her jeans and pulled them off. He had expected that she would be wearing warm underclothes, but she was not, or even a bra and panties, maybe because of her assignation with Hammerhead. He took her by the hands and pulled her to sit close to the fire. Then he picked up Mandrake and laid him in her lap.

"Put your arms around him," Monks said. "It'll warm you both up. I'm going for more wood."

He made three more trips, scouring the dry areas under trees and overhangs, stoking the fire each time he returned to the cave. Finally, he decided that they had enough firewood to last another couple of hours.

He sank back against a stone wall and pulled off his own sodden clothes. Marguerite was cradling Mandrake like a Junoesque Madonna with child, her long black hair spilling down over both of them. Her eyes were closed, her head still sagging in lethargy, but her skin was starting to take on the flush of returning warmth. The lure to warm his own half-frozen flesh was too much to resist. He knelt and clasped her—just for a few seconds, not long enough to risk that the chill might set her back.

Then, astoundingly, he felt the tickle of arousal in his groin.

He moved away in quick embarrassment and got to the other side of the fire.

It brought a whole new level of meaning to the term *survival instinct.*

* * *

Monks squatted at the cave entrance like a savage, gazing out into the quiet night, the rifle resting across his thighs. It was just past five A.M. The fire was subdued to embers, which he kept at a careful level, evenly filling the space with warmth and helping to dry the clothes that he'd spread out on rocks and sticks. Marguerite was more animated, helped by the heat and a couple of candy bars that he had coaxed her to eat, the high-sugar fuel that her depleted body needed. He hadn't been hungry himself, although he should have been ravenous, and he realized that his appetite was killed by the methamphetamine. But he knew he needed food, and forced himself to chew the tasteless bread and baloney.

Rested, he worked to balance the complex equation of factors and probabilities they faced. The storm seemed to be subsiding, at least temporarily. The visible fire was a risk, the more so as the snow diminished, but the heat was essential, and the longer their clothes could dry, the better. But if the snow stopped, they were going to leave a trail that, come daylight, would be highly visible. A man on a vantage point, with optics, could probably see it from miles away.

If Marguerite was feeling strong enough, it was time to move on again.

He set the rifle upright against the wall and got out the insulin and syringes. He drew a three-unit shot and knelt beside the little boy nestled in her embrace. She had been wetting his mouth every so often, and she watched with anxious eyes as Monks pinched up a fold of skin over Mandrake's abdomen and slid in the needle.

"Are you up to starting again?" he asked her.

"I guess so."

"If you're not sure, we'll wait."

"No. I'm okay now. This helped a lot."

"Then let's pack up."

Monks gathered her clothes and gave them to her. They were far from completely dry, but at least they were no longer soaked. Without the pelting rain and wet snow, body heat would help to dry them further. He got his own shirt and jeans, and then realized that she hadn't moved. Her head was bowed, her face hidden by her hair.

"What's the matter?" he said.

"He's looking for us." Her voice was muffled and tremulous. "He's getting into my head. That's how he'll find us."

Monks stared at her in disbelief. "You mean Freeboot?"

"He's telling me I should just wait here. He'll come get me."

He knelt beside her and gripped her wrist.

"Marguerite, you're imagining this," he said. "You're stressed out, maybe feeling guilty. But Freeboot's not getting into your head. He might have made you believe he can do that, but he can't, not really. Nobody can."

"You don't know him."

It was the same insane conviction that Monks had heard from Glenn.

"You can't stay here, are you kidding?" Monks said. "If he *doesn't* find you, you'll die. If he does, he'll—God knows what he'll do."

She shook her head, with childlike stubbornness. "No. It's all okay, he forgives me."

Monks squeezed the bridge of his nose between his thumb and forefinger, trying to think of a way to cut through the invisible spiderweb that Freeboot had strung around his followers.

"What about Hammerhead?" Monks said. "You think he'll forgive you?"

"He wouldn't dare cross Freeboot," she said, looking up scornfully. "Besides, I can make Hammerhead do anything I want."

"But you'll have to start sleeping with him again. And the other *maquis*. Right? Anybody who wants you, isn't that the deal?"

She bowed her head again, averting her eyes.

"But you only want Freeboot, really," Monks said. "He uses you like a whore for his men, and he plays around with other women."

For thirty seconds, she was silent and still. Monks was abruptly aware of the piney fragrance of the fire, the dark flush that the heat had brought to her skin, the golden-downed bumps of her spine the length of her long graceful back.

Then, in a low voice, she said, "He says he has the right to every woman he wants, because he's the alpha male. He was fucking around tonight. I knew he was going to. I got pissed."

"Was that the business he had to take care of?"

"He does it all the time. There's these big parties every couple of months. Everybody from camp goes down to the flats to score dope."

Monks had figured out by now that "the flats" referred to the rest of the world outside the camp. But while he didn't know much about drug deals, he had never thought of them as social events.

"What kind of parties?" he said.

"People around here get permits to grow medical marijuana. It's supposed to be for their own use, but other people come up from the cities. Bikers, black gang guys. They bring crank, crack, whatever, and everybody trades. And there's always young girls around," she added venomously.

So that was where Freeboot had been while his son was dying.

"Did Motherlode go, too?" Monks asked.

"Yeah," Marguerite said, still caustic. "She kept saying that as soon as she stocked up, she was going to come back and be with Mandrake. She's full of shit. All she cares about is her dope."

There was no point in asking if Glenn had gone. Monks knew the answer.

"Marguerite, you did the right thing," he said. "For Mandrake, for me, for yourself. Keep on doing it. We just have to make it a little farther, and then Freeboot can never touch you again."

She shook her head. "I was wrong. I belong to him. You go on, I'm staying here."

Options flashed through Monks's frayed mind, including herding her at gunpoint. But what could he do if she refused—shoot her? He decided on one more try at reason. If that didn't work, he could only hope to make it out himself and send back help.

"What can Freeboot do to you from far away?" he said. "How can he hurt you?"

She finally met Monks's gaze. Her eyes were wet with frightened tears.

"It's not even like being scared of dying," she said. "It's like he'll be in your mind forever, making you live in hell."

"Then how come he's not doing it to me?"

She shrugged warily, her full breasts rising and falling.

"Because it's all just something he's made you believe," Monks repeated emphatically. "We'll get him out of your head for good, I promise." He squeezed her wrist, managing one of his crocodilian smiles. "I always hate to see a pretty girl put her clothes back on, but we've got to move."

She smiled back, a quick, timid twitch of her lips. Monks seized the moment.

"Here, this will jump-start us," he said. He reached for his jacket and pulled out the little jar of meth. Mixing speed and hypothermia might be a bad idea, but at this point, he was willing to risk anything. Marguerite was slow to accept it, maybe sensing that it would goad her out of her passivity. But then she unscrewed the lid and bent over it to inhale.

Monks did the same. It occurred to him that this was, in all probability, the only time in his life that he would crouch naked beside a fire in the wilderness with a lovely young woman, doing illegal drugs.

He pressed his palm against her cheek.

"Now come on," he said. "The kid needs you."

She wavered for another several seconds, but then nodded. She set Mandrake down and started pulling on her clothes.

Monks closed his eyes in relief.

Twenty-one

His feet hurt like hell. The wet, loose pull-on boots had chewed them into blistered lumps of flesh that he picked up and put down, one in front of the other, in a dull, trudging cadence without end. Marguerite slogged along silently ahead of him, so he could keep her in sight in case she weakened again. The snow had stopped, and what was on the ground had lightened to a film of slush, but the terrain was still rough. At least he could be sure now that they were traveling in a straight line.

It was just after noon. He estimated that they had made it twenty-some miles from camp, now descending a series of ridgebacks in a direction he was pretty sure was west, where Marguerite thought the nearest highway lay. The clouds had lifted enough for him to navigate by a general sense of the terrain sloping down toward the ocean, moss growing on the north side of the trees, and an occasional glimpse of faint lighter streaks behind the dark shifting tapestry of gray, indicating the path of the sun. But they still obscured any long-range vistas, and they presented the kind of threat that kept experienced outdoors people uneasy. He looked up constantly, trying to gauge what was coming. It seemed to him that the clouds were thickening again, suggesting another storm moving in. Often, several of them lined up out on the Pacific like batters in a dugout, waiting for their turn to step up to the plate and lash the countryside.

Monks knew that both he and Marguerite were getting close to collapsing again. Even if they could find shelter, he wasn't at all sure that they would recover this time. But there *had* to be a road before too much longer.

There was nothing to do but keep lifting up those feet and putting them down, one after the other.

Marguerite stopped abruptly, raising her head.

Monks had heard it, too—a human voice.

He stood motionless, listening hard, trying to convince himself that the sound had been a tree branch snapping under its snow load, or a raven's caw.

But he knew the truth, and a few seconds later, it came again—a man's voice, shouting, as if calling to someone else.

Marguerite swung to face him. Her eyes burned with fear and accusation.

"I told you he'd find us!" she half-sobbed.

Monks shushed her angrily with a wave of his hand, and stepped close.

"Come on, keep moving," he whispered hoarsely. "Stay in the trees. And stay quiet."

She turned and hurried on. Monks followed, with disbelief washing through him—along with rage, the feeling of being cheated. He had started to believe that whatever their other troubles might be, they had finally eluded pursuit, that last night's heavy snow and today's melting had wiped out their trail. He didn't believe for a second that Freeboot had zeroed in on Marguerite's thoughts, like a radar beam. The *maquis* had probably spotted some tracks from a vantage point, as he had feared, and found enough vestiges to follow.

In this vast rugged landscape, it still seemed astounding.

There were at least two voices, maybe more. They continued to sound at intervals, no doubt following the clear line of tracks in the snow. The distance was hard to gauge—at least a mile, he guessed, and hoped to Christ farther. In a silent alpine forest, voices could carry a very long way.

But one thing became clear within the next hour. They were gaining, fast.

Monks turned his head, listening over his own panting breath. He was sure that the pursuers were within a half-mile by now.

When he turned back, he saw that Marguerite had stopped on top of a rise and was pointing a shaking finger ahead, like an ancient explorer, long lost at sea, finally sighting land.

He hurried to her side. Below, cutting across the mountain bases, lay the dark curving scar of a paved road.

He put his hands on his hips and bent over, breathing deeply, trying to relax and think. The distance to the road looked like about two miles. Staying on the ridgeline, they could make it in an hour. But that terrain was wide open, and a half-mile was easy shooting range for high-powered rifles.

The only other way that he could see was to drop down into the ravine that lay to the north—just the kind of situation that he had been trying to avoid. It would be choked with undergrowth and deadfall, and he could see the dark glimmer of a stream at its bottom, water that might be too deep and fast to cross. But the thick brush would provide cover, and without that, they were dead.

"We're going to make it," he told Marguerite, gripping her shoulders. "I'll go first now. Stay close."

Then a gunshot cracked through the silent air, the sharp echoing boom of a large-caliber rifle. A man yelled something. Monks could not make out the words, but the tone was menacing, and Marguerite flinched.

Without doubt, the voice was Freeboot's.

The ravine's bottom narrowed into a gorge with sheer granite walls twenty feet deep. What was probably a lazy stream or even dry in most weather had become a small river, tossing dead branches along its frothing course at the speed of a man trotting.

Monks stared down at it. He had led them into the trap he had been fearing. Unless they found a ford close by, there was no way they were going to get across this one.

The gunshots behind them were frequent now, some of them full automatic bursts, crashing through the thick tree branches. None of them were coming close—Monks didn't think that the *maquis* had seen them yet. The rifle fire was intended to scare them into giving up, and Marguerite looked ready to. She was lagging behind, forcing him to wait for her and hiss encouragement. Physically, they were both on their last legs. But he knew that she was giving in to Freeboot's imagined psychic power, too.

Monks bulled his way through the brush along the gorge's narrow granite shelf, looking back every few seconds to make sure that she was still behind him, snapping branches with his hands to clear them out of her way. They passed one place where a section of bank had caved into the stream to form a stepping-stone bridge. It invited tormentingly, but extended only halfway across.

After fifteen minutes, he realized that some of the gunshots were coming from ahead of them, not behind. The *maquis* had fanned out on the ridge above. When they started dropping down into the ravine, it would be like a closing fist, with their prey in the middle of it.

He turned back, gripping Marguerite by the wrist and yanking her along to the rockslide they had passed. The half-dozen boulders that stuck up above the water's writhing suface would get them halfway. That was the best they were going to find. He pulled her close and clamped his arm around her waist. This time he couldn't trust her to hang on to his belt.

He waded in with her, staying upstream of the rocks, using them to brace himself against the icy current. When they got to the last one, he yelled into her ear, "We're going!" and lunged toward the far bank. The waist-high wall of water slammed into him, splashing up to blind him and spinning him around. His flailing free hand found the slippery branch of a fallen tree. He clung to it, fighting to get his footing back, and pulled them forward another yard. Then he saw that a leg-sized chunk of dead wood was tumbling downstream toward them. He managed to throw one leg over the trunk of the fallen tree, then let go of the branch to fend off the rushing log, but it swung around with his push and gave him a hard blow to the ribs.

Gasping, he worked his way along the tree, straddling it to anchor them. It ended within six feet of the far bank, but that was six feet of seething torrent, and his numb right arm was losing its grip on Marguerite.

"Get there and grab something!" he screamed at her. "I'll hold you!" He pulled her in front of him and shoved her forward with everything he had left, lunging along downstream of her to brace her. Her hands clawed at the slick rocks of the bank, slipping and pulling several loose.

Monks got his feet under him and heaved her forward again. This time, she got both hands on a solid chunk of granite. With him pushing, she crawled up enough to wrap her arms around it. Gripping her jacket, he pulled himself up, too. On hands and knees, they scrambled to solid ground and fell flat.

The a burst of gunfire from the opposite bank stitched across the cliff above them, showering them with shards of granite.

"*Move*," he yelled, slapping at Marguerite's legs. He yanked the pack off and clutched Mandrake in front of him, running to dive into the bank's thick brush. Keeping cover, they clawed their way up the bank, with gunfire spraying around them.

Finally, they pulled themselves over the top and into the shelter of trees.

Monks set Mandrake on the ground and lay down beside him. The little boy's face was pale as frost and looked crumpled, like a paper mask that had gotten soaked. But he was breathing.

Monks rolled onto his back.

"You okay?" he said to Marguerite.

She nodded slowly, like someone not yet completely awake from an intense dream.

He wormed his way behind a tree close to the bank. He could see the stream for half a mile in each direction. The rockslide they'd crossed was the only possible ford. He reckoned that the road couldn't be more than a mile from here, over open, almost level forest. Now it came down to getting there before the *maquis* could cut them off.

This was a hell of a lot better chance than he had been expecting.

He scooped up Mandrake and thrust him into Marguerite's arms.

Her eyes were shining, with water or tears.

"You've got to get to that road fast," he said, turning her to face it. "I know you're whipped, but it's not far. Flag down a car and call the sheriffs."

"What are you going to do?" she asked anxiously.

"Put a stopper in the bottleneck."

He gave her a gentle push, then crawled back to his vantage point and scanned the opposite bank with the rifle's scope, searching for signs of movement. Within a few seconds, he saw a small fir twitch, a hundred yards to the west and halfway up the bank. He trained the scope on the spot. A man wearing camouflage was sliding cautiously downhill under cover of the brush.

Monks looked for others. His peripheral vision caught a small tumble of rocks and mud, this time to the east—another man coming down the slope. The two of them were advancing in a sort of pincer movement, with the stream ford between them. He couldn't see either of their faces, but he could see their rifles.

He judged that it would take them three or four minutes to reach the ford. Then they would be exposed. A litany of doubts started in his brain. He was not expert enough to deliberately wound. It was either fire warning shots or risk killing. He had only ever killed one man, in desperate self-defense, and he had fervently hoped never to come close to that again.

But he shoved the worries aside. They were not something he

could afford right now. Then he remembered the amoral euphoria that the meth induced. He unscrewed the container, dipped in the knife, and sucked up a solid jolt.

With the rush blossoming through his brain, he took the extra ammunition clips from his belt and arranged them next to him, set the rifle's selector switch to single shot, and clicked off the safety.

Through the scope, he watched the nearer *maquis*, the one to the west, stretch out his right leg and brace his boot against a tree stump, lowering himself another step downhill. His thigh made a good-sized, clear target. Monks braced his elbows on the ground. Slowly, squeezing, he touched off the round.

The rifle boomed and kicked hard against his shoulder. Above the roaring of the stream, he thought he heard a shriek. Quickly, he sighted in again. The man had his right knee pulled up to his chest, with hands clutching his ankle and blood spilling out from his boot between his fingers.

Not a great shot, but it had done the job.

He would have been easy to finish off, and Monks was thinking about it, when a burst of return fire smashed through the trees above him.

He flattened himself and wormed his way ten yards to another tree. The second *maquis* was hidden, but Monks remembered where he had been a few seconds ago. He flipped the selector switch to full automatic and touched the trigger again.

A half-dozen rounds burst from the barrel with blistering speed, spraying the brush on the ravine's opposite bank like an invisible whiplash. The area remained still. Probably Monks had missed. But now that man knew he was spotted, and that might stop him from advancing.

There were other *maquis*, other ways they could get to Monks or around him. But a strange realization came to him, almost like being touched by something outside of himself. His fear was gone, and his fatigue had become a kind of relaxation that was casual, even pleasant—

the sense of a long, hard journey almost over, just one more rough spot to go. He had done everything he could, and there was nothing left but to abandon himself to fate. He decided to stay where he was for an hour, giving Marguerite time to get to the road, and shoot anyone he saw. If he was still alive, he would try to make it there himself.

He was jerked abruptly from this comfortable state by realizing that a man had appeared across the stream.

It was Freeboot. Barefoot.

Monks shook his head hard, thinking that the meth had him hallucinating. But when he looked again, Freeboot was still there. Once again, he had materialized out of nowhere.

He was standing in full view at the rock bridge, making no attempt to hide. He carried an assault rifle in one hand, barrel angling down toward the ground. Although there was no *way* that he could see Monks, he was staring directly at where Monks lay.

Monks raised his rifle barrel an inch at a time. He planted his elbows again and centered the scope on Freeboot's chest. The selector switch was still on full auto. His finger touched the trigger and slowly started to tighten.

Then stopped.

He lowered the rifle, climbed to his feet, and stepped out from behind the tree. Now Freeboot could see him.

For thirty seconds, the two men stood with gazes locked.

They had each other's sons.

With feral quickness, Freeboot swung his rifle up, the muzzle pointing to the sky, and fired off a long, shuddering burst that spoke all the words that would never be told of rage, defeat, admiration—a challenge to the next duel.

He turned and loped back up the ravine's bank, vanishing into the brush.

Monks turned, too, and started for the road. There was no need to stay, now.

He had been right, it was an easy hike of not much more than half an hour. A woman with a child should have had no trouble flagging down a ride. He stopped on top of the last small rise, watching for flashing lights, listening for sirens or a helicopter.

But there was no sound but the restless wind, no vehicles or human beings in sight in this deserted place on this desolate afternoon.

New fears entered his heart: that Marguerite had gotten turned around in the forest, or worse, been picked up by someone dangerous.

After a few minutes, civilization finally appeared in the form of a passing car, a recent-model Nissan or Toyota. A minute or two after that, a delivery truck went by in the other direction. Monks assured himself that Marguerite and Mandrake were fine. He had been in Freeboot's camp too long. The world outside of it was filled with normal people, not violent psychotics, and the odds that she had run into trouble were a million to one. Getting help was just taking longer than his impatient imagination was allowing.

But as more time passed, and the sky faded toward dusk, he started to suspect that wherever Marguerite had gone, whatever she had done, she had not sent any sheriffs his way.

Twenty-two

The logging truck slowed at Monks's waves, then pulled over fifty yards down the road. It was the fourth vehicle that he had tried to flag down. The others had swerved and accelerated past him. He couldn't blame them—he had stashed the rifle behind a tree, but still, no one was likely to stop in the middle of nowhere for a man who looked like he did. But loggers tended to be bolder than ordinary citizens.

He ran to the truck with stiff, heavy steps. It was grime-spattered, the big tires caked with reddish brown mud, the load of fir trunks crusted with snow. The driver, a full-bearded man wearing suspenders and a baseball cap, rolled down his window warily.

"Call the sheriffs," Monks shouted. He slowed to a walk, breathing hard. "There's armed men up in those woods. They were hunting me."

The driver studied him for a few seconds, as if trying to gauge just how crazy Monks was. Then he reached forward to the dash and came back with his CB radio handset.

"Tell them to send a helicopter," Monks said. "There's a camp up there, twenty miles in. A group of people, run by a man named Freeboot."

This seemed to get the driver's attention. "The Harbine camp?" he said, holding the handset poised.

"I don't know what it's called. A dozen old log buildings, at the end of a dirt road."

The driver nodded curtly, then spoke into the handset: "Breaker, this is Dahlgren Logging truck eleven. Got an emergency on Highway 162, near mile marker seventeen. Do you copy?" The language was a weird echo of the *maquis*' pseudo-military code. Monks reminded himself that he was back in the real world.

A static-laden, squawking reply came from the radio. Monks couldn't make out the words over the diesel's steady rumble. The driver turned away from him and spoke with his voice lowered. An SUV with a young couple and skis on the rack passed by, giving the truck a wide berth.

The driver leaned out the window. "They want some more information."

Monks flogged his exhausted brain for the right thing to say, to convince law-enforcement officials to send out a helicopter on the word of a disheveled, shouting lunatic standing in the middle of a road.

"There's a young woman with a sick little boy, who were with me. She should have called them by now."

The driver relayed the information, then shook his head. "They ain't heard anything like that."

Monks pressed the heels of his hands to his eyes. "Tell them to call the area hospitals, ambulance services, any medical facilities. The kid's almost dead from diabetes. Maybe she took him straight in."

The driver eyed him distrustfully, but spoke into the handset again. "It's going to take a minute," he told Monks when he finished.

Monks paced, bracing himself to learn that Marguerite and Mandrake had disappeared.

But almost immediatly, the driver got a callback, then looked at Monks with cautious respect.

"An ambulance got called about forty minutes ago to pick up a little boy with diabetes, down near Longvale. But nobody said anything about coming out here."

Monks closed his eyes in relief—Mandrake had made it. There was no telling about Marguerite, but that was another worry he couldn't afford right now.

"Look, my name's Monks, I'm a doctor," he said to the logger. "I'll give the sheriffs the whole story when they get here. But those people up there are going to try to escape. There need to be roadblocks, and for Christ's sake, get that helicopter moving. Somebody might get killed."

He decided not to add that the somebody might be his son.

The driver finished speaking to the sheriffs, then hooked the handset back on the dash.

"They say they'll do it, but you better be right."

"I'm right," Monks said. "I wish to hell I wasn't."

Unexpectedly, the driver said, "You look like you could stand to warm up. Come on, hop in."

Monks walked around to the truck's other side and swung himself up onto the running board, then into the cab. It was more like a den than a vehicle. The passenger seat was torn out, replaced by a crate of worn mechanic's tools. The driver handed him a greasy brown duck jacket to put on top, and Monks squatted on that, finding a place for his feet amidst a pile of ropes, come-alongs, saw chains, rigging shackles, a battered metal Thermos, and a plastic lunch cooler. The smell wrapped him like a blanket, a combination of diesel fuel, solvent, tobacco, and, most of all, man.

"Chew?" the driver said, offering a foil packet of Red Man.

Monks shook his head. "Thanks for stopping. Sorry to trouble you."

"Hell, I'm glad to be in on this. Them people up there—they kept to themselves and never caused any problems, but everybody had a bad feeling about them. They *hunted* you?"

"I've just been in a gunfight with them. I shot a man in the ankle."

The driver's face turned cautious again, or maybe skeptical. "Where's your gun?"

"I'll get it," Monks said wearily. He climbed out of the truck and walked to where he had stashed the rifle. He walked back, holding it high over his head with both hands, in a clear position of surrender. Still, when he got close to the truck, he saw that the driver was holding a pistol, barrel braced on the window ledge—not exactly aimed at him, but ready. It was a large-caliber revolver, a .357 or .44 Magnum.

"Go ahead, take it," Monks said, handing the rifle butt first up to the window. The driver gripped it and pulled it into the cab. It might have strengthened his belief in Monks's story, or convinced him that Monks was not only crazy but dangerous. The pistol disappeared from sight, but Monks was sure it was still close at hand. The driver did not invite him back inside.

Monks watched for the helicopter that, finally, he knew was coming. Within ten minutes, he could feel its distant vibrations, quickly rising into a deep staccato drumbeat. It sped across the gray gap of open sky like a faraway hawk yawing with the wind, heading up into the mountains that Monks had fled.

The radio's speaker squawked. The driver picked up his handset again.

"The hell—after all that rain?" Monks heard him say, his voice loud with disbelief. He swiveled in his seat to stare down at Monks.

"They're saying that camp's on fire," the driver said.

Twenty-three

"Dr. Monks? Time to wake up."

The voice dimly penetrated Monks's veil of sleep. He tried to open his eyes, but they were crusted shut. He knuckled at them until he managed to pry the lids apart, and sat up.

His immediate take was that he was in a nightmare conjured from some medieval vision of hell. The sky around him was dark, but beneath it a field of glowing embers stretched into the distance, flaring into flames and spouting small volcanoes of sparks. Misshapen, humpbacked figures prowled the outskirts, expelling hissing bursts of liquid onto the fires.

Then Monks remembered, groggily, that he was in the backseat of a Forest Service firefighters' van, looking at what was left of Freeboot's compound—the place known locally as the Harbine camp. The humanoids were a hastily mustered hotshot crew, not used to being called out this time of year, dressed in protective gear and spraying flame retardant. Two water trucks with fire hoses stood by.

The next thing that came into his mind was good news that he had learned from the sheriffs: Mandrake had been stabilized at the hospital in Willits, and he would soon be moved to a larger facility that specialized in juvenile diabetes. He had, in fact, contracted a viral infection that had weakened him severely and might have turned to pneumonia. But indications were good that he was going to recover.

The only thing that they would tell him about Marguerite was that she also had been picked up and was being questioned.

"It's getting toward dawn," his awakener said, standing in the van's open door. "We'll be wanting you to walk us through it as soon as it's light."

Monks recognized him as a walrus-mustached Mendocino County sheriff lieutenant named Agar who had been in charge of the several-hour grilling that Monks had gotten yesterday evening. The deputies hadn't believed his story at first, and there had been no sightings of Freeboot or his followers in spite of roadblocks. It had even been hinted that Monks might have started the fire. But after he pulled up his pants legs to show them his savaged shins, they had started to come around.

He had told them that his son was with the group, that he feared that Freeboot would take revenge on Glenn, and he had passed up the offer of a warm bed to drive up here with them last night, hoping and dreading that there might be some sign of Glenn. But the fire was still a football-field-sized inferno that could blister skin from twenty yards away. Monks had watched it helplessly for a while, then borrowed a sleeping bag and crawled into the van. He was aware that crashing after extended meth use tended to be immediate and deep, and sleep had slammed down on him like a collapsing brick building.

"So I'm Dr. Monks now?" he said to Agar. "You sure?" His identity was another thing that the hard-faced deputies had been skeptical about.

Agar smiled. "Pretty sure. We've checked around, and we haven't found anybody else pretending to be you, at least not *yet*."

"Can't imagine why anybody'd want to be," Monks muttered.

"What's that, sir?"

"Nothing. There any coffee around?"

"Right over there at the roach coach."

Monks climbed stiffly out of the van. He saw that TV news crews had arrived during the night, and had set up cameras and equipment behind a yellow tape that the deputies had strung up, a safe distance from the fire.

"They're foaming at the mouth to get hold of you," Agar said. He watched Monks, gauging his response. Like most older cops that Monks had dealt with, Agar was on the beefy side, polite, and professionally bland—a characteristic that sometimes disguised shrewdness, and sometimes not. Agar was one of the shrewd ones.

"I'm not making any public statements until I talk to my lawyer." Monks didn't know if that made any sense, but it seemed to work for other people, at least on television.

Agar nodded approval. "We'll keep them away."

Monks followed the deputy to the "roach coach," a catering truck set up for the firefighters. Its open side panels displayed urns of coffee and hot water, trays of sweetrolls and doughnuts, and a steam table with scrambled eggs, bacon, and sausage. His belly reminded him that he had hardly eaten in the last couple of days. He decided that he'd better fuel up while he had the chance. He filled a styrofoam cup with black coffee—predictably weak, but hot. The powdered eggs and greasy bacon tasted pretty damned good.

He stood off to the side, eating and watching the pageant around him, while the sky slowly lightened. The firefighters were starting to sift the ashes now, wading around in the areas that had cooled enough, searching debris and scattering embers with rakes. Several leather-jacketed deputies paced the perimeter or talked on radios.

He had overheard enough last night to know that the fire had exploded so suddenly and burned so hot, there was no doubt that accelerant had been used—a lot of it. Probably the log buildings had been soaked with gasoline, then lit from a distance by electronic detonators. It had been done fast and efficiently—as if according to a preexisting plan.

Then Freeboot and his people had slipped away. A search was slated to start at first light, in case they were still in the woods. Monks doubted it.

He scanned the field, trying to identify from the smoldering remains which buildings had stood where. The lodge was easy to recognize because of its large rock foundation. He oriented himself by it and located other sites—Glenn's cabin, the washhouse, several other cabins and sheds reduced to smoking heaps of debris. Toward the field's far end, the roof had caved in on a barn that had stayed closed while he had been there. Now he saw that it housed the smoke-blackened remains of a D-6 Cat and other heavy equipment.

"They had themselves quite an operation here," Agar said, coming to stand beside him. "I've got a feeling we're going to find some surprises."

Monks nodded distractedly. His gaze kept returning to the firefighters, prodding and dragging the ashes with their rakes—

Probing, first and foremost, for bodies.

More vehicles were arriving, headlights piercing the early-morning gray, bringing more deputies and volunteers for the search through the woods. Some of the pickup trucks had dirt bikes or ATVs in the beds or on trailers. Most parked up the road, discharging men in hunting gear, carrying rifles.

But one four-wheel-drive sheriff's SUV drove all the way into the camp. When the two people in the backseat got out, Monks noticed that they were women—then, that one of them was Marguerite.

Multilayered emotions bristled in him: happiness at seeing her safe, gratitude for her help, anger that she had gotten him into this mess in the first place—and mystification at why she had left him to stand by the roadside.

"That's the young woman who helped me escape," he said to Agar.

The deputy nodded. "Her story checks out pretty good with yours."

"Why's she up here?"

"Same reason as you. We want her to show us around, tell us everything she knows."

"Okay if I have a word with her?"

"I don't see why not. Let me make sure." Agar walked over to the deputies who had brought the women and spoke briefly with them. Then he turned and beckoned Monks to come on over.

Marguerite watched him approach, her hands shoved deep into her coat pockets and her face emotionless—no happiness, no remorse. Monks could have been a mailman, coming to deliver a flyer about a tire sale. Her emotional shock had to be huge, with the trauma of all that had happened—and the shattering of her bond of loyalty, passion, and something mysteriously deeper still, to Freeboot.

He put one arm lightly around her shoulders. "I want you all to know that she's a hero," he announced to everyone standing around. "Saved that little boy's life, and mine, too. Went through hell to do it."

The words didn't seem to unlock any warmth in her. She stayed passive, neither responding nor resisting, not even looking at him. Monks let her go. The gesture had been clumsy, but he wanted her to know that he was on her side—that in his mind the good that she had done far outweighed the bad. He hoped she would absorb that in time.

The other woman watched anxiously, but she seemed relieved at Monks's goodwill. She was older, mid-forties, and had the same black hair and olive skin as Marguerite. He guessed that this was her mother, or maybe an aunt.

Agar said, "Lia, before our men start spreading out, you got any ideas which way those folks might have gone?"

He was looking at Marguerite as he spoke, and Monks was puzzled for a few seconds. Then he remembered that it was Freeboot who had given her the name Marguerite. Apparently, her real one was Lia.

"There's a hidden road," she said, still with almost trancelike somberness.

"Where?"

"It starts over by the security station. The men connected it to logging roads." She pointed at the big Cat in the smoldering barn. "They'd work at night, then scatter brush around to cover up."

"Where's it lead, do you know?" Agar asked.

"Where the highway starts, near Elk Creek."

"Christ, all the way down there?"

"They had ATVs. They'd radio ahead for people to meet them with cars."

There was much pushing back of smokey-bear hats and shuffling of booted feet among the deputies. The *maquis* had probably gotten out of the forest yesterday afternoon before the fire had even been discovered.

Looking aggravated, Agar asked, "Lia, why didn't you tell us this yesterday?"

"I was too freaked, okay?" She lashed out the words, suddenly animated, wet-eyed with anger—or panic. "You got any fucking idea what this is like?" She walked away quickly, hugging herself. The other woman hurried after her.

Monks said nothing. But her real reason had come clear to him—the same reason why she hadn't called immediately for help. She had wanted to give Freeboot plenty of time to escape.

Agar sighed and hiked up his gun belt. "Let's get somebody to check it out," he said. "And hold off the search. If she's right, there's no point in sending those boys out."

The older woman had caught up with Lia and was talking to her quietly but sternly. Monks walked over to them.

"You've got to quit trying to shield Freeboot, Lia," Monks said. "This has gone way past that."

Her flat affect had returned, but there was a hint of resentment when she spoke—maybe at his use of her real name.

"He *let* us go," she said. "You know that, don't you?"

Astonishment, then anger flared in Monks—that after all this, she was still clinging to the image of Freeboot as superhuman.

"He let us go because I had an assault rifle leveled at him," Monks said.

Her eyes went uncertain, but then quickly cool, even pitying, as if he couldn't possibly understand the deeper truth. She turned and walked away again. This time, the older woman stayed with Monks. She looked almost lost in a big raglan turtleneck sweater. Like Lia, she was attractive without being pretty. Her eyes were large, a little sloed, and very dark. Her face was drawn and anxious.

"I'm her mom," she said. "I was afraid you'd hate her."

Monks shook his head. He was all out of hate.

"She helped," he said. "My own son refused to."

"It's that man Freeboot," she said with sudden heat. "He turned them into zombies."

"Maybe. But they let him."

She sagged a little, and nodded. "I *did* try to talk to her. Probably not very well. She sure didn't want to hear it."

"Don't I know," Monks said.

There seemed to be a strange mutual comfort in that. They stood without speaking again for a moment longer, until Agar called to him.

"Dr. Monks, you ready to show us what happened to you?"

Monks joined the deputies and started telling his story, while a technician with a camcorder followed. For the next half-hour, they moved around the fire's fringes, while he described everything he could remember.

He had just finished recounting being assaulted and getting his hair hacked off, when the moment came that he had been dreading.

"Over here!" a man yelled. It was one of the firefighters, in the part of the smoking field where the small cabins had stood. He had set his rake aside and was bent over something, brushing it off with his glove.

When he stepped back, Monks got a glimpse of greasy, charred bones, lying like wreckage in the ashes.

Agar glanced quickly at Monks, no doubt with the same thought. This could be Glenn.

"You better stay here, sir," Agar said.

Monks watched from the sidelines while the firefighters and deputies conferred. He felt disembodied, as if something deep within him had grabbed hold of his already raw emotions and shoved them into a locked compartment, not daring to leave them near the surface.

Then Agar came hesitantly toward him. He had put on firefighter's protective boots and carried another pair.

"Doctor, I hate like hell to ask you this," he said. "But we'd appreciate it if—you know, if there's anything you could identify."

"I don't know anything about forensics," Monks objected. Then he sat abruptly on the ground and pulled on the boots.

The ashes were hot around his sore feet and calves. When he got close to the corpse, the smell of roasted meat blended with the woodsmoke and flame retardant. It was lying prone with arms outstretched, turned slightly onto the left side, as if sleeping. There was no evidence of contortion from pain, or of an attempt to escape. Whoever it was might already have been dead when the fire reached here.

Monks hoped so.

It appeared to be of medium height, maybe a little more. That eliminated Hammerhead, but left most of the others that Monks had seen. There were no obvious injuries or identifying marks. Jewelry would have been destroyed, and dental fillings melted. Only remnants of charred flesh clung to the bones. Skin and hair were gone entirely.

He glanced at the firefighter who had found the corpse and said, "Give me your glove. I'll be careful."

Monks crouched and very gently swept the film of ashes off the skeleton's pelvis. Its heart-shaped cavity was wide, and rounded on the insides of the ilial bones between the sacrum and the pubic symphysis.

He closed his eyes, knowing that he could be tricking himself. He counted to ten, then looked again. His impression was the same.

"I think it's a woman," Monks said. "That's all I can tell you, and I'm not at all sure about it. You'd better get an expert."

He handed the glove back to the deputy and waded out of the ashes—somber with guilt because his pity for the victim was overcome by the ugly wash of relief that it was not his son.

"Doctor, are those human remains?" someone shouted. It was a newswoman, shoving a microphone past the restraining tape, while a man beside her focused a camcorder on Monks.

He thrust his hand out at them, palm flat, and walked on past.

Part 2

NEW MURDERS INCREASE PANIC

Wendy Reicher
Tribune staff reporter
Published March 10, 2004

Chicago—The latest in a series of more than a dozen multiple murders tentatively linked to the "Calamity Jane" killings was discovered early this morning near Lake Forest.

Walter R. Krieger and his wife, Nancy, were found shot dead in their home in the exclusive gated community of Avalon Greens. Krieger was an executive who sat on several major corporate boards and an influential industry lobbyist. His status in the business world, along with the killers' penetration of heavy security and the lack of any apparent motive, fit the pattern of previous crimes.

Police confirmed that items were taken from the home but refused to say what. In the past, stolen items have been dumped out in inner cities and homeless camps, among them expensive jewelry and the rare golf clubs that gave the murders their name. This has given the killers a growing Robin Hood image in some areas. Baseball caps and T-shirts with the "Calamity Jane" logo have even appeared, sparking outrage and demands for swift police action from citizens' groups.

"We're aggressively pursuing a number of promising leads," FBI spokesman William Joslin told a press conference earlier today. "It's only a matter of time before these people are brought to justice."

But a Chicago police official, speaking on condition of anonymity, said, "It's almost like they're thumbing their nose at us—trying to prove there's nothing anybody can do to stop them."

With no suspects in custody, widespread concern is on the rise.

Twenty-four

Monks cut the last of the pressure-treated two-by-ten deck joists with a Skilsaw and laid it on a stack with the others, then paused to rest, wiping a film of sweat from his forehead. He glanced out to the hazy Pacific horizon for signs of incoming weather, as he had gotten in the habit of doing. It was early March. Spring came more slowly to the North Coast than to other parts of California, and storms were still frequent. But this was a clear day, and the afternoon sun was warm on his shoulders.

He had found out why Lia—he still thought of her as Marguerite—had recognized tools like bolt cutters and pipe wrenches. Her mother, Sara Ferraro, was a professional builder, with her own all-female construction company. She lived in the hills above a little town called Elk, about fifteen miles south of Mendocino and a two-hour drive from his own home in Marin County. He had spent quite a bit of time here over the past couple of months, and had volunteered to rebuild the deck behind her house, one of those things that she had been meaning to get to for years but never had the time. His carpentry skills were decent, but nowhere near Sara's level, and he was feeling under the gun, performance-wise.

His watch read 4:43 P.M. Sara often worked late, but this was Friday, so she'd be home soon. He figured he had just enough time left to set the joists in place. Then he would have the completed substructure to show off to her.

Standing in the middle of the deck's twelve-by-sixteen-foot rectangle, he fit the two-by-tens, one by one, into the metal hangers he had nailed at twenty-four-inch intervals along the rim joists. He was careful to keep the lumber crowns pointing up—that was important, he had learned from her, for load-bearing members.

When he finished, it looked pretty good, and he was feeling pleased with himself.

Then he noticed that some of the joists were as much as a quarter-inch higher than the rim joists where they met.

"What the *fuck*," he said. When he got his tape measure and checked, he found out that the two-by-tens varied from about nine inches in depth to almost nine and a half inches. The bigger ones were sticking up too high. He dropped the tape back into his tool belt, feeling disgusted, ripped off. What the hell kind of world was this when you couldn't trust lumber dimensions?

He could hardly leave the joists as they were—that would create humps in the decking. He supposed he would have to pull them out again and notch them underneath—a major, and time-consuming, pain in the ass.

But not today. He got a cold bottle of crisp Kronenbourg beer from the kitchen, then went back out and sat on the lumber pile. The beer was cold and rich, and that dry pilsner taste was just right for the end of a sweaty day of physical work.

In the weeks after the fire at Freeboot's camp, Monks had dealt extensively with law-enforcement authorities, and had lobbied hard to get Marguerite a deal without jail time. The courts took into account her brainwashing and her help in escaping, and agreed that there was nothing to be gained by punishing her. She had been sent to live with relatives in Phoenix. Privately, Monks thought her cooperation seemed more dutiful than wholehearted, but as long as she kept her job and stayed out of trouble, the law would consider her on probation.

Monks had driven her and Sara to San Francisco airport to send her off. When the boarding gate closed, Sara, tough and fiery through the entire ordeal, had collapsed against him and said, "Now take me home and fuck me, will you?"

That first coupling had been more combative than gentle, and it had lasted some time. He had his own tensions to work out. He had battled with guilt about taking a lover while his son was still missing, and with the fear that both he and Sara were in brittle states—using each other for the wrong reasons, which could come around to harm them. It might have been better to cut clean. But it was also really good, and as those things will, it kept happening.

Mandrake was in a long-term care ward for juvenile diabetics, and much improved; tests had found him free of HIV or other serious complications. Monks had been to see him once—an official visit to consult with medical and social services authorities. Mandrake's reaction to Monks was one of wariness and withdrawal. Psychologists had decided that it would be best if Monks faded from his memory, along with all the trauma that he represented. Monks agreed, but it hurt.

There had been no news about Freeboot, or any of the others—including Glenn.

The human remains found at the fire scene—the only ones—were, in fact, female. They belonged to Mandrake's mother, aka Motherlode, whose real name was Alexandra Neville. All indications were that she was unconscious, perhaps already dead, when the fire got to her. Given her addiction, she might have passed out, or even overdosed, and been overlooked by the others until it was too late.

But the possibility of murder existed, and Monks couldn't help suspecting that Freeboot had killed her because of his insane conviction that she was responsible for Mandrake's illness.

If this were true, then killing Glenn to get revenge on Monks seemed an all too likely possibility. That fear ate at Monks like a sarcoma, keeping him awake for hours at a time in the middle of most nights. Rationally, he had over and over again justified leaving Glenn there. But when it came to something like this, rational thought didn't cut it.

When Sara's beat-up Toyota pickup truck pulled into the driveway, Monks got up to greet her. She leaned out the window and eyed the deck approvingly.

"Good boy," she said. "You're due for a reward."

"I screwed up." He pointed to one of the uneven joints.

"Oh. You should set the hangers low, then shim. There's no ceiling underneath, so it doesn't matter down there."

"Now you tell me."

"Hey, I can't be giving away all my secrets too fast. You already know plenty of them."

She got out of the truck, dressed in blue-collar drag—boots whitened with drywall dust, faded jeans stained with construction adhesive and caulk, and a torn sweatshirt. Her dark hair was pulled back in a loose ponytail. It was a look that wouldn't have worked for a lot of women, but on her it was sexy. The hard labor of her job kept her taut and lithe—she could touch her palms flat to the ground without bending her knees. In bed, she liked to clasp her ankles behind his neck.

He saw that she had groceries, and went to help carry them inside.

"Shrimp, scallops, and rock cod," she said, handing him a plastic sack filled with cold paper-wrapped parcels. "We're going to have seafood pasta. *Frutti di mari.* Okay?"

"Wonderful," Monks said.

She frowned. "What's the matter?"

"Nothing," he said, but then realized that his uneasiness must be showing. "Do I seem out of it?"

"Like you're carrying a granite block on your back, baby. More and more."

"Sorry. I'm fine. Really."

"Yeah?" she said, and smiled, maybe a little sadly. "I know it's tough for you, Carroll. I can't even imagine. At least I know where my kid is." She kissed him lightly on the cheek and went inside.

Monks gathered up the rest of the groceries and followed her. The kitchen was small and neat, smelling of herbs and garlic, its butcher-block counters scarred and the Creuset cookware much used. Like the deck, it was something she intended to redo if she ever got the time. He liked it as it was.

"You pour us a drink and shell the shrimp, I'll do the rest," she said. She liked to get everything ready in advance, then kick back, and do the final cooking when they were good and hungry.

"Done," Monks said. He opened the bottle of Guigal Côtes du Rhône that she had brought—seafood or not, Sara was a red wine drinker, with a keen sense for good inexpensive varietals—then poured himself his old standby of Finlandia vodka on ice, touched with fresh lemon. This was the time of year that he had planned to be in Ireland, but that had been put on indefinite hold.

He dumped the big tiger prawns into a bowl. Sara turned on the TV news, and Monks half-listened as he pried apart the carapaces. They were barely thawed, the shells' icy edges stiff and sharp against his thumbs. While his hands moved automatically, his senses drank in the pleasantness around him—the lovely woman, the cozy place, the savory food and drink. He had enough money, enough of everything. What he needed was to feel more useful, he decided—not *too* useful, just a little.

His mind started going over employment options. He still worked as an investigator for a malpractice insurance firm in San Francisco. His case load had been light lately, but only by his choice. He could let them know that he was willing to take on more. There were also many hospitals and clinics that would gladly hire him for temporary *locum tenens* work, including a couple around here. He could arrange a schedule that would satisfy him and still leave him plenty of free time. That would be the ticket.

"... this country better be ready for a wake-up call, because it's about to get one," a man's angry voice said on the television. In the background came the shouts and mutterings of a crowd.

Monks paused, his attention caught by something he could not quite identify.

"It's bad enough they don't give a damn about us, but then to come in here and treat us like *this*," the speaker fulminated. "Those politicians better start realizing, there's twenty million people out here who got nothing. Outlaws, or damned near."

Monks dropped the shrimp he was holding and strode to the TV. Sara glanced at him in surprise.

"What—" she started to say, but he held his hand up for silence.

The television screen showed a fiftyish white man with the look of the homeless—thin and bearded, wearing a greasy parka and mismatched pants and shirt—stabbing a forefinger with violent emphasis as he spoke. A mob hundreds strong was grouped behind him, murmuring and erupting in shouts of anger and menace. The background looked somehow familiar—a slum in an older city, four- and five-story brick buildings with rickety back porches hung with laundry.

"There's an army already out there, and it's ready to fight *back*." The speaker thrust his fist into the air in a Black Power salute. The crowd repeated the gesture, pumping fists up and down and raising its collective voice to a roar.

The TV screen switched back to the studio anchorwoman, well groomed and professionally poised.

"Again, Chicago police came down hard on an urban homeless camp after items were discovered there that might be linked to the 'Calamity Jane' killings," she said.

Chicago. That's where he'd seen those buildings—on the South Side, where he'd grown up, down by the Rock Island Railroad tracks.

"Officials deny that any brutality was used, but a videotape has surfaced of police rampaging through the area, evoking outraged comparisons to the Rodney King incident in Los Angeles," the announcer went on. "Authorities say they're looking into the matter.

"Up next, a look at the weekend's sports. Stay with us."

Sara's face was questioning.

"Freeboot said the same thing to me, in almost those same words," Monks said. "The same number, twenty million outlaws. The riff about the army already being out there."

He flipped to a different channel and this time caught the story as it was starting.

". . . now we'll hear how a shocking murder in an Illinois gated community has led to a near riot in a homeless camp," another anchorwoman said. "Here's Ted Derrick in Chicago. Ted?"

The screen flashed to a good-looking young man with a microphone, standing at the fringes of the same slum and crowd that the earlier newscast had shown.

"Kelly, events have taken a strange and even uglier turn here, since the murder yesterday of Walter Krieger and his wife," he said. "This morning, items of Mrs. Krieger's lingerie, believe it or not, started turning up in this urban homeless camp—very expensive stuff, Italian silk and what-have-you, not the kind of thing you'd expect to find here."

Sara was watching now with dismay, holding a chopping knife in a posture that looked unconsciously defensive.

"They stole her underwear?" she murmured. "*That's* creepy."

"Police received an anonymous tip about the lingerie, is that right?" Kelly, the anchorwoman said.

"Correct. There's speculation that the tip came from the killers themselves, wanting to link this to the previous Calamity Jane murders."

"*Why* are they doing this?" she said, leaning forward suddenly and slapping her hand down on her desk, with the petulance of a teeange girl.

Not just petulance, Monks thought. Fear. It could happen to *her*.

"Nobody seems to have any answers yet, Kelly."

She leaned back, regaining her composure. "And there are complaints of brutality when police searched the camp?"

"Yes. Residents say they ran amok, with violence, threats, and racial slurs. Here's a video that was taken by a bystander."

The screen changed again, this time to a scenario that looked like it could have been from a movie of a postapocalyptic world. Unsteady and amateurish, surreally lit by the garish flashing lights of squad cars, the footage showed a dozen policemen in full riot gear charging through an alley, tearing apart cardboard shelters, kicking men in bedrolls and clubbing those who tried to stand.

"There's a sense that the police were taking out their frustrations on the homeless," Ted's voice cut in. "Blaming and punishing *them* for the murders."

The screen switched to the same homeless spokesman who had been on the earlier broadcast, repeating his strident shout:

"It's bad enough they don't give a damn about us, but then to come in here and treat us like *this*—"

Monks felt Sara's hand touch his arm. The concern was in her eyes again.

"How about we turn this off and get in the hot tub?" she said.

"There's an army already out there, and it's ready to fight *back*," the angry face shouted.

Monks switched off the set. "Let me just clean up," he said. He peeled the few remaining shrimp, put them in the refrigerator, and washed the counter.

Since the fire, he had checked out some of Freeboot's claims and found them accurate. Official estimates put the homeless population at over three and a half million, more than a third of them children. That was probably on the conservative side, and didn't take into account the many more who were marginal—one short step away.

More than three million jobs in industry had disappeared over the past couple of years. There was a pervasive perception of the homeless as lazy and irresponsible, but a whole lot of them were staunch, hardworking citizens who couldn't pay their bills after the factory doors slammed shut. The few jobs that were "created" to replace those lost tended to be either high-end technical—beyond the reach of people without higher education—or minimum-wage. Thousands of soldiers were coming home from overseas deployment and finding that out.

And the big rock of poverty that dropped into the national pond spread other ugly ripples. The FBI estimated twenty-four *thousand* violent gangs. Prisons were overcrowded to the bursting point, their population over two million, with millions more ex-cons and parolees also on society's fringes.

The total might not add up to twenty million, but it was a hell of a lot of people. How many more were that one short step away, who weren't showing up on any economic-indicator charts? Outwardly doing all right—but in fear of losing their jobs, facing power bills that suddenly tripled and surging gasoline prices that hammered commuters and other escalating expenses, unable to afford health insurance and knowing that a sickness or injury would wipe them out. Literally a paycheck or two away from losing everything. If you went another rung down the socioeconomic ladder, you were talking people who worked for minimum wage, who would never own a house, who were condemned to a semidesperate life with the talons of drugs and crime clawing at their children.

When Monks was growing up, the lucky kids had a chance at college. Others went into jobs in factories or the trades, not glamorous, but stable and adequately providing. If you were responsible, you could live decently, buy a home, and hope that your children would have it better—the American dream. His own father had been a laborer, and his mother, a grade school teacher. He had been one of those lucky kids.

Now that was pretty much gone. *Lucky* was more and more equivalent with *affluent*, and for the others, that stable life was edging closer to extinction all the time.

For all of Freeboot's madness, he had pinpointed a major weakness that had crept into society over the past couple of decades—a huge mass of rage and desperation. Monks thought of it in terms of basic chemistry. If you put water in a pot and turned up the heat and pressure, the molecules got more and more agitated until they finally boiled over.

It had been eerie, watching Freeboot's words come out of a stranger's mouth. But the really surprising thing, Monks realized, was that he was not really surprised. The three months of constant worrying and looking over his shoulder had been building, not receding.

He had been waiting for something.

Twenty-five

Sara's antiquated hot tub dated back twenty-some years, to when she and her coke-dealer ex-boyfriend had first lived here. It was an indulgence, even a caricature of California decadence, but nice for chilly nights and watching the ocean, calm and starlit, or ominous under an incoming wall of fog, or wild with a storm.

"It's just a word-of-mouth thing, don't you think?" she said. She was leaning back, water up to her chin, calves draped across Monks's thighs. Her hair was a damp, dark cloud. "What that homeless guy was saying, that sounded like Freeboot? Something that gets passed around between street people. Maybe Freeboot wasn't even the first one who made it up."

"You're probably right."

"I can understand why it upsets you, but—I think you're seeing Indians behind every tree."

Monks realized that she was working to soothe him, as she often did. He caressed the back of her knee appreciatively.

"You didn't know you were taking on a full-time job, trying to keep me calm," he said.

"Listen to you—finding something else to feel guilty about."

"What do you mean, something else?"

"All kinds of things. Thinking Glenn inherited your bad side."

"I don't exactly *think* that," Monks said. But it brought back the unhappy memory of his conversation with Shrinkwrap at the camp.

"But you're afraid of it. Every parent is—the honest ones, anyway. You think I don't worry that Lia grew up like me? Sex, drugs, hooking up with a guy who ran her life?"

"You turned it around," he said. "So will she."

This time it was Sara who looked distracted by her own thoughts. She had been a good girl, the pride of her blue-collar family, attending UC Berkeley on a full scholarship. Then, home for the summer before her senior year, she'd started living with the area's ranking coke dealer, a man almost ten years older. She never went back to school. For a while, they'd lived the high life. But the drug business started changing, with rougher competition moving in and her boyfriend getting paranoid and erratic.

Then she got pregnant. Ostensibly, it was unplanned, but on some level she understood that it was a desperate move to ground herself. She had quit the drugs, leveraged her ex out of the house, and borne Lia—and then started to face the reality of paying for a child and a life. An uncle in the construction business had hired her to do book work. She had started cleaning job sites for extra cash, picked up skills quickly, and eventually parlayed them into the novelty of an all-female crew, backed by a reputation for quality work.

But she alluded to times, during those intervening years, of bad relationships, lapses back into drug use, and almost abandoning herself to the downhill crash of that earlier life that she had barely pulled out of.

"She'll find her own way," Sara finally agreed. "You ready for a refill?"

"Sure." Monks drained the bit of vodka left in his glass and handed it to her.

She went to the kitchen and came back a minute later, carrying the full glasses like a waitress, except that she was naked and dripping wet. Monks watched her the entire time. He loved to look at her—

her smooth olive skin, dark-nippled breasts soft and etched with the lines of mothering, lush black V disappearing between her thighs. Although he had witnessed many births, he would clasp her slim hips and touch the soft petals of her labia in near disbelief that a child could have passed through. The older he got, the more fascinated he became by the beauty and resilience of women.

She knew it, and took her time getting back into the tub.

"You feel guilty about us, too," she said.

Monks started to deny it. But, like most of her insights, it bore truth.

"There's a part of me that says I don't deserve anything this good."

"Maybe it's an Irish-versus-Italian deal," she said. "You brood about things forever. We just do them, then we scream at each other, or go to confession, and it's over."

"I don't think it's that cut and dried."

"Okay, it never is. But—I don't know exactly how to put this. You're a tough guy in some ways, but you've never really gotten down."

"Gotten down?"

"Compromised yourself, to get what you wanted."

"I've done plenty I'm not proud of," Monks said.

"I mean really down and dirty, hon. Like, there were a couple of times I blew guys for coke." She watched his face. "Shocks you, huh?" she said.

"A little," he admitted, annoyed with himself for his prudishness.

But she seemed amused. "It helps you learn to get over things. You realize it's not the end of the world. So what about fucking in a hot tub? Does that slam you with extra guilt?"

Monks slid his hand up the inside of her thighs to their wet, furry juncture. She closed her eyes and scooted her rump forward, pressing into him.

"Sometimes guilt makes things sweeter," he said. "Any mick can tell you that."

* * *

It was the strangest apartment building that Monks had ever been in, an old brick tenement hung with laundry, but the front walls were missing, so he could see right into the rooms. He was talking with a pixie-ish young woman, standing where the doorway would have been. She was pretty, her skin very pale, her hair orange.

That will be fine, then, *she said earnestly. Monks agreed, but her features started changing, becoming bearded and disheveled, and she was speaking angry, accusing words. Disturbed, Monks drifted on, through a vaginal labyrinth of deep purples and reds.*

Now there was something behind him, following, that he didn't like at all. A name was coming into his head, with an "F" sound. Federico. Francesco. Freefreefree—

He ran, but the world around him had thickened into an endless swamp. His legs were like chunks of lead, his steps agonizing. He clawed at the decayed cypress knees that thrust up around him, pulling himself along, but it was way too late, because whatever had been following was not really behind him at all, it was already in *him*—

Monks said, "*Haaah,*" and struggled to sit up. His eyes were open. He was in Sara's bed, with her sleeping beside him. He put his hand on her flank. Her breathing was undisturbed. Glad that he hadn't awakened her, he settled back again and closed his eyes.

But a page from *Pilgrim's Progress,* its Gothic etchings forever seared into his childhood memory, opened in his mind.

. . . he had gone but a little way before he espied a foul fiend coming over the field to meet him; his name is Apollyon.

Monks got up quietly and carried his clothes to the living room to dress. There was no chance of getting back to sleep.

The green LED readout on the microwave read 3:13. He opened the liquor cabinet and looked at the vodka bottle. But he knew that if he started, he wouldn't stop, and come dawn, he would be wide-awake drunk. He started heating water for coffee instead.

His own dream had fit a pattern that was common for him—images that had recently been in his mind, blended with elements of absurdity, and ending in a helpless attempt to escape. The young woman's face, melting into an ugly blur that recalled the homeless man on TV. The comforting birthlike passage giving way to a world that was harsh and dangerous. Federico and Francesco, Italian names stemming from his earlier talk with Sara, his mind groping for the "F" that it linked to the threat.

Freeboot.

In the aftermath of the fire, law-enforcement authorities had quickly identified Freeboot. His real name was James Reese. He had grown up semiferal in the northern California backwoods, part of a loose clan of dope growers and outlaws. As he had claimed, he'd spent a lot of his later life in prison. It also seemed true that he had experienced some kind of conversion—not religious, but intellectual and political—that had turned him from a run-of-the-mill loser into a serious figure who won the respect of other inmates. He had cleaned up his act, even getting his prison tattoos filled in to symbolize his turnaround. With his last sentence in Folsom served without incident, he faded off the radar of the criminal-justice system.

But there was another factor in the equation—a psychologist with the all-American name of Mary Jane Wilson, and an unsavory past of her own. Twice, as a high school counselor—once in her home state of Ohio, and later in Missouri—she had been dismissed for seducing teenage boys.

Hard-pressed to find work, Mary Jane had ended up as a counselor in the California prison system. She had her own ax to grind against authorities now, and, like many of the convicts, she felt at heart that she had been perfectly within her rights to do what she had done, that it was the law that had wronged her.

One of her clients at Folsom was James Reese. It was during that time period that he had his "epiphany." The two of them bonded, him taking the name Freeboot, and she Shrinkwrap. The details of what followed were unclear, but an overall picture emerged from what solid information was available, what Marguerite had contributed, and guesswork.

About four years ago, Shrinkwrap had moved to the North Coast, where she falsified her record, deleting the dismissals, and set up shop. Here in the heart of pot-growing country there were plenty of troubled kids. She quickly became popular with them, although this time there were no reported incidents of sexual misconduct. If she was at it again, she kept it well hidden. She bought an isolated run-down farm near Lake Pillsbury and turned it into an informal retreat for her young clientele. Using intuition and her skills as a psychologist, she determined their susceptibility.

When Freeboot got out of jail and joined her, he brought with him a rhetoric-charged agenda and a training program cobbled together from his superficial reading of history, folklore, and paramilitary creeds. The chosen candidates were carefully brought up through levels, their loyalty constantly tested, their personalities systematically broken down and rebuilt along fanatical lines, with the reward of belonging to a secret, super-powerful elite. Drug use was encouraged, especially of methamphetamine—which, Monks had learned, had been given to kamikaze pilots and Nazi soldiers to make them more alert and aggressive, enabling them to function up to ten days without sleep. A popular form of manufacturing the drug was even known as "the Nazi method."

Freeboot also acquired Motherlode, who had the extra qualification of being a wealthy heiress. Besides a hefty trust fund and other investments, she happened to own the property up in the wilderness north of Lake Pillsbury. He married her and set up a second camp there—the place where Monks had been held.

Shrinkwrap's farm served as both a cover operation and a base, providing physical needs and a closer link to civilization. The mountain camp was for the elite—the training place for the few who were selected to be *maquis* and brides. Everything was kept scrupulously legal on the surface—taxes paid, no obvious drug use or welfare fraud, or any other reason for authorities to come around. As the logging truck driver had told Monks, people in the area knew that the group was there and didn't much like it, but everybody left everybody else alone.

Days of careful searching through the camp's wreckage had revealed little. The fire had destroyed almost everything. Computers found in an underground bunker had been stripped of their hard drives, and explosives had turned what was left into a chaos of junk. Police had done their best to track down the fugitives, but the fugitives had vanished. The identities of some were traced, but with no results—they were drifters, runaways, throwaways. Others, like Taxman, remained wild cards, their legal names still unknown.

It seemed that Freeboot's boastful intentions about righting social injustices and changing history had gone up with the smoke. Now he was a fallen idol, an ex-con on the run, wanted for a host of crimes that would put him back in prison for life. But even here, he had provided for himself with alarming foresight. He had acquired power of attorney over Motherlode's inheritance, dismissing the outraged trustees that her parents had put in charge. Investigators had discovered that roughly twelve million dollars of that money then had been siphoned off, apparently into numbered overseas bank accounts.

Now Motherlode was dead and Freeboot was rich.

Much as Monks had tried to write him off, he had not been able to. Freeboot's level of organization, together with his personal power, were too disturbing. Now he seemed to be turning up in Monks's imagination—getting into his head, as Freeboot's devotees claimed he could. All of Monks's scientific training scorned any such notion. But he recalled uneasily two separate instances when he could almost have sworn that people had made psychic contact with him. Both of them had been trying to kill him at the time.

The coffee water was boiling. He ground up a cup's worth of French roast, dumped it into a filter, and poured the steaming water slowly through, in stages. The result was strong and bitter, the way he liked it.

He was starting to think about making breakfast when he heard a car door slam outside. There was no reason for anyone to be coming here at this hour.

He stepped to a window away from the kitchen light just in time to see the vehicle's taillights as it pulled away, leaving a thin white plume of exhaust in the chilly night. It looked like an older-model van, the kind that were popular in the 1970s. Someone was walking toward the house, shouldering a backpack.

Monks got a dizzying lurch in his gut, like when flying and the airliner dropped suddenly in rough weather.

It was Lia.

Sara hadn't said anything about her coming home. He was quite sure that Sara didn't know—and that this was a violation of Lia's probation. He unlocked the door and opened it.

"I knew somebody that was coming up here and I caught a ride," she said, stepping past him and unslinging her pack onto the floor. "We drove all night." She seemed neither glad to see him nor surprised. She knew from phone talks with her mother that he had been staying here sometimes, and his Bronco was parked in the driveway. Her movements were jittery and her pupils seemed dilated. He wondered if she had been using meth—another probation offense.

"Welcome home," he said. "I'll get your mom."

Sara was already hurrying down the hall, tying the belt of her robe. She must have heard the car, too. She gave Monks a quick, distraught look, but then put on a big smile as she came into the living room.

The two women embraced, with Sara murmuring, "Oh, baby, it's so good to see you." She stepped back, clasping Lia's shoulders, still smiling but looking perplexed.

"But you're not supposed to be here," Sara said.

Lia pulled away. "Don't start, okay, Mom?" she said sharply. "There's just no way I can live in that straight world."

"What are you telling me?" Sara said. "You're not going back?"

"No way," Lia repeated emphatically.

Monks stayed in the background, silent. Lia hadn't been happy about going to Phoenix; but, then, she hadn't been happy about anything. He waited, expecting Sara to remind her of her probation terms. Leaving Phoenix was not her decision to make.

Instead, Sara said, "Okay, we'll work it out. What about Joe and Ellie?" Those were the relatives that Lia had been staying with.

"What about them?" Lia retorted.

"Do they know about this?"

"What do *you* think, they'd have let me go? I told them I was going to spend the weekend at a girlfriend's."

Sara sighed. "I'd better call them."

Monks was taken aback by her swift acquiesence. He told himself that it was none of his business, but that wasn't true. When he had lobbied to get Lia the deal, he had implicitly staked his word that she would stick to it. And allowing her to stay here would constitute something like harboring a fugitive, even if in a very small way.

But now was not the time to bring it up.

"I was about to make breakfast," Monks said. "How about it, Lia? You hungry?"

She swung around to face him, with her edgy, defiant gaze.

"Call me Marguerite," she said. "You know that's my real name."

Twenty-six

Monks's relationship with Gail, his ex-wife and Glenn's mother, had become distant over the years, but it had intensified during the past three months—since their son had once again become a focus of their lives. In fact, they hadn't had so much interaction since finalizing their divorce.

This afternoon, Monks had agreed to meet her for lunch. There was no news of Glenn, no aspect of the incident that they hadn't already discussed dozens of times. But she needed to take her anxieties out on Monks, and while he usually received an emotional beating, in a twisted way he got some satisfaction, too. It was somewhat like giving blood.

Gail had a pleasant face and an athletic figure, a little on the big-boned side, like their daughter, Stephanie's. Her hair was short and gingery, like Glenn's. She kept herself trim by playing tennis and taking treks to remote places around the globe with her second husband, Sawyer, an environmental-sciences professor at UC Davis. She was intelligent, goodhearted, politically correct, and vaguely hostile to abstract thought.

"*I* think the police aren't looking hard enough," she said.

The fact was that Freeboot, with his illicit wealth, could be anywhere in the world. Monks answered with a noncommittal "Hmh," chewing on a club sandwich. The restaurant was in Sonoma, at the corner of the old town square. It wasn't the kind of place that he particularly cared for—it was small and cramped, with a sort of forced chichi ambience, and passersby gaping into the big plate-glass windows made him feel like an animal in a zoo. But Gail had chosen it.

"Every time the phone rings, I jump," she said. Her gaze was reproachful, as if he were to blame.

He nodded empathetically. Only since the fire had she confessed that before then, Glenn had been calling her regularly—and that she had frequently wired him money, to whatever bank he specified. She knew that he had moved from Seattle to northern California about two years ago, but he had refused to tell her exactly where. She kept sending money anyway. Monks had long since realized that the relationship between mother and son—especially an only son—was of a profundity beyond his grasp. And he suspected that Glenn's emotional problems only made Gail's attachment stronger.

"You don't think those sheriffs know something they're not telling us, do you?"

"I don't see what good that would do them," Monks said. "But I suppose it's possible."

"That's comforting."

"There's nothing we can do about it, Gail. Nothing but wait."

She picked at her salad and watched him eat his sandwich with a hint of disdain, like a well-bred lady forced to share her table with an ill-mannered serf. When they were courting, Gail had been a fun-loving free spirit. But in the course of their marriage, she had became caught up in the role of a doctor's wife. By the end, she seemed more interested in their social standing and the square footage of their house than in her sometimes contentious husband.

He accepted the lion's share of the blame. She had wanted a smooth, stable, affluent life. He had felt the much less reasonable need to rattle cages. He supposed it was a common situation—both partners waking up one day, after a number of years, to find that they no longer recognized the person they were married to, while probably unaware how much they themselves had changed.

"I know you had to leave him there," she said, suddenly laying down her fork. "But I still can't believe it."

He exhaled. This was one of the conversations they had had many times before, Gail always understanding and agreeing with his reasons—above all, the need to save Mandrake—but finally not accepting them. And every time, his own anguish crashed back down on him.

"I'll take care of the check," he said, standing.

He had expected her to stay at the table, but she waited for him at the restaurant's door. She wasn't yet done with him. Outside, the afternoon was warm with spring sunshine, but he could see the graying line of a fog bank beyond the coastal mountains to the west.

"How are you and your new friend getting along?" Gail asked.

"Just fine."

"How many is this now, since we split?"

"For Christ's sake," he said wearily, "are you keeping a scorecard?" In a dozen years he'd had two semiserious affairs and a few flings. He still wasn't sure which category Sara would turn out to be in.

"Just wondering if you're getting into a second adolescence, like so many men. Trying to prove your virility."

"Second?" Monks said. "You're the one who spent years telling me I never grew out of my first one."

Her lips twitched in a quick, grudging smile. "You'll call me if you hear anything?"

"You know I will," he said.

They exchanged a dry, formal kiss and walked their separate ways.

Monks climbed into his Bronco and drove north on Highway 12, passing through the small settlements of Boyes and Fetters Hot Springs, on his way to Sara's. He had spent the last three days at his own house in Marin, taking care of necessities and trying to appease three cats that were pissed off by his absences. He was distracted and had to remind himself to keep his accelerator foot light through Sonoma's long stretch of its twenty-five-mile-per-hour speed limit.

The hardest thing about dealing with Gail was the inevitable aftermath of Glenn coming to the forefront of his mind again, along with all the ways that Monks feared having failed him.

He had talked extensively with law-enforcement authorities about what would happen if Glenn did turn up. The issue of his criminal culpability was murky. At Monks's urging, the courts would probably overlook Glenn's role in the kidnaping, along with his drug use if he agreed to enter rehab. There was the troublesome possibility that he had used his computer skills to help drain off Motherlode's inheritance, but at least that was white-collar crime.

Whatever anger Monks had felt toward him was gone, especially as he'd come to realize the extent of Freeboot's influence. Mostly, Monks nursed the tormenting hope that Glenn would get shaken enough to come home and start turning his life around. But as the weeks had turned to months, it seemed more likely that he was still in deep with Freeboot.

Either that or he was dead.

Twenty-seven

Monks had been right about the incoming fog. It started to thicken when he turned off Highway 101 at Cloverdale and turned into dense gray gloom in the coastal mountains west of Booneville. Everything in sight was coated with a fine sheen of moisture—the trees, the road, the Bronco's windshield. His sense was of driving through a rainstorm that was trembling on the edge of cracking wide open.

He arrived at Sara's house a little before four P.M. Both of her vehicles were gone—the pickup truck that she drove to work, and the Nissan Altima that Marguerite had been using.

That reminded him unhappily of another situation that he wasn't dealing with well. Marguerite had been home for almost two weeks now. He had talked to Sara privately about her probation issues. Sara had soothed him as usual, assuring him that she would work things out as soon as Marguerite calmed down. But that never happened, and it looked to Monks like Marguerite was settling in. She came and went as she pleased, apparently hanging out and partying with friends she had grown up with. Without doubt, she was drinking and using drugs. But no one else seemed concerned, so he had decided to let it ride. At the least, it was a major improvement over her being under Freeboot's domination.

He poured himself a vodka in Sara's kitchen, put on a jacket, and took the drink outside. Marguerite's homecoming had deepened his sense of foreboding, and he had spent the past two weeks in a limbo of drifting from one inconsequential task to another, tense, irritable, and not getting much done.

The fog rolled in like a tide, advancing in swirling clouds and filling the deep ravines that converged down at the ocean. He liked watching it, liked this kind of weather; he supposed that it aroused something atavistic in his gloomy Celtic soul. He thought again about the canceled Ireland trip. Maybe *that* was what he needed to do—just get the hell out of here for a while and let people and events take care of themselves. Nothing he was doing was helping, that was for sure.

He was starting his second drink when he heard a vehicle pull into the driveway. He walked over to where he could see around the corner of the house. It was the Altima—Marguerite was home. He went back to his fog watching, a little uncomfortable with her presence.

She hadn't done anything that troubled him directly. For the most part, she politely ignored him. But it was still a bizarre situation—sharing a house with a woman who had helped to abduct him, and sleeping with her mother. He was pretty sure that he wouldn't have begun the affair if he had known that Marguerite would be around, and he didn't know if he would be able to sustain it on those terms. That was another thing that he was on the fence about, waiting uneasily for a push one way or another.

The door to the kitchen opened and Marguerite stepped out onto the deck. Monks turned to her inquiringly, assuming that there was something she had to tell him. But then he saw that she was carrying a bottle of beer, one of his Kronenbourgs.

She raised it, as if saluting him. "You won't turn me in for this, will you?" she said teasingly.

He was surprised. This was the first time that she had been anything like sociable.

"I don't know," he said with mock severity. "What's the reward money up to now?"

She laughed and tipped the bottle up, taking a long drink. A little of the foamy liquid spilled from her lips. Then the bottle slipped from her fingers, bouncing on the deck and spraying beer.

"Shit," she said. "Would you get me another one? I'll clean this up."

He hesitated, suspecting that she had already drunk quite a bit.

"Sure," he said. "But how about only *one* more?"

She made a face, an exaggerated pout. That was unlike her, too.

He went into the kitchen and opened another one of the Kronenbourgs, not happy about his own judgment. But if he had refused, she would probably just go back out to the bars.

When he got outside again, she had disappeared. The beer bottle still lay where it had fallen. Then he saw that the styrofoam lid of the hot tub was off. Marguerite's jeans and blouse were lying beside it in a tangle on the deck. She was in the tub, leaning back, arms spread luxuriantly along the rim behind her, toes just peeping over in front.

"Why don't you come on in?" she said. "It's fucking freezing out there."

Monks stopped walking and tried to think of an appropriate response. Nothing came.

"Hey, why be shy?" she said. "We've seen each other's skin before." She pushed away from the hot tub's wall and slid toward him through the water.

"Marguerite, what's going on? This is—silly."

"I think you're sexy," she said mischievously.

Monks was quite sure that whatever was prompting her—an attempt to establish control over him, or assauge her guilt, or wound her mother, or even a reversion to her time with Freeboot, when she had held the exalted status of temple prostitute and been the object of men's desire—it had nothing to do with his being sexy.

"That's flattering, but I doubt it," he said.

"You'd love to fuck me, admit it," she taunted. "Doesn't every guy have a fantasy about a mother-daughter team?"

"I've got my wrinkles, honey, but that's not one of them. No offense."

She stood up suddenly, a long, dewy sheen of smooth skin and wet hair. But her smile was glassy, her eyes wide with false innocence, or maybe just dope.

He turned away hastily. "Here's your beer," he said, setting the bottle on the deck and retreating.

"If you bring me that, I'll tell you something you want to know," she called after him.

"Put your clothes on," Monks said, pulling the kitchen door open. "Then tell me."

"It's about Coil."

Monks wheeled back around. Her smile faded under his stare. She dropped down into the water again, sinking up to her chin.

He walked to the tub and knelt beside it. She backed away as far from him as she could get.

"If this is some kind of game, tell me now," he said. "I'll walk away and it's over. But you'd better not lie about my son."

"I'm not lying," she said. Her voice was very small now and her eyes were scared.

"What is it you know?"

"He's okay."

Monks gripped the tub's rim hard.

"*How* do you know?" he demanded.

"I can't tell you yet."

He bristled. "What the hell do you mean, you can't tell me?"

But she had recovered some composure, knowing that she held the cards.

"You have to do things just right, and you can talk to him," she said.

"Do *what* things just right?"

"I'll let you know."

"You'll tell me *now*, goddamn it!" He lunged toward her and grabbed a fistful of her wet hair, twisting it hard.

"I don't *know* yet. Let me go!"

Her yelping voice pierced the cloud of anger in his brain. He relaxed his hand and she jerked free.

Monks took a mental step back. The implications of what she was saying were sinking in.

More gently, he said, "Are you telling me you've been in touch with Freeboot?"

"He never left me, not for a second," she whispered. "I could feel him around me all day, and in me all night."

Monks was stunned. He had assumed naïvely that she had been getting over her obsession. Instead, it sounded like she was in deeper than ever.

"And you've talked to him?" he said. "Is that how you know about Glenn?"

She didn't answer, and her gaze slid away from his.

"Marguerite," he said, choosing his words carefully. "If you know where Freeboot is, you *have* to tell the police. This is very, very serious."

"No cops," she said emphatically. "Nobody else, period. He says it's between you and him, that you'd understand that."

"He sent you to tell me that? He wants to work out some kind of a deal?"

She nodded, her gaze still averted. And that, Monks thought, was the reason that she had tried to seduce him—on Freeboot's orders. Monks would be unlikely to go to the police if he had just had sex with his lover's daughter.

"Marguerite, you can't be serious about trusting him again," Monks said.

"He's forgiven me. He needs me."

"How can you believe that? Remember what everybody agreed on—you, the police, the counselors? Freeboot *used* you. That's all it was. If he says he's forgiven you, he just wants to use you again."

She shook her head almost sadly, and repeated words that he had heard too many times: "You don't know him."

"What about him leaving Motherlode up there to die in the fire? Maybe on purpose?"

"Bullshit, man, that was an accident," Marguerite said angrily. "She was passed out and nobody knew it until too late."

Monks gave up trying to reason with her.

"Get dressed," he said. "We're going to the sheriffs."

"No! I'll deny it. I'll say I was just goofing. And then you're shit out of luck."

He hesitated, afraid that she was right.

"I'll let you know," she said again. "Just stay cool." Then, glaring at him, she slid one arm across her breasts and her other hand between her thighs, in the time-honored gesture of a nude woman covering herself from unwanted eyes.

"You better get out of here before my mom comes home and sees you hanging around me like this," she said haughtily.

Monks stood up, reeling from the dizziness of blood rushing from his head, and made his way back into the house.

Twenty-eight

Monks stood in Sara's kitchen, breathing deeply, trying to get a handle on what to do next. There didn't seem to be any good choices. He decided to stay out of Marguerite's way for the moment—give her privacy to come in and get dressed. Then he'd try to talk to her again. He walked into the living room, thinking hard for a line of reasoning that might make her listen, and waiting impatiently for the sounds of her coming inside.

Instead, he heard a car's engine starting up.

He strode to the nearest window and looked out just in time to see her backing the Altima out of the driveway fast. Her right hand was pressed against her ear, as if she were talking on a cell phone.

More red flags went up in Monks's brain. Marguerite must have pulled her clothes on still wet and gone straight to the car, in a hurry, intent on avoiding him. She didn't have a cell phone, and Sara always took her own to work.

His immediate suspicion was that Freeboot had given her one, in order to communicate with him.

Monks trotted out to the Bronco and took off after her, west on the county road toward the little town of Elk. He left his headlights off, taking the risk in spite of the fog, and drove fast until he spotted her taillights ahead. He dropped back out of sight, accelerating every minute or so to make sure that she was still there ahead of him. From the glimpses he got, she was still talking on the phone, probably paying no attention to her surroundings.

It was just four miles to the intersection with Highway 1. Marguerite turned north, up the coast toward Fort Bragg. Monks let another vehicle get between them. He turned on his headlights now, trying to blend with the stream of traffic that would be in her rearview mirror, but pushing to stay close enough so that he would notice if she turned off.

Which she did almost immediately, into the parking lot of the state beach right there at Elk. The move was so fast and sudden that Monks almost missed it. He made the snap judgment to drive on past rather than pull in right behind her, then immediately started fretting that she already *had* spotted him—that she was turning around and would shake him before he could get back. He slammed on his brakes, skidding on the roadside dirt, and spun the Bronco in a U-turn.

But when he drove past the beach, he could see the Altima, a dim shape in the otherwise empty parking lot. He cut his lights and pulled over to the roadside again, in a spot where he didn't think that she would see him even if she was looking. He yanked his binoculars from the glove box and stared at the car through the fog, willing her to do something that would signal her intentions. She might only have come here to get away from the house—make phone calls to friends, or calm herself down, or get high.

But she might be meeting someone, too, and that someone could be Freeboot.

Monks got out the 7.65-mm Beretta that he kept in the Bronco, locked in a hidden safe deposit box welded under the console, and slipped it into his jacket pocket.

She had only been out of his sight for two minutes at most, but he was starting to worry that she might have jumped into a waiting car and sped away. Then the gray swirls of fog parted enough to give him a look at the beach.

He could just make out a dim shape close to the ocean's edge. It might have been a rock, but it was human-sized, and he was pretty sure that it was moving. He shoved open the Bronco's door and ran for the parking lot, staying low.

There was nobody inside the Altima. But something on the passenger seat caught his eye—a gold chain with a pendant, deep green against the car's tan upholstery, lying there carelessly, as if it had fallen unnoticed. Monks leaned close. It was not the sort of inexpensive decoration that women sometimes hung from their rearview mirrors. The pendant was the size of a silver dollar, jade or some other green stone, beautifully carved in the shape of a dragon. It looked like a genuine Asian antique.

A memory flashed into his mind of the morning at the camp when he had seen Hammerhead give something like this to Marguerite. Monks had only gotten a glimpse of it then—had assumed that it was a trinket, and hadn't thought about it again.

But he suspected that this was it, and it was no trinket. Where the hell had Hammerhead gotten it? Had Freeboot been that generous with Motherlode's money? Did the *maquis* have a sideline of theft?

Something troublesome was stirring around in his head. Something about jade . . .

He tried the door, but the car was locked. He hesitated, trying to think of a way to get in, but Marguerite was getting farther away every second. He started running to catch her.

Visibility was down to less than a hundred yards. He wasn't sure which way she had gone, and there were no clear footprints in the loose sand near the highway. But when he got to the water's edge, he found a fresh trail heading north. The surf was high, crashing into shore in seething gray-green waves and spraying his face. His loafers filled with sand and slipped on slimy bunches of kelp, quickly tiring his legs.

Then, in the gloom ahead, he got a glimpse of a hurrying figure.

He cut inland to stay close to the cover of the dunes, watching her shape vanish and appear again through the gray clouds. He had the sudden eerie sense that he was following a specter through a dream. But to where? There was nothing ahead—only the bluffs at the beach's end.

She kept on going when she reached them, quickly climbing a tight switchback trail up the cliff face. She was over the top and out of sight by the time he got to the base. He followed, slipping and sliding on the hard, pebbly soil, forcing his aching legs and lungs as hard as he could up the steep trail. Clutching at bunches of sea oats, he pulled himself up the last few feet—

Just in time to see her jump into a pickup truck that was waiting on the deserted headlands.

Monks ran forward, pulling out his pistol, but the truck was already moving away. Within a few seconds, it had faded from sight.

He strode on to where it had been parked, in the faint hope that some clue might remain. There was nothing, not even tire tracks. The spot was desolate, cut off from the highway by dunes, with only the ocean to the west, pounding against the huge ocher rocks, and more headlands to the fog-shrouded north. There was no road in, but the ground was flat, easy for a four-wheeler to manage. No doubt the locals knew how to get on and off the highway. He thought the truck was a Chevy or GMC, but it could have been a Ford or Dodge, or even one of the bigger Toyotas. It was relatively new, light gray or off white. There were thousands like it around.

The wind was much harsher up here than on the beach, rising from moan to howl as it tore at his clothes and hair. The fog had obscured the process of dusk, and now, suddenly, it was almost dark. He did not think that he had ever felt so alone.

Hands shoved into his pockets, bracing himself against the blasts of wind, he turned around and started trudging back.

Then he stopped.

Jade. Antique Chinese jewelry. Stolen from the victims of one of the Calamity Jane killings.

He searched his memory for details. He recalled clearly the uproar when the Calamity Jane golf clubs had been discovered, and he knew that the killers had tossed other valuable or personal items into Dumpsters. Like the Chicago woman's lingerie—that seemed to be their signature. But he was less clear on the jewelry incident. He remembered that he'd been caught up in his own obsession with Freeboot at the time—that he hadn't even heard about that particular murder until days after it had happened, and that he'd still been too concerned with the aftermath of the fire to worry about the rest of the world.

That placed it during the time when he had been Freeboot's prisoner—just when he had seen Hammerhead give the pendant to Marguerite. The victims had lived in Atherton, south of San Francisco, a drive of several hours from the camp.

His gut took that queasy twist that it did when something in him started to grasp that an already bad situation was much worse than it seemed.

He started trotting again. He'd have to smash the Altima's window—the Bronco's jack would do it. He needed to get hold of that pendant.

But when he got to the parking lot, the car was gone.

Twenty-nine

Monks approached the Bronco warily, fearful of men lying in wait, or even a planted bomb. If it *had* been Freeboot or his people in the pickup truck, then they had been right here in this area—no telling for how long or how many times. While he'd been following Marguerite, they could have been following him.

The Beretta was back in his hand, held close to his thigh, a round chambered and ready. His gut and brain both told him that if Freeboot had wanted him taken or killed, it would have happened by now. Back there on the headlands would have been an ideal setup.

But when it came to Freeboot, Monks would never assume anything ever again.

Nothing moved except the brush, branch tips and leaves rippling in the wind. The Bronco looked untouched, but he hesitated, fearful of going up in an explosive swirl of flame and jagged metal. Then he clenched his teeth, yanked open the door, and swung himself in. The engine caught instantly and settled into its deep, comforting rumble. He turned up the fan and held his chilly hands over the warm air flooding up through the dash vents.

Seeing the angry homeless man on TV a couple of weeks ago, spouting rhetoric that sounded like Freeboot's, had forced Monks to the uneasy conclusion that Freeboot's plans to incite violence might be more than just talk.

But Freeboot's possible involvement in the Calamity Jane murders was a different order of business.

They think they can hide in their gated communities and nobody can touch them. They're gonna get spanked hard.

Marguerite knew that Monks had seen Hammerhead give her the pendant. Monks remembered her reluctant, even frightened response. Did *she* know where it had come from? Had she accidentally-on-purpose left it in the car for Monks to see? Subconsciously hoping that he would make the connection, and save her again from her helpless submission to Freeboot?

The police had to be contacted immediately. But something deep within Monks resisted, warning him to stay silent—

Because now he was slammed by the fear that Glenn might be involved in the murders.

The hypocrisy was terrible. If it had been someone else's son, Monks would have blown the whistle without hesitation.

But it was not someone else's son.

Whom did he owe more to—CEOs who reaped huge profits by gutting domestic industries, exploiting subsistence labor in Third World countries, even ripping off their own employees and investors, selling out the very real lives of working people—or his own flesh and blood?

He knuckled his eyes, trying to shake off this insane calculation. Maybe Freeboot *was* getting into his head.

A sudden chirping sounded nearby. He tensed, glancing around in bewilderment, thinking a tree frog or locust must have gotten into the vehicle. Then he recognized the coy summons of his cell phone. He kept it in the Bronco when he was traveling, in case of vehicle trouble or other emergencies, but he almost never got called except during investigations.

Certainly not at a time and place like this.

He reached into the glove box and got the phone.

"This is Monks," he said.

"Marguerite told you we'd get in touch, man. What part of that don't you understand?"

Monks closed his eyes at the sound of Freeboot's sardonic voice.

"I wanted to find out what she knows," Monks said. "For Christ's sake, we're talking about my *son*."

"You want your son? You got him. Hey, Coil, it's your old man." The last words were a sharp summons, spoken away from the mouthpiece. There came a few seconds' pause, and a fumbling sound as the phone changed hands.

"How's it going, Rasp?" The voice was young, insolent—unquestionably Glenn's.

Monks swallowed drily. "Glenn, are you all right?"

"Number nine," Glenn crooned mockingly. "Number nine, Number *nine*—"

"Okay, get out of here," Freeboot told Glenn, cutting back in. "Me and your dad got to talk in private."

"Freeboot, I don't hold any grudge," Monks said. "I don't have any desire to send you to jail." Those were lies, but he was making the swift and frightening realization that he *was* willing to stay quiet about the pendant. "I'll never tell anybody I heard from you. I just want my son safe."

Freeboot answered conversationally, like one old friend catching up with another.

"You look like you recovered pretty good from your hike. Grew that patch of hair back. Put on a little weight."

"All right, you've been watching me," Monks said. "I figured that."

"You've seen me, too. Within the last two weeks, fifty feet away. Looked right at me."

Freeboot waited, letting the point sink in—he had altered his appearance to the point where Monks wouldn't recognize him. It might not be true, but Monks's gut told him that it was.

Freeboot was on the loose and invisible.

"Now let's talk about *my* son," Freeboot said. "He's in Sacramento, at that Coulter Hospital, right?"

Warily, Monks said, "What makes you think that?"

"Marguerite told me that's where he got took. Then we helped ourselves to their records. They didn't exactly give their permission." Freeboot sounded smug, throwing out another boast—hospital records security and computer firewalls tended to be top-notch.

Monks winced, wondering if Glenn was involved in this hacking, too. It was no big secret that Mandrake had been taken to Coulter. But then he had been officially discharged and placed in the long-term care ward under a changed name, precisely for fear that Freeboot might come looking for him. Probably the hospital had kept the same ID number or other telltale data, not dreaming that his father would be able to penetrate that far.

"I want to see him," Freeboot said. "And they ain't exactly going to give me visiting privileges, are they? So, being as how you're the one that took him away, you're going to give him back. We trade—your kid for mine."

"*What?*"

"Let's quit fucking around and get down to business." Freeboot's voice was steely now. "Coil's doing fine. At least, that's what he thinks. But the truth is, I'm sick of the little shit. He's whiny and cocky, both—thinks we can't get along without him because he's so fucking smart. He's wrong, dude."

The threat was flat and matter-of-fact.

"He'll stay fine," Freeboot said. "Long as I get my own son back. Tonight."

"That's"—Monks started to say *insane*, but the memory of Freeboot's explosive ego stopped him. "Impossible."

"I don't want you to have time to get yourself in trouble. Sacramento's not that far. You leave right now, you can be there by eight, nine P.M."

"Whoa, hold on. I can't just walk in and ask for him."

"How you do it is your problem," Freeboot said coldly. "You know your way around those hospitals. Figure something out. Then you and I are done. You'll never hear from me again. Your kid stays safe, he never knows anything about this."

"What about Mandrake?" Monks said. "*He's* going to die if you treat him like you did before."

"No, no, man, I'm going to take him someplace where he'll have a great hospital and doctors." Freeboot was earnest now, in his persuasive mode. "I got it all set up. See, I learned some things from you. I'm admitting you were right. But I want him *with* me, you know?"

"Freeboot, don't do this," Monks said, the words rushing out in a plea. "The police aren't looking hard for you now. But if one of those kids dies, that changes everything."

"Nobody's going to get hurt unless *you* fuck up."

Monks clamped his jaw tight, recognizing the psychopath's logic at work again. If anything bad happened, it would be his fault.

"If I can get Mandrake, what am I supposed to do with him?"

"I'll be calling you," Freeboot said. "You better understand something real clear—you get this one chance. You try to pull anything, it's all over."

The connection ended.

Monks set down the phone with a shaking hand. His concerns that had seemed so earth-shaking a minute ago were ancient history now. All that mattered was being in the vise of sacrificing either Glenn or Mandrake.

Monk was sure that Freeboot was lying about continuing Mandrake's medical care, and that crystallized his suspicions about Motherlode. Freeboot had murdered her, to wipe away the stain that she had brought to his imagined genetic superiority.

And he intended to do the same thing to his son.

"I should have killed you when I had the chance, you son of a bitch," Monks whispered, and jammed the Bronco into gear.

Thirty

He drove east toward the town of Philo, in the direction of Sacramento, moving as fast as he dared. It was night now, and the road through the coastal mountains narrowed down to one lane in places, with a lot of steep slopes and tight curves.

The impossible choices hammered his brain. On top of everything else, there was no reason to think that Freeboot would keep his word about Glenn. Monks thought again about trying to use the jade pendant as a bargaining chip—promising to stay quiet about it in return for having Glenn delivered safely to him. But threatening Freeboot was likely to get Glenn killed.

The only faint hope that Monks could see was to throw out a net and hope that Freeboot slipped up.

Monks picked up his cell phone, but hesitated. Freeboot knew that he had the phone and might call for help; he had to have planned for that possibility. The *maquis* would be watching him from moving vehicles or stationary ones posted along the way. They would vaporize at any sign of police. They might even have bugged the Bronco while he had been at the far end of the beach. He looked around helplessly. It was the size of a shortbed pickup truck, its rear compartment packed with the traveling gear he carried, its massive undercarriage thick with years of grease and mud. There were thousands of places to hide microphones that could be as small as pinheads. But stopping to use another phone would be a red flag to anyone who was watching.

He punched 0.

"Operator, this is an emergency. I need your help," he said to the woman who answered.

"You can dial nine-one-one, sir."

"No, I can't," Monks said quickly. "Listen to me, please. I need you to call the San Francisco office of the FBI, *now.* Tell them—"

"Sir, I'll give you that number and you can make the call."

"Ma'am, I'm driving fast on a mountain road, and I'm dealing with a serial killer who's at large. This is a matter of national security, and if you don't help me out here, you're endangering that. Do you understand?"

There was a three-second pause. No doubt she was activating whatever alarm or recording device was used for lunatics.

"Look, I know how this sounds," he said. "My name's Dr. Carroll Monks. Ask for an agent named Duane Baskett. If he's not there, tell them it's about Freeboot, okay? *Freeboot.* I repeat, this has to happen very fast, and in absolute secrecy."

"All right, sir," she said, maybe with a trace more respect. "I'll connect you. Stay on the line."

The FBI had been aware of Freeboot's group for a couple of years, but considered them relatively inconsequential—in a league with hundreds of other little enclaves that had paramilitary leanings. Monks's kidnaping, the camp's conflagration, and the possible murder of Motherlode had put them on the map in a much bigger way. Baskett was a Special Agent in Charge who had come up from San Francisco to investigate after the fire. Monks had spent a fair amount of time talking with him, and hadn't much cared for him. He was good-looking, athletic, in his early thirties, with the condescending air of a cop who thought he knew far more about what was going on than anyone else. His youth made it a notch harder to take. But he seemed efficient, he knew who Monks was, and it was his case.

"This is Baskett," a crisp voice said over the phone. "First off, Dr. Monks, are you in danger?"

"Not immediate. At least, I don't think so."

"This has something to do with Freeboot?"

"Yes. I have to assume he's having me watched. I also may be bugged, but I don't see any way around taking that chance."

"Do you want police assistance?"

"*No* cops," Monks said. "This has to stay invisible."

"All right. What have you got?"

Monks took a breath. It wasn't going to sound much better to Baskett than it had to the operator.

"That Calamity Jane murder in Atherton, a few months ago? Where the antique Chinese jewelry was thrown in the Dumpster?"

"Yeah?" Baskett said cautiously.

"I just saw a very expensive-looking jade pendant of that type. Freeboot's girlfriend, Marguerite, had it. And I'm almost sure I saw one of the *maquis* give it to her, up at the camp, right about the same time as that murder."

When Baskett spoke again, his voice was edged with skepticism, maybe even amusement. "Let's run through all that again. You think Freeboot might be connected with the Calamity Jane killers? He *might* be watching you? And you're basing this on seeing a piece of jewelry?"

"I'm basing it on a lot of things," Monks said heatedly. "And right now there are lives at stake. For Christ's sake, work with me."

Baskett's tone made it clear that he did not appreciate being given orders. "Let's start with you describing this pendant."

"Dark green jade, carved into a dragon, very fine workmanship. On a gold chain."

"Hang on," Baskett said. Monks heard him repeat the description to someone in the background.

The other man's reply was muffled, but when Baskett spoke into the phone again, his tone had gone from skeptical back to cautious.

"One of the prize items in that collection fits that description," he said. "Chinese, Ming dynasty. It's still missing. But there's probably a thousand others around that look like it."

"Out there in the boonies, with a bunch of dopers and runaways? Turning up at exactly that time?"

"Why the hell didn't you tell me about it back when we were talking?" Baskett demanded.

"I didn't get a good look at it the first time. I thought it was just junk. But when I saw it up close, the jade connection clicked. Look, I understand you don't want a false alarm, but can I tell you *why* I'm on the run right now, and we'll worry about the back story later?"

"Go ahead," Baskett said.

Monks gave a terse explanation. When he finished, he could hear other voices in the background. It sounded like this was attracting attention.

"Give me your vehicle description and location," Baskett said.

"Blue Ford Bronco, '74. I'm on the Philo-Greenwood Road, south of Mendocino, a few miles east of Elk. I'll be turning north to Ukiah at Booneville, then over to I-5 and south to Sacramento."

"We'll have a tail pick you up. Don't worry, they won't get spotted. Maybe we'll get a break. But if not—you're going to have to go through with this, Dr. Monks. Get the little boy and hand him over to Freeboot. That will be our chance to move in."

Monks had seen this coming, but he still shook his head in denial, an absurd gesture over the telephone.

"We can't risk getting Mandrake hurt," he said.

"We can't *not* risk it. Think about it. You believe Freeboot, don't you, that he'll kill your son?"

Monks hesitated, then said, "Yes."

"So do I. And God knows how many others, if we don't nail him now."

Monks stayed silent. There was no way that he could think of to argue.

"Are you familiar with Coulter Hospital?" Baskett asked.

"I've been there."

"Any suggestions on how to proceed? It's got to *look* like you're doing it for real, and trying not to get caught."

"Can you get undercover people in place?"

"There's a rapid response team already on the way. Tell us what you want."

Hospitals differed physically, but the basic operations were similar, and Monks remembered Coulter's layout reasonably well. He also remembered an incident that he had been involved in a few years earlier, when a prisoner had been smuggled out of a mental hospital in a laundry cart.

"Have Mandrake's doctors sedate him lightly," he said. "Something like half a milligram of Ativan, to keep him sleepy for ten or twelve hours. Get your own people on the wards so nobody stops me, and set up a laundry cart down in the service area. I'll go in as a maintenance man and take him out in that."

"All right, we'll get right on it."

"I might come up with something better. I'll keep thinking."

"Did Freeboot say anything about where he wants you to deliver the boy?"

"Nothing. Only that he'd let me know."

"Okay, Doctor. I'll check back with you."

As Monks clicked off the phone, bile rose in his throat at the thought of putting Mandrake in the middle of what could turn out to be a violent confrontation.

He forced himself to concentrate on practicalities. He needed to check in quickly with Sara, to keep her from getting alarmed. She was probably home from work by now. He punched the house's number.

When she answered, he said, "Honey, I hate like hell to do this to you. Emil just called—you know, the guy who watches my place? There's a pipe leaking in the kitchen. I have to get back and take care of it before it floods."

"Do you know where Lia is?" she said, as if she hadn't heard him. Her voice was fragile with worry. "Her stuff's all gone."

Monks bared his teeth in a grimace, hating himself for this deception. But it would be worse to tell her that Marguerite had gone back to Freeboot—and there was the chance that Sara would panic and do something that might compromise this.

"She probably just took off with her pals for a few days," he said. "Maybe she met a guy. Let's face it, she's done it before."

"She cleaned out everything. Like she's not coming back."

"She'll work it out for herself, Sara. Just like you said."

"I suppose. It's just—different now."

"I know it's tough."

"Yeah," she sighed. "I know you do. Well, looks like I'm a bachelorette for a while." Her voice lightened, in a brave attempt to sound coquettish. "Guess I'll go out trolling the bars."

He tried to think of some bit of banter to return, but came up empty.

"I won't be long," he said. "I've got to get off now, I'm getting into some bad curves. I'll call you soon."

The part about the curves was true, especially in the fog. He put the phone back on the seat and gripped the wheel at ten and three. The gas gauge read just over half-full, and the Bronco had an auxiliary twenty gallon tank that he kept topped off. That would get him easily to Sacramento, with another few hundred miles to spare. There was the issue of his bladder, but he always carried a couple of plastic containers of water. He could empty one out the window and use it as a trucker's jug if he had to.

He returned his mind to searching for a way to lure Freeboot into view without exposing Mandrake. That was one thing about spending twenty-five years in the ER—he had learned to clamp down on his emotions and deal with the business at hand.

Thirty-one

Mercifully, the fog lifted as he got inland. When it was bad, it could blanket the Central Valley in blindness, causing pile-ups of dozens, even hundreds, of vehicles on the freeways. Traffic thickened as he approached Sacramento, the drivers fast and aggressive and sure of where they were going, or at least acting like they were. He picked his way through them with tense caution, along with his unseen escorts—probably Freeboot's men, and definitely FBI agents. It was eerie, sitting alone in the dark, rumbling Bronco, knowing that others were nearby, watching—that he was a minnow, being followed by piranhas, with alligators hunting for them.

There was still no sign of Freeboot, and neither Monks nor the FBI agents had come up with a better plan.

Sacramento was a big spread-out city, with grids of lights stretching as far as he could see, cut by the dark, winding paths of the rivers. The freeway interchanges were bewildering to an outsider. But he remembered how to find Coulter Hospital. It was a fairly straight shot, off I-880 near McClellan Air Force Base.

He was within three miles of there when his cell phone rang.

"It looks like a go," Baskett said. "Any questions?"

"Not right now. I'll think of plenty when it's too late."

"You came out on top last time, Dr. Monks. Hang in there, we're with you."

Monks muttered thanks, distantly aware that it was the first positive thing that Baskett had ever said to him. Maybe impending disaster brought out the agent's inner child.

Monks knew that by now the hospital was under intense FBI surveillance, with agents inside disguised as personnel. Mandrake had been sedated. Then, in a macabre twist, he had been injected with a microtransmitter the size of a grain of sand, just under his skin. If Freeboot managed to get away with him, the agents would have a means of tracking him. Monks knew that it made sense, but using a four-year-old as bait was evil enough, without treating him like a piece of meat besides.

He saw the green freeway sign for his exit, Plumas Road, along with a blue HOSPITAL sign, and moved over into the far right lane. A stream of other vehicles took the same exit, lining up at the stoplight at the ramp's end. Plumas was a busy four-lane strip, lined with stores, mini-malls, and gas stations. He turned left onto it and drove another mile and a half north, where the area changed to small office buildings and apartment complexes. He turned left again into the hospital's parking lot. This time, no other vehicles followed him.

The players here, he knew, were already in place.

Sacramento's Coulter Hospital was a relatively new sprawling complex, three stories, and spread out like the city itself. The juvenile-diabetes ward was around the back, on the first floor of the northwest wing. The maintenance department where the laundry cart was waiting was in the basement at the east end, next to the receiving area where the hospital took in its supplies. A driveway led down to loading docks there. It was a busy area, with maintenance, repair, delivery, and other personnel coming and going at all hours. No one would pay attention to a man who looked like he knew what he was doing.

At night, this far from the hospital's main entrance, the parking lot was almost empty. Monks picked a spot away from the argon lights. He rummaged through the gear in the back of the Bronco for jeans and a work shirt, then peeled off his dressier clothes and changed clumsily in the tight space of the front seat. He exchanged his loafers for running shoes. He took his keys from the ignition and hung them on his belt. It was not the multikeyed ring on a lanyard that maintenance men favored, but it gave that impression. He put on the Giants baseball cap he used on occasions when he didn't want to be seen clearly, and pulled the brim low over his face.

Freeboot almost certainly had his own surveillance going. It was critical that Monks make this look real.

He got out and walked to the loading dock's steel man door, trying to affect the look of a worker on his way to a job he didn't particularly want to do. Inside, he met the familiar sultry warmth of the hospital's physical plant, the sharp smells of disinfectant and cleaning fluids, and the less definable scent of human bodies, some decaying and some on the mend. The room was large and open, with concrete walls and floor. There was no one else around. He kept walking toward an area where several janitorial carts were lined up against a wall. One of them was piled with freshly folded bedding.

A sleeping little boy would easily fit in the bottom bin, draped with pillowcases and sheets.

He gripped the cart's tubular steel handle and pushed it out into the hallway, keeping his head down and shielding his face with the cap's brim.

A large black man came walking down the hall toward him, wearing a gray uniform with a name patch sewn on. He had the competent look of someone who belonged here, and would know who else did and didn't. Monks tensed, fearing that this was a slip-up and he would be challenged.

But the man only raised a big hand in greeting as he passed, saying, "What's happening, baby?"

Monks muttered, "How's it going," and walked on, feeling a little better—suspecting that he had just seen his first FBI agent of the night.

He took a service elevator to the first floor and trundled the cart toward Mandrake's ward, passing several more people with a glance or nod, classifying them automatically—hospital attendants, a harried intern, a phlebotomist pushing a cart of blood samples, a middle-aged woman in a dress who might have been a visitor or an administrator. At least that was who they seemed to be.

When he got to the ward, the charge nurse was at her desk, making notes on charts. She gave him a smile and murmured "Hi," then bent back to her work. Probably she was an agent, too.

The hallway from there on was empty, as it usually would be this time of evening. He knew from Baskett that he was looking for room 163. Still, he played his role, pushing doors open and glancing inside as if he was checking the laundry situation. When he got to 163, he glanced furtively up and down the hall, then pushed the cart inside. Mandrake was asleep on his belly, mouth slightly open—the picture of helpless innocence.

Monks's hands shook and his teeth almost chattered as he lifted the limp, warm weight out of bed. Staged though this was, the guilt and shame of abducting a child burned through his veins with his hammering pulse.

This time, the charge nurse did not look up as he pushed the cart past her.

Thirty-two

Monks buckled Mandrake in the Bronco's passenger seat, quickly arranging pads to make him comfortable.

"Buddy, I feel like absolute shit," he whispered to the sleeping child. "After all we've been through together, to do this to you—I just can't tell you."

His cell phone chirped. He grabbed for it, fumbling in his haste.

"All right, we seen him," Freeboot said curtly. "You just drive back the way you came. Keep that phone handy. Oh, and tell my little boy he's going to be with his daddy soon." The connection went dead before Monks could speak.

Hope surged up in him. Freeboot's men had been watching, but not overhearing. They didn't know about the FBI agents.

There was still a chance.

Monks pulled out of the parking lot and drove back to the freeway, easing carefully into traffic. Driving along this mundane road on this ordinary March evening, surrounded by mothers in minivans anxious to get their children home, strings of truckers cutting swaths to make their schedules, complacent businessmen on their way to conferences or trysts, he found it hard to imagine all the human activity seething behind the scenes.

Monks had gleaned enough from Baskett and from his own previous experiences with the FBI to have a fair idea of it. The Critical Incident Response Group had hundreds of personnel on alert by now. Several vehicles were following him, leapfrogging, with drivers taking turns at dropping back, changing into different disguises, then catching up again. A microphone and tracking device had been planted on the Bronco, shot from a gun as one of the tailing cars passed him. Monks hadn't even been aware of it. Hidden roadblocks were ready to slam shut, and helicopters were poised to drop SWAT and hostage-rescue teams. Probably, top-level officials across the U.S. and even worldwide had been informed that the Calamity Jane killers were in the crosshairs.

This was going to be very big news, very soon—however it turned out.

Monks and Baskett had agreed to talk as little as possible, and to try to keep it to moments when Freeboot's men weren't likely to be watching. Monks spent a couple of minutes maneuvering on the freeway, changing lanes and speeds, then punched the number that Baskett had given him.

"Freeboot just called," Monks told him. "They know I got Mandrake. He told me to drive back the way I came, and keep the phone handy."

"O-*kay*, we're *in* this," Baskett called out to the people around him. "Dr. Monks, we'll assume the situation's unchanged until we hear from you. When we do, we're ready to move."

Monks drove on, thinking about the next question:

Move where?

Just over two hours later, he was on Highway 20, passing the west end of Clear Lake. The road was two-lane with little traffic, making things tough for his FBI shadows. But headlights would appear in his rearview mirror and turn off after a few miles, then quickly be replaced by different ones. Probably some of the oncoming vehicles were also part of the team.

He hadn't talked to anyone in the interim. With the little boy asleep beside him, driving back into the coastal fog, he had been lulled into a sense of unreality.

That was shattered by the chirp of his phone. He jerked so hard at the sound that his teeth clacked together.

"When you get to Upper Lake, turn right," Freeboot's steely voice said. "You know where you're going from there?"

Monks realized, with an ugly jolt, that Freeboot knew exactly where he was.

Then, with another one, that that road led to Freeboot's burned camp—his home turf, where he would be at maximum advantage.

"The camp?" Monks said.

"That's right. Now, I got this feeling you might have talked to somebody."

"I called Marguerite's mother, that's all. I had to give her a story about why I left."

"Yeah, well, you better be all alone from here on. We got you covered all the way. If anything else *twitches* out there, this is history." Freeboot paused, a silence filled with menace that Monks could feel over the phone.

"What do I do when I get there?" he said.

"Just come walking on in, and call my name out *loud*." Freeboot gave a sudden little snort that sounded like laughter.

That was all.

Thirty-three

The last fifteen miles of road to Freeboot's camp were gravel and dirt, almost impassable in places, twisting and crossing in an unmarked labyrinth. Someone who didn't know the way could drive around lost for days, but Monks had come up here enough times with the sheriffs to remember it. The earth was washboarded and rutted, still soggy from the winter rains, slick enough in places to make him spin his tires and drift sideways, even on slight inclines. After the first couple of miles, he locked the Bronco into four-wheel-drive and left it that way.

But for all that he could see, he might as well have been on another planet. The fog thinned into patches as he gained elevation, blanketing him one minute, then parting to reveal a nightbound landscape of rocky crags and forest lit by a gibbous moon, then closing in again. There were no FBI vehicles tailing now, no lights but the Bronco's, no signs of human life.

Monks heard a sound, a plaintive little yowl like the plea of a trapped cat. His head swiveled toward it.

It was Mandrake, starting to cry.

"*Christ,*" he hissed, hitting the brakes. The sedative that the hospital had given Mandrake wasn't strong enough—the jouncing ride had awakened him. He looked up fearfully into Monks's face, a face he already associated with nightmare.

And now he was in a new one.

Monks unbuckled Mandrake's seat belt and cradled him, doing his best to smile. "Everything's okay, buddy," he said soothingly. "You're just having a little dream, but you'll be back to sleep in no time."

"Mommy!" Mandrake screamed, struggling and flailing with his tiny fists.

Monks sagged in despair, then crooned nonsense while he fumbled in the back for his medical kit. He flipped on the dash light, found a vial of Ativan and a syringe, and drew off a half-milligram dose, holding it above Mandrake's head, out of his view.

Mandrake probably didn't even feel the needle, but it hurt Monks plenty.

The crying stopped. Mandrake's head rolled to the side.

Monks made up his mind. He cut the Bronco's ignition and lights, and picked up the phone. The connection was weak and static-laden, just at the edge of fade-out range.

"Freeboot's never going to let me get to the camp," he told Baskett. "He'll stop me along the way, grab Mandrake, and disappear."

"We've anticipated that, Dr. Monks. Recon teams are moving in on foot right now. There are helicopters, and paratroopers ready to drop."

"I'm not going to let him have Mandrake."

"You *have* to. That's our beacon on Freeboot."

That was the contingency plan that Baskett had put into effect. Monks would hand Mandrake over to Freeboot. When he took off, FBI surveillance would recognize that the implanted microtransmitter was moving apart from the tracking device on the Bronco. That would be their signal to move in. But the transmitter's range was limited, a maxmimum of a couple of miles even in open terrain. Once Freeboot was outside that, he was gone.

"There's a thousand square miles of wilderness out there, and it's his backyard," Monks said.

"Our men are the best, Special Forces–trained."

"You haven't seen him in those woods. He's like a cougar."

There was a brief pause. Then Baskett said, a little too kindly, "You've been doing fine, Doctor, and you'll be done very soon, which I think is good. Sounds like you've had enough."

Monks's eyes widened in outrage. "I know landing Freeboot would make your career, Agent Baskett. But you're not going to risk that little boy's life to do it."

"*You* are going to follow orders, Monks," Baskett said, with icy anger. "If you compromise this operation, you don't know what trouble *is*."

"I'm the one who's out here with his ass on the line, while you're sitting on yours in an office," Monks snapped. "So spare me the tough-guy act."

"You know he'll kill you if you don't have that kid."

"He's going to kill me anyway," Monks said. "I'll try to get some shots off—that will be your new signal to move in. I'm stopping right now to leave Mandrake in the woods. Have your men get him quick, there's critters."

He clicked off the phone. It chirped again instantly. He rolled down his window and threw it into the roadside brush, then tugged off Mandrake's pajamas.

He wrapped Mandrake in a sleeping bag and put that inside a nylon duffel, making knife slits to let in air. Outside, he stayed still for half a minute, listening into the darkness. There was nothing moving, no sound but the prickly stillness of a vast forest at night. He trotted twenty yards into the woods and hung the duffel high on a sturdy pine stob. The agents would find him by means of the implanted microphone, probably within half an hour.

Back in the Bronco, Monks quickly stuffed the pajamas full of his own spare clothes, padding them into the shape of a little body, then pulling a wad out of the neckhole and covering it with a white T-shirt to simulate a face. He buckled the doll into the passenger seat and awkwardly patted it into shape to look like a sleeping child. At night, it might fool somebody for a few seconds.

Whatever happened, Mandrake was out of it now.

Monks hefted the cold, comforting weight of the Beretta, then tucked it under his right thigh. The round that he had chambered hours earlier at the beach was still in place, ready to fire.

He started driving again, expecting at every bend to find the road blocked and armed men moving in—praying that the stuffed pajama dummy would lure Freeboot close enough for a clear shot.

Thirty-four

But no ambush came. When Monks got to the camp, a little more than an hour later, there was still no sign of a living soul.

He was shaking with dread.

He stopped the Bronco fifty yards short of the scorched clearing where the fire had been. He opened the door and stepped out onto the soft wet earth, holding the Beretta pressed against his thigh. He waited, watching, listening. The collapsed buildings were as desolate as ancient ruins. The night breeze still carried the faint smell of charred wood.

Just come walking on out and call my name out loud.

Monks walked slowly forward to the edge of the burn.

"Freeboot?" he said. The wind caught his voice, carrying it like an echo.

Call my name out *loud.*

"*Freeboot!*" he yelled, and this time something tiny changed in the periphery of his vision. He swiveled toward it, raising the pistol.

A light had come on—small, dim, on top of a pile of soot-crusted rock that had been part of a foundation.

Glenn's cabin, Monks remembered. That was where Glenn's cabin had stood.

He trotted toward it, stumbling through the soggy foot-deep ash that still covered the earth.

As he got close, he saw that it was a small scalloped bulb, sitting in an open guitar case, like a candle illuminating a shrine.

But Glenn's guitar was not inside. Monks slid to his knees, staring at what was:

A human ear, with dark blood congealing along its severed edge.

The lobe was pierced by the skull-shaped earring that Glenn had worn.

Monks looked up to the sky, his face streaking with the first tears that he had wept since watching young soldiers die under his helpless hands thirty years ago.

Part 3

Thirty-five

Monks's home telephone rang five times. He let the answering machine take the call.

"Carroll?" Sara's voice said, with brittle sweetness. "Will you pick up the phone, please? I know you're there."

He raised his glass blearily and swallowed more vodka. It was sometime after dark; he didn't know or care when. He was sprawled on the couch in his living room, surrounded by squalor—clothes on the floor, unwashed dishes, half-eaten food. Like a man evading creditors, he hadn't answered the phone for the past two days. The only reason that he left the phone on at all was because the severed ear was being DNA tested and he still harbored a whisper of hope that it wasn't Glenn's.

"We *have* to talk," Sara said imploringly. "You can't just keep your head buried in the sand. I understand why you had to lie to me, and I'm over it now."

His cats prowled the mess happily, one or another of them occasionally settling on his chest to comfort him. A dying fire in the woodstove kept the chill away. The television was playing an old episode of

Have Gun, Will Travel. Richard Boone had just finished thumping a couple of mouthy young punks in a frontier bar. That was a world that made sense.

"You prick," Sara fumed. "You selfish asshole. Pick up the goddamn *phone.*"

There was silence for ten seconds or so, then an abrupt deadness that had a sound of its own.

Monks swilled more vodka. She was absolutely right, he was a prick and a selfish asshole. But she was determined to nurture him, and he had already explained to her, as gently as he could, that if he encountered any nurturing just now he was going to kill somebody.

He was walking the perilous line of that somebody being himself.

The phone rang again a few minutes later. This time the voice was a man's. Monks listened without interest, expecting it to be another reporter.

"Dr. Monks? This is Andrew Pietowski, with the FBI."

Monks stiffened.

"I'd appreciate it if you'd give me a call ASAP," Pietowski said. "There's something important I'd like to discuss with you. Let me give you a couple of numbers where I can be reached."

Monks heaved himself to his feet and walked unsteadily to the phone, getting it in time to interrupt Pietowski reading out the numbers.

"This is Monks," he said.

"Doctor, glad you're home. I don't know if you remember me."

"Yes," Monks said. Pietowski was a Washington, D.C.–based domestic terrorism specialist who had followed the Calamity Jane murders from the beginning—a hefty man in his fifties with a big balding head, big nose, and big ears, a look that was reminiscent of former president Lyndon Johnson. He had flown to California immediately on learning that Freeboot might be involved. Pietowski listened more than he spoke, seeming to prefer staying in the background, but he had the kind of imposing presence that Monks had noticed.

"I'd like to drop by your place, but I thought I'd better call first,"

Pietowski said. "I gather you, uh, had a run-in with some newspeople."

"It was nothing personal. I never actually shot *at* anybody. I just wanted privacy."

"I think they got that message."

Monks braced himself and said, "Is this about Glenn?"

"No. Those results won't be back for a few more days."

He sagged with the miserable relief of bad news postponed.

Pietowski broke the silence. "Okay if I come on in?"

"Sure. How soon are we talking?"

"I'm at the foot of your driveway."

Monks blinked. "I'm not exactly at my best right now."

"I'll take my chances."

It was almost one A.M., he saw with vague surprise. He eyed the wreckage around him with a notion of a hasty cleanup, but decided there was no point in pretending. He poured another drink instead, and waited at the door for Pietowski.

Freeboot had gotten away clean, again. The sad and sordid truth was that the Bronco had, after all, been bugged. The FBI had found three devices, probably planted by Freeboot's men while Monks had followed Marguerite on the beach, just as he had feared. Freeboot had known from the start that the FBI was coming in. The kidnaping and the agonizing drive to the camp had been a sham to torment Monks, and the FBI's huge wasted effort, a way of insulting them. Freeboot probably had gone to the camp hours before Monks got there, and left the ear in the guitar case, with a voice-activated light.

Call my name out loud.

And then Freeboot had stayed in the forest long enough to stalk one of the recon agents, disarming him and beating him unconscious with his own rifle—a contemptuous message that he could easily have killed the man. He had worn a ski mask, bolstering the thought that he'd altered his appearance and didn't want his new face seen. But his bare footprints were easy to identify. Dogs had followed them for two miles. After which, the prints had simply vanished.

Baskett and other agents had given Monks a thorough raking over the coals. They had finally conceded officially that he wasn't to blame, but it was clear that they blamed him anyway. A lot of attention had focused on Glenn—how deeply he might have been involved in hacking computer information that was instrumental in the selection of the murder victims and facilitating the killings. The fact that Glenn, by all indications, was dead, did not figure in. He was still a criminal in their eyes, and the heavy weight of guilt by association had landed on Monks.

With Freeboot now linked to the Calamity Jane killings, the media furor had been explosive. After the FBI had tossed Monks away like a drained husk, satisfied that he had nothing more to give them, packs of journalists fell upon him. When he finally got to his home, bone weary and heartsick, a crowd of them was waiting.

He might have been able to endure even that, but he had come to realize that the media's main interest in him didn't lie in what had happened—it was in fashioning some tawdry story about a dysfunctional family with a renegade son.

He had shoved his way through them into his house, then walked back out with his shotgun, emptying the five-round magazine over their heads amid a shower of leaves and branches from the overhanging trees. After the last of their vehicles spun out of his drive, he had politely carried all of their dropped equipment down to the county road and left it there in a pile. The incident had brought him a warning phone call from the local sheriff's office, along with several threatened lawsuits from the offended news folk. Other calls were still jamming his line—requests for newspaper and magazine interviews, invitations to appear on national television, feelers from talent agents and film producers for books and made-for-TV movies. But no one had dared come onto his property again.

There was one upside to it all: this time the authorities had hidden Mandrake genuinely and well. The odds of Freeboot's finding him now were practically nil.

Pietowski's headlights appeared, coming up the driveway. He

parked and got out of the car, a newish generic sedan that was probably from an agency pool. He was wearing a light jacket and slacks, looking more like a realtor on his way to a Kiwanis Club dinner than a man who made a living tracking killers.

"Nice place," he said. "I see what you mean about liking your privacy. Ever think about putting in a security system?"

"I keep meaning to."

"You're not worried about Freeboot paying you a visit?"

"He's not going to kill me, not any time soon," Monks said. "He wants me alive, thinking about Glenn."

Pietowski gave a curt nod. His meaty ears seemed to flop slightly.

"I hate to say it, but you're probably right," he said.

Inside the house, Pietowski glanced around with the bland expression that Monks had seen on other FBI agents, absorbing all the information that the room offered. He stepped through the junk on the floor and picked up the open bottle of Finlandia vodka, raising an eyebrow appreciatively.

"Good stuff," he said. "How long you been going at it?"

"Couple days."

"Mind if I have one?"

"Help yourself," Monks said. He waved a hand toward the kitchen. "There's clean glasses in there someplace. Ice. All that."

Pietowski moved to the kitchen with his deliberate, almost lumbering walk, and started opening cubboards. His jacket parted as he reached for a glass, giving Monks a glimpse of the leather sling of his shoulder holster.

"So, you're a Chicago boy," Pietowski said. He chunked ice cubes into the glass and filled it with the Finlandia. "Me, too. Where'd you go to high school?"

"Saint Leo. Down on the South Side."

"Sure, I know it. I'm from Saints Cyril and Methodius, myself, up north. Wall-to-wall Polacks."

Monks got a piece of split oak from the woodbox and knelt in front of the stove. He stirred up the embers with the log, shoved it all the way in, and closed the iron door. He turned back, still on his haunches, then sat on the floor, hard, like a toddler.

Pietowski watched him, with a twist to his mouth that might have indicated sympathy.

"I know you took a hell of a beating," he said. "You did what you had to. So did we. That's how you've got to look at it."

Monks exhaled, then nodded. Pietowski extended a hand. Monks took it, and used it to pull himself laboriously back to his feet.

"There's just been another killing that looks like a Calamity Jane," Pietowski said.

Monks nodded again. He was too numb to be shocked.

"Happened a couple hours ago, it's just now crossing the wires," Pietowski said. "A Sutton Place penthouse, right in the poshest part of fucking Manhattan. Security like Fort Knox. They got up on the roof somehow and rappeled down an outside wall. But this time we got the shooters."

A flare of grim excitement cut into Monks's sluggishness. *Finally,* something to go on.

"Have you identified them?" he asked.

"We don't have a clue, which is why I'm here. When they knew they were trapped, one of them dove out a window. Hit the pavement face first, from twelve stories. The second one was right behind him, but a police sniper creased his head and knocked him back inside."

Pietowski took a six-by-nine-inch manila envelope from his jacket pocket and tossed it on the coffee table.

"This is the one that's still got a face. I thought maybe you'd recognize him, from the camp."

Monks remembered the *maquis* well, even the ones he'd only seen by firelight. He opened the envelope and pulled out several high-resolution black-and-white photos of a man's face taken from slightly different angles. He was about thirty, clean-shaven, with short, neatly styled hair. It was the same businessman's look sported by Freeboot's other *maquis,* except for the bloody jellied mass of blood and brain where the sniper's bullet had clipped the right parietal bone, above and behind the ear.

But Monks had to shake his head. "I'm ninety-nine percent sure I never saw him," he said, tossing the photos back on the table.

"That's too bad."

"Sorry I can't help."

"I don't mean you. I mean, that tells us that the ones you saw aren't the only ones. There's more of them out there than we thought."

While Monks ingested this unsettling information, Pietowski started pacing with slow, heavy steps that were like the systematic plodding of a draft horse.

"I'm guessing they were under orders not to be taken alive, so they wouldn't break down under questioning," he said. "Maybe even to destroy their faces, to make them harder to identify. Their fingertips were scarred, too, like the ones you saw. Now, what the hell kind of people are willing to sacrifice themselves like that?" He seemed to be asking himself, rather than Monks. "Religious fanatics, suicide bombers, okay. Or somebody in a jealous rage that pulls a murder-suicide. But highly trained operatives do *not* commit extremely risky crimes, give *away* what they steal, and then off themselves when they're cornered. That's not how they think. Those guys are survivors."

"Freeboot talked about the assassins," Monks said. "Their absolute loyalty. The night of that scalp hunt, he told a story about how the Old Man of the Mountain could point at a man and snap his fingers and that man would jump off a cliff to his death."

Pietowski grunted. "Telling a story's one thing. Getting people to actually do it—" He shoved his hands into his pockets, then stopped walking and turned back to Monks.

"I've got something else to ask you. There's a buzz, about Bodega Bay. You know the place?"

"I've driven through it a fair amount," Monks said. Bodega Bay was a small, pretty town on the coast about twenty-five miles north of his home—an old fishing harbor that had adapted more and more to recreation, and recently to condos.

"That's where they filmed that Hitchcock movie *The Birds,*" Pietowski said. "Remember that, mid-sixties?"

The Birds was the town's claim to fame as a tourist attraction, although mention of it tended to make residents roll their eyes. Monks recalled, oddly, that early advertisements for it had read: THE BIRDS IS COMING.

"Sure," he said. "What do you mean, a buzz?"

"The undercover people we've got working the streets—they've heard a rumble that there's something coming down there, April 1. We don't know *what.* But that 'Revolution Number 9' riff is in the air, like it's some kind of a theme."

Monks recalled what Marguerite had told him about Freeboot's cultivating contacts with elements more sinister than the homeless—gangs and big-time drug dealers, via wild parties that centered around the medical marijuana trade.

"So you think Freeboot might be involved?" he said.

"That's a long shot. And the whole thing might be complete bullshit. It's April Fool's Day, for openers. But we can't ignore it. What I'd like you to do is be there. We'll have undercover agents, too, but you're the only reliable witness we've got who's actually seen those people. You go in disguise and hang around. You spot anybody, you alert us."

"I don't know that I could do you any good," Monks said. "They're going to be in disguise, too. Freeboot told me I looked right at him."

"Yeah, but you weren't thinking about him then. If you're *looking,* you might see things you recognize. Even the way somebody moves."

Monks nodded hesitantly. "I'll try."

"I'll call you tomorrow. We'll figure out the details."

Pietowski turned toward the door, then picked up the bottle of vodka and hefted it. The room had gotten warm from the added firewood, and his big doughy forehead was gleaming with sweat.

"For what it's worth, I've crawled into one of these plenty,"

Pietowski said. "Last time it happened in a big way was after Waco. I got called in there, after the ATF fucked it up. There were plenty of ways they could have walked up to Koresh and slapped cuffs on him. Instead, all those people burned. Kids."

He set the bottle back down. "I'd love to jump in right now, believe me, but I can't afford it. Neither can you."

After he left, Monks saw that he had barely touched his drink, if at all. Monks had the sudden sense that Pietowski had come to him as a sort of priest, offering absolution, giving him a chance to set aside the past days and move on to action that might be of actual benefit. Ashamed, Monks dumped out his own glass in the sink.

He went to the kitchen calendar and pieced together that today was March 30. Tomorrow was going to be ugly and penitential, filled with sweat and pain—splitting wood, lifting weights, and working the heavy bag to a base line of pain throbbing in his head like the rap music blasting from a passing car.

Then, the wait to find out if this rumor was an April Fool's Day joke or the next outrage that Freeboot planned to throw in the world's face.

Thirty-six

Monks was in a hotel room in Bodega Bay just coming out of a restless half-sleep when the phone rang. It was 5:33 A.M., the morning of April 1. He located the phone's red LED in the darkened room and picked up.

"Monks," he said.

"This is Pietowski. Turn on the TV, any news channel. Call me back." He sounded enraged. Monks finished waking up instantly, fearing that he'd done something wrong.

He found the TV's remote and started flicking through channels. His finger stopped at the fourth one he hit. An attractive blond anchorwoman was at her desk in the foreground, with the CNN logo on the backdrop.

". . . was emailed to millions of computers around the nation, from an unknown source, early this morning," she said. "A list of five hundred names and addresses, titled—apparently, with vicious sarcasm—'The Fortune 500,' includes prominent members of the business community, legislators, and government officials—among them, *all* the victims of the Calamity Jane killers.

"Initial response from law-enforcement agencies is that the list is an April Fool's Day prank. But the people whose names are *on* the list are alarmed that it's a warning—that they're intended targets, too.

"We'll have more on this *explosive* new development after this short break. Stay with us."

Monks punched the number of Pietowski's cell phone. They had talked enough times during the past two days that he had memorized it by now.

"I only got part of the story," Monks said.

"Freeboot just stomped on the panic button, is the story. Sent out a mass e-mail that looks like a piece of spam, except it could only have been compiled by some highly sophisticated hacking."

"The news announcer said the police were treating it as a joke."

"Joke, my aching ass. They got the addresses of people that are harder to find than Osama bin Laden. Cracked firewalled corporate and government databases, identified people who operate way, *way* behind the scenes."

Monks swallowed a dry lump at the back of his throat. That pointed to Glenn, and the FBI agents knew it. Yet it fanned the flicker of hope that he was still alive.

"We're already spread thin, and now we've got five hundred of the world's most influential people screaming at us about what we're going to do to protect them," Pietowski said sourly. "Anything happening there?"

Monks walked to a window and opened the curtain. The view looked west over the town along Highway 1, and down the long spur of Doran Beach farther out, a favorite spot of windsurfers and body boarders. It was just dawn, and the vast expanse of ocean and sky was a pale gray-blue that would soon turn to azure. The highway was empty. The sea was calm, the surf hardly more than ripples. Toward the harbor's north end, the fishing fleet and recreational boats floated in the marina like beasts of burden grazing in a peaceful pasture, waiting to be put to use.

Informants had confirmed a rumor on the streets of San Francisco, Oakland, and other cities all the way to L.A. and Seattle, that some sort of mass party was supposed to take place in Bodega Bay today, and that "Revolution No. 9" seemed to be the motif. But the odds of finding Freeboot here seemed tiny, and Pietowski even feared that it might be a diversion from something serious, like another Calamity Jane killing.

"Right now, the place looks quiet as a tomb," Monks told him.

"I guess that's good, except it means we're going to waste a lot of manpower. Call me again when you're ready to hit the bricks. We'll run a test on your microphone."

Monks got a cold bottle of orange juice out of the room's mini-refrigerator, then started making coffee, using half the specified amount of water. He shaved in the shower, mirrorless, a habit he'd carried over from his navy days.

When he came back out, he poured a cup of the thick black brew and stepped to the window again, still grappling with his hope that the "Fortune 500 List" might mean that Glenn was still alive—and his fear that if so, it deepened his involvement in the killings even further.

Outside, the sky was lighter, but things remained as tranquil as before. Local police and sheriffs had been alerted, but everyone agreed that it would be best to stay quiet, rather than alarm residents over what might amount to nothing.

A single car came into sight, driving into town on Highway 1 from the south. Monks kept watching it. It was a big old sedan, an Olds or a Buick, 1970s or even sixties vintage, dented and crusted with dirt that looked as permanent as paint—not the kind of vehicle that was common around upscale Bodega Bay. He could hear its rumble all the way up to his room. It moved slowly, giving the sense that it wasn't in a hurry to get to anyplace in particular—it was just cruising.

As it drove past his window, an arm flopped carelessly out of the rear passenger-side window and flicked a cigarette butt that skipped a few times on the pavement, throwing off sparks.

The car kept going north on the highway, then turned left on Westshore Road, which led down toward the marina and campgrounds.

Thirty-seven

By noon, Bodega Bay's marina was thronged with people—close to five thousand, Monks judged, with more still pouring in. Parking areas were jammed with vehicles, a lot of them junkers, along with a fair number of chopped Harleys. The newer arrivals were parking some distance away and walking in, since vehicle traffic was almost impossible. The strip of Highway 1 through town, with its shops and restaurants, was clogged.

It was looking like *The Birds,* all right—only this time it was thick with human beings.

Monks wandered around the fringes, wearing the disguise that Pietowski's makeup specialists had provided—ragged jeans, worn-out boots, a threadbare army field jacket. His wiry black hair was dyed gray, then worked with pomade to straighten it and give it a greasy, matted look. One of his incisors was blacked out to appear missing. A thick beard and mustache, along with a weathered baseball cap pulled low over sunglasses, hid most of his face. A tiny receiver was planted in his left ear and a body bug microphone was sewn inside his collar, giving him two-way contact with an FBI listening post set up in a phony delivery truck parked nearby.

The day was pristine, clear, warm with sunshine but cooled by a light ocean breeze. The scene was outwardly festive, something like the mass concerts or happenings of the late sixties—but Monks percieved an undercurrent that was disturbingly different. These weren't kids who had come to party, to soak up the music, grooviness, peace, and love. These were fully formed adults, most of them well past their teens and many pushing middle age and bearing the hard look of years on the streets or in jails. Even the younger faces tended toward an uncaring cynicism, a sense that nothing they saw was of value or even interest.

He eavesdropped on conversations as he cruised, trying to get a sense of what this gathering was all about, but nothing became clear. There didn't seem to be any kind of central event planned. All that he could glean was that some mysterious groundswell had named today as the day, and Bodega Bay as the place, for a party. There was a lot of beer and screw-cap wine. Marijuana smoke drifted through the air, and he was sure that there was plenty of hard dope around, too.

So far, all was peaceable. But several police cars had moved into the marina, inching their way through the crowd, which parted, grudgingly, to let them pass, then immediately closed to swallow them like a giant amoeba engulfing its prey. A white-and-red Coast Guard patrol boat was hovering just outside the mouth of the harbor's channel, and Monks had seen three different helicopters—a Coast Guard Dolphin, a dark green Bell sheriffs' search-and-rescue craft, and a small one he couldn't identify that was probably the media. Not surprisingly, the local residents looked alarmed.

The cricket-like chirp of Monks's cell phone in his coat pocket startled him. He had brought it as a backup in case radio contact failed, but he hadn't expected it to ring, and he didn't want to be seen using it. He angled his steps away from the crowd with covert speed, shielding the phone with his hand to talk, as if he were coughing.

"This is Monks," he said.

"Oh, God, you've got to *help* me." The woman's voice was shaking, the words spilling out in a fearful rush.

But Monks recognized Marguerite. This was the first time anyone had heard from her since the night that she had slipped away from him on the beach.

Startled, he said, "Yes, of course, honey. Tell me what you need."

"You were right, he killed Motherlode, and he wants to let Mandrake die. I know that now. What if *my* baby's not perfect? He'll do the same thing."

"*Your* baby?" Monks said, with swiftly deepening surprise.

Then he understood.

"Jesus, Marguerite, are you pregnant?" he said. "By Freeboot?"

"He chose me to start his new dynasty," she sobbed. "Then I found out the truth. Now he doesn't trust me anymore. I'm just a, a *thing*, like a cow. Breeding stock. He's keeping me here. Please, come get me and hide me."

Monks strode deeper into the scrubby headland vegetation and raised his voice, knowing that Pietowski would hear at least his end of the conversation.

"Where are you?" he asked her.

"He won't tell me. Somewhere back in the woods, like always. He's gone now, but there's others around. I'm sneaking this call, I can't let them see me."

"Do you know where he is?"

"Bodega Bay. Him and some others."

Monks's scalp bristled. "What does Freeboot look like now?"

"I don't know. They're all wearing disguises and I didn't see them leave. Oh, God, I can't believe this is happening."

"Come on, Marguerite, *think*. There has to be something that will help us find him. Then you'll be safe."

There was a several-second pause. "Callus," she said tremulously. "He's the one you shot. He'll be limping."

Monks had a grim flash of satisfaction. He hadn't known until now that Callus, the *maquis* who had beaten his shins, was the man he had shot. But a glance at the teeming crowd mocked the hope of finding a single limping man among the thousands.

"Keep talking," he said. "Think out loud. What else?"

"Someone's coming." Her voice sharpened with panic. "I have to go."

"Marguerite, call back and stay on the line," Monks said urgently.

But a man's voice cut harshly into the background on her end. "Hey, what the fuck you doing? *Give* me that."

"Chill out, man," she said shrilly. Then she squealed in fear or pain.

"Marguerite!" Monks yelled.

There was a brief scuffling noise, a *clonk* as if the phone had hit the floor, more of her squealing and unintelligible words. Then the connection went dead.

Monks clenched the phone in his fist, willing it to ring again, knowing that it would not.

"Andrew, did you get that?" he said into the transmitter.

"Some of it." Pietowski's voice was tinny in Monks's ear, but his vexation came through. "We're already looking for the limper. You got any more description on him?"

Monks remembered Callus, all right—his ruthless face and brutal efficiency.

"Five-ten to six feet, athletic, hard-looking. Very clean cut when I saw him, like the others. Nothing that stood out."

It wasn't much help, but Pietowski said, "All right, now we know they're here. Let's go rip some new assholes."

Monks moved back toward the crowd, his rage at Freeboot and the *maquis* boiling up afresh. With it came a weight of worry for Marguerite. It seemed that she had finally come to her senses—but at what price.

Thirty-eight

Traffic moved at a crawl along Highway 1 through Bodega Bay, choked by the thousands of pedestrians and hundreds of cars parked illegally along the roadside. A forty-foot Bounder RV edged along in the stream, another bewildered and frightened tourist trying to get through this wild mess. But then it pulled over into a space conveniently vacated by two cars, just as it arrived. The passing crowd swirled around the big rig like water around a stone, but not without offering up plenty of jeering, hostile glances, and occasional raised fingers to this symbol of leisure and wealth.

Shielded behind the smoked windows, Freeboot watched them stonily, with the mixture of pity and contempt that rare men like him—men of great vision and ability—had always held for society's losers, whose asses had first to be kicked into realizing the power they held, and then into using it. In fact, the RV was just the opposite of what it seemed—a command post for an army that didn't yet know it existed. And the first battle in the war was coming together out there on the streets right now.

The RV's parking spot, secured early that morning by the *maquis*, was a vantage point on high ground, with a clear view of the marina below. Within a couple of minutes, Freeboot saw a California Highway Patrol motorcycle cop approaching, navigating slowly but steadily through the throng. Tension and disdain were obvious in the faces he passed, but no one was ready to take on The Man.

Yet.

Freeboot moved to the RV's passenger door and opened it. Anyone who saw him would have taken him for a middle-aged tourist. He looked completely different than he had three months ago. He had spent a lot of that time in Panama. *That* was a great place—mescal, cocaine, pretty women, and plastic surgeons who didn't ask questions. His cheeks and nose had been thickened, a chin implant added, and his ears angled forward to give him a bearlike look. His hair and beard were short, white, and well trimmed. He wore a padded shirt and a fanny pack across his belly to accentuate a paunch. But underneath it, his ferally strong body was the same.

The cop pulled up to the door, straddling his big BMW motorcycle. His brawny forearms and biceps stretched the short sleeves of his tan shirt. A Smith & Wesson .40-caliber automatic rode high on his right hip. He wore knee-high black boots, tight black gloves, and aviator sunglasses.

Behind the glasses, Freeboot knew, Hammerhead's eyes were bloodshot and crazed with meth.

The passing crowd drifted away from this exchange—a cop probably checking on the safety of the RV's well-off passengers, maybe offering them an escort out of here.

"It's going to start real soon," Freeboot said quietly. "Get it done, and ride out like a son of a bitch. You'll be gone before they know what happened."

Hammerhead's lips were set in a tight line—the tough look of a cop in a tense situation. But they moved in a sudden tremor, and a little froth of saliva spilled out of one corner of his mouth.

"You talked to her again?" he said.

Freeboot assented, a slow, assured raising of his head.

"Just a little while ago," he said. "Marguerite's had some wrong ideas, but that's all over. She'll be waiting when you get back."

Hammerhead's corded forearms flexed as he put the bike in gear and accelerated away.

Taxman stepped from the RV's rear section, carrying a long nylon duffel bag, the kind that athletes used for equipment. Inside it was a Remington model 700 .308-caliber rifle with a Leupold scope. He lowered the passenger-side window a few inches and raised the gun to his shoulder, keeping all of it but the scope inside the bag, slipping the tip of the muzzle out through a slit and bracing it in the window opening. The crosshairs found Hammerhead's white helmet and followed it.

"You going to be able to pick him out?" Freeboot said.

"As long as everybody's where they're supposed to be." Taxman stashed the bag in a cabinet.

"If they're not," Freeboot said, "get creative."

He kicked off his shoes and stripped off the padded shirt, replacing it with a Kevlar vest.

Inside the RV's bathroom, Shrinkwrap was putting the finishing touches on her young lover's disguise, kneeling before him and dabbing Mehron stage makeup on his face while he sat on the closed toilet lid.

"Perfect," she said, holding up a compact mirror in front of him.

Glenn Monks stared into it, looking like he had stage fright. His lips parted, showing his blistered teeth and gums.

"Don't be scared, baby," she said softly. "I'm very proud of you. I know how much it's hurt you, everybody thinking you're just a computer geek. Today, you make full *maquis.* Remember, as soon as it starts, clean up with these"—she tapped the packet of moist towelettes in his shirt pocket—"and get your ass back here."

He nodded, swallowing dryly.

"What's the first thing you're going to say when you get up there?" she asked in a teasing voice.

"People, y'all *listen* to me." His voice was shaky, and it cracked.

"Don't panic, try it again," she coaxed. "You're *cool,* baby, you're the coolest rapper I've ever heard. Just be *you.*"

"People, y'all *listen* to me," he cried out, with strained force. "We here today to talk about gettin' *back* what The Man been takin' *away* from us."

"*Perfect*," she said again, rubbing his thighs through his pants, comically baggy jeans worn with the waistband just above his pubis and the cuffs dragging on the ground.

Her hands moved to the zipper. "Now lean back and close your eyes," she whispered. "I'm going to give my brave soldier a good-luck present."

A few minutes later, she walked with him to the RV's cab and watched him slip out into the crowd. It hurt. He had touched that deep, sweet spot in her. But Freeboot was right—the meth had been getting to him, making him petulant, unreliable, tiresome to be around, and a risk if he got caught. It was a hard truth of all successful politics that sometimes, individuals had to be sacrificed for the greater good.

There were plenty of other lovely boys out there, younger ones, with bright white smiles.

Thirty-nine

Striding back to the marina, Monks was jolted by the fear that it had caught on fire. What looked like a wave of flame was sweeping through the crowd.

Then he realized that he was seeing several hundred garish T-shirts, colored nuclear sunset orange, worn by the oncoming partyers.

A closer look stunned him even more. The T-shirts' central logo was a cartoonishly ugly vulture with an evil grin, pinning the neck of a squealing lamb with one taloned foot, while ripping out its guts with the other. Above that, in large bold letters, was printed: THE BIRDS IS BACK, BABY!

And below it, bloodred and shaped like jagged lightning flashes driving into the scorched earth, were the characters *REV # 9*.

"Are you seeing these T-shirts?" he said into his hidden microphone.

"There's cars with trunkfuls of them—they're handing them out free," Pietowski growled. "The caps, too."

Monks hadn't yet noticed those, but now he saw that most of the T-shirt wearers were also sporting dark blue or black stocking caps, pulled down low over foreheads and ears, hip-hop style.

"Now they all fucking look alike," Pietowski said. "We're going to disperse them. Watch yourself, this could get rough."

Monks was starting to hear the faint, faraway sound of sirens over the clamor of the many-thousand-limbed beast that prowled around him. The crowd heard it, too, and the noise level dropped as people turned to look toward Highway 1. Seaward, the throbbing pulse of helicopters thickened as they moved closer. Another swift, purposeful Coast Guard cutter was approaching from the direction of San Francisco. The local police and sheriffs, helmeted and wearing riot gear, were getting out of their cars, trying to start moving the crowd off the marina and back toward the highway. Knots of confrontation were forming, the partyers reacting with anger and taunts.

"People!"

Monks swung toward the sound, shouted over a megaphone. It came from a young black man wearing a stocking cap and one of the garish orange T-shirts. He had climbed up on top of a fish-processing shed at Spud Point, where the crowd was thickest.

Holding the megaphone to his lips, he yelled again.

"People, y'all *listen* to me. We here today to talk about gettin' *back* what The Man been takin' *away* from us."

Monks absorbed instantaneous and disturbing impressions. The accent didn't sound quite right—it had the ring of a white man trying to imitate black speech. The voice was high-pitched, strained—

And yet, even over the megaphone, familiar.

"Oh, *Christ*," he breathed, and took a running step to throw his arms around his living son. Then he stopped just as fast and hovered, breathing hard, torn between the need to get to Glenn and the fear of what was going to happen to him when the police got him.

"Now I want y'all to look around you," Glenn called out. He pranced on his perch, starting to gain confidence. "There is strength in *numbers*. Yeah! Look how *many* of us there are."

As more heads turned toward him and the crowd's noise quieted further, the sirens and thunder of the chopper rotors rose, as if a giant volume knob was being turned up. The Coast Guard patrol boat was discharging armed men at the harbor's mouth, and the sheriffs' helicopter was landing on the headlands to the west, dropping what looked like a SWAT team. Red and blue lights were lining Highway 1, popping like flashbulbs at a celebrity wedding.

"Now, when the Man put on his *uniform*, he think it give him the right to walk all over us. But when we put on *our* uniform—" Glenn pulled the T-shirt away from his skinny chest and patted himself on the head in demonstration— "well, he don't know who we *be*. So that give *us* some rights, too. Y'all see where I'm coming from?"

"Cease and desist!" a much louder voice interrupted. This one was coming through an amplified microphone mounted on a Sonoma County sheriff's truck, not just a handheld bullhorn. "This is a police order. You with the megaphone—come down and walk forward with your hands up. People in the crowd, start dispersing peacefully."

"You think they gonna arrest us all?" Glenn shouted scornfully. "Where they gonna put us? The jails are already full, baby! Full of people who smoked a joint, or stole some food 'cause they was starving! While the motherfuckers who stole your jobs and your homes and your *dignity*, they flying around in private jets! Yeah!"

A different kind of murmur was starting to rise from the crowd, with a tone of angry assent. Monks saw several clenched fists raised into the air.

"This is an unlawful assembly," the police microphone bellowed. "I *repeat*, disperse yourselves peacefully."

The cops on foot were shoving their way toward Glenn now, but the crowd was shoving back. Nightsticks started to flail. Monks fought his way along, his hesitation gone—in a panic to get to Glenn and drag him out of this insanity.

"Andrew, that's my son up there. That's Glenn!" Monks yelled into his microphone. "I need help getting him safe!"

"Ten-four that," Pietowski said. "We're coming."

Monks was twenty yards away from the shed when a California Highway Patrolman on a motorcycle came charging through the tangled mass of people, running straight into whoever got in his way and kicking them aside. Monks got a glimpse of his bull neck and broad back.

As the cop passed in front of the shed, he slowed and unholstered his pistol, raising it to aim at Glenn.

Monks stared, rigid with disbelief.

Then he yelled, "*No*," and threw himself forward, grabbing shoulders and handfuls of clothing to claw his way through the crowd.

A man with the look of a biker snarled, "*Watch* it, fucker," and punched him hard in the side of the head, knocking his sunglasses flying. Monks reeled, tripping over legs—

Hearing the terrible thumps of high-powered gunshots.

When he fought his way to his feet again, Glenn was gone from sight. The motorcycle cop was riding on, waving his pistol. Now people screamed and trampled each other to get out of his path.

And then, a black spiderweb the size of a half-dollar appeared on the back of the cop's white helmet, like an eggshell shattering. It slammed him forward over the careening bike's handlebars.

"Eleven ninety-nine, officer down!" the police microphone roared. "Code Three for all law-enforcement personnel!"

Monks struggled on toward where Glenn had been, now trying to keep from getting knocked down and stomped to raw meat by the fleeing human torrent. People were surging in all directions, even swarming over the marina's moored boats and leaping into the channel. Through the yells and screams around him and the pounding in his own ears, he was aware of more gunfire, and he caught glimpses of shouting cops with raised weapons. A cordon of police had formed around the fallen Highway Patrolman, shielding him from the stampede.

". . . return fire!" he heard the microphone boom. "There are snipers in the crowd! Repeat, officers are authorized to return fire!"

Monks made it to the shed where Glenn had been perched and clambered up the webbed iron frame of a derrick to the roof. Two cops were already up there, crouched, swiveling tensely with pistols ready, watching the chaos below.

Glenn lay off to one side, prone and still.

Monks jumped from the derrick onto the roof. Both cops swung to face him, aiming at him with two-handed combat grips.

"Stop right there!" one bellowed.

"That's my son," Monks shouted, and kept coming.

"I don't give a fuck! Turn around and get out of here."

"Wait a minute, you saying you know this kid?" the other one said. He yanked his handcuffs from his belt and started toward Monks. "Get down, asshole. On your face, hands behind you—"

"I'm FBI and that man's a doctor!" a hard voice broke in, yelling up at them from below. "Stand back and let him work."

It was Pietowski, striding toward the shed with a pistol raised in one hand and his FBI badge in the other. He was flanked by two men who looked like undercover agents, dressed like Monks in funky outfits, but also brandishing guns.

The cops on the roof hesitated, looking at each other. Monks pushed past them and dropped to his knees beside Glenn. His fingers smeared the greasy blackface makeup as he checked for vital signs. Glenn was breathing, and the pulse in his carotid artery was faint but steady. There were no obvious wounds. Monks turned him carefully onto his back.

Glenn's half-closed eyes opened a little wider in recognition or surprise. He tried to say something, but only blood came from his mouth, bubbling between his lips.

"Hush," Monks said. "Don't try to talk."

He could hear Pietowski behind him, up on the roof now. "This situation's under control," Pietowski told the two policemen. "You men can get on down and help your buddies."

"If this guy's really a doctor, he should be taking care of cops, not this maggot," one muttered.

"With all due respect, officer, you don't know zip minus shit about it," Pietowski said harshly. "There's still shooters out there. Go find them."

Monks's fingers located an entry wound in Glenn's chest, below the sternum and a couple of inches to the right. His mouth bleeding almost certainly meant that the bullet had punctured that lung, but the lung hadn't yet collapsed, and there were no indications that his heart or spine had been hit. Monks's hands kept searching over the rest of Glenn's body. He had heard the motorcycle cop fire at least three shots. But there seemed to be no other wounds. Probably, the first round had knocked Glenn spinning away and down, and the others had missed.

He eased the stocking cap off Glenn's head, dreading what he'd find. But both of Glenn's ears, minus the earring, looked just fine.

"How is he?" Pietowski asked.

"Lucky."

"Paramedics are on their way. We'll get him on a chopper."

Monks kept his hands on Glenn, reading his instant-by-instant condition through them, automatically making small adjustments—keeping his nostrils clear, loosening his clothing. With good prompt care, Glenn was going to make it.

A team of two paramedics arrived within minutes, carrying a backboard. Monks helped them ease Glenn onto it, and watched them closely as they strapped him down and lowered him to another team, waiting on the ground with a gurney. They seemed competent, but he intended to go with them to the hospital, and he started to follow them off the roof.

Pietowski caught his arm. "There's people lying on the ground who need you here," he said, pointing at the havoc below.

The crowd was thinning at the marina by now, most of it surging up into town. Monks didn't hear any more gunfire, but there was still plenty of panic. Cars were ramming each other, driving over curbs, through yards, into buildings. The metallic crunch of collisions pierced the air, and shards of splintering glass from windshields and storefronts sprayed out here and there, glittering in the sunlight. Thousands more were fleeing on foot, swarming like locusts along the highway, through the shops and restaurants, up the streets and into the clusters of condos on the hills. Police helicopters hovered close overhead, megaphones bellowing warnings, but it looked like nothing short of napalm could stop the frenzy. At least a dozen people had fallen and were lying motionless or struggling feebly. A couple of them were wearing police uniforms. Monks remembered that he had heard the words over the police bullhorn: *There are snipers in the crowd.*

The paramedics with Glenn had reached a Life Flight helicopter and were loading him on.

"Don't worry, we're not going to let anything happen to him," Pietowski said.

Monks nodded, but he knew the bitter truth behind that concern. Glenn was a big prize, the only one the FBI had apprehended so far in connection with the Calamity Jane murders. He was also the best hope they had of tracking down Freeboot.

The nearest of the fallen bodies was the Highway Patrolman who had shot Glenn. Several angry-looking cops were hovering around, and another team of paramedics had arrived, but Monks was quite sure even from a distance that he was dead. The crash had dumped him in an ugly sprawl, with one jackbooted leg still tangled in the handlebars of his bike.

"Stand aside," Pietowski said again, flashing his badge. "This man's a doctor." The cops and paramedics moved back.

Monks knelt beside the man who had tried to kill his son. He had been shot twice. He might have survived the round to the helmet, but the second one, just below its rim, was lethal. Monks knew that that was a preferred target of SWAT-team and military snipers—through the spinal cord into the medulla oblongata.

Then he recognized the thick-featured face, and his rage turned to shock.

"This isn't a cop," he said to Pietowski. "He's one of Freeboot's men. Hammerhead—the one who had that jade pendant."

Monks was still crouched there, trying to grasp this new insanity, when one of the FBI undercover agents stepped away from the group, pressing his hand against his ear, listening.

Then he yelled, "They spotted a guy with a limp, up on the highway!"

Agents and cops took off running, the younger men at a sprint. Monks and Pietowski followed, lumbering and panting. Other uniformed men with raised weapons were running on Highway 1.

"He's getting into that RV!" someone yelled.

Monks saw the vehicle, a huge white box on wheels, almost the size of a bus. There was no way that it was going anywhere in this jam. Anybody inside it was trapped.

"Attention! Inside the RV!" the megaphone on the sheriff's truck bellowed. "Come out with your hands up!"

Dozens of cops, Coast Guard, and SWAT-teamers ringed the RV, taking cover behind parked cars.

"Everybody stay the hell back," Pietowski yelled. "That thing could be rigged to explode." He looked pleased but wary. There was still plenty of risk, and the possibility of a drawn-out siege.

Monks started to hear a bizarre sound that seemed to be coming from inside the RV—a screaming whine like a dozen chain saws being revved. The others heard it, too. Talk stopped and the megaphone went silent.

Then the RV did explode, the entire barn-door-sized back panel bursting free with a gut-wrenching *kuh-whump*, spinning through the air like a giant tin can lid showering shrapnel. A cloud of thick smoke billowed out with it, sending the nearest cops spinning away and clawing at their faces.

In the midst of that, several MX-type dirt bikes came flying out of the RV's rear section. The gas-masked, helmeted riders hit the pavement, submachine guns slung across their chests, spraying full automatic bursts that hammered into the parked cars and buildings. The bikes tore through the smoke, splitting off in different directions. Cops fired back furiously, and one bike went into a skid, sliding into a curb and throwing the rider hard against a car.

Monks saw that another of the riders, incredibly, had bare feet.

"That's Freeboot!" he screamed. "The barefoot one!" He ran forward into the acrid reek of the gas, covering his nose and mouth with his sleeve, pointing with his other hand. Through burning eyes, he saw the barefoot rider jerk suddenly, in the convulsive spasm of a man hit by a bullet. But he recovered, popping the bike up in a wheelstand and skidding around in a half-circle. Front wheel still raised, he tore back through the heart of the smoke cloud and appeared again a few seconds later, weaving and leaping like the others through the jammed traffic. Helicopters thundered overhead in pursuit.

Pietowski watched them go, his face taut with controlled rage.

"He looked like he got hit," Monks said.

Pietowski nodded grimly. "That makes me feel a little better."

They walked to where the fallen rider lay, surrounded by glowering cops, red-eyed from gas. The body was crumpled and motionless against the car it had struck. The torso looked padded, and Monks realized that the rider was wearing body armor. Probably all of them had been, along with bullet-resistant helmets. But blood was seeping from under the jaw—a lucky shot for the cop that had fired it, the end of luck for the rider. Monks knelt to feel for a pulse, but he already knew, again, that life was gone.

"He's dead," Monks said, standing. "You can move him."

"Let's see who we got," Pietowski said.

A deputy knelt and eased the helmet off, revealing soft auburn hair and a thin, almost pretty face. He stepped back in shock.

"Jesus," he said, "it's a woman."

"Shrinkwrap," Monks said. This time, he felt neither anger nor pity, and by now, not even surprise.

Pietowski nodded. "Nice catch, gentlemen," he said to the cops. "She was a kingpin."

Highway 1 looked like a mile-long junkyard, crammed with vehicles too impacted to move. The remnants of the crowd were still spiderwebbing out in the distance, over the headlands to the north, across the crescent beach south, and up into the coastal hills to the east. At least another thousand still lined the streets, many huddled on the ground or crouched behind shelter, and there were new casualties from the motorcyclists' gunfire, explosion, and general mayhem.

"I'd better get to helping," Monks told Pietowski, and walked out into the chaos, scanning the injured, doing triage in his head as he decided where to start.

Forty

Thirty hours later, Monks walked into Queen of the Valley Hospital in Napa to see Glenn. Most of the serious casualties from Bodega Bay had been taken either to Santa Rosa Memorial or to Bayview, in Marin County. But the FBI wanted their star witness separated from the pack, and the Queen was known for its top-notch trauma center. He was under full-time guard by teams of two armed agents, in case Freeboot's *maquis* came looking for him to silence him.

Glenn wasn't yet strong enough for serious interrogation. So far, the impatient agents had been limited to a few brief sessions. But he was able to talk a little, and, knowing now that Freeboot had set him up to be killed, was cooperating fully. He had already given them valuable information, including details on hideouts and communication systems, and a description of what Freeboot looked like now.

And he had tactily admitted hacking the computer information on the "Fortune 500" list.

Via Pietowski, Monks had arranged to get a few minutes alone with Glenn. The agents on guard were expecting him. He identified himself to them, stepped into the room, and closed the door. He glanced approvingly at the medical arrangements—EKG monitor, saline IV with antibiotics, nasal oxygen tubes. It was just the kind of setup he would have used.

Glenn was sitting up in the adjustable bed. He looked uncomfortable and scared, but intact. The severed ear had been another of Freeboot's mental tortures. He had demanded Glenn's earring and Glenn had handed it over, without any idea of what it would be used for. Whose ear it was that Monks had found might never be known.

"You getting enough pain meds?" Monks asked.

Glenn nodded, and pointed to the call button on the bed arm. "They come right away." With the strain of the injured lung, his voice was a husky whisper.

"I'll keep this short, Glenn," Monks said. "I need to know the truth about some things. Just between you and me. No one else will ever know." He pulled a chair up to the bedside and leaned close, watching Glenn's face intently.

"Did you know that Freeboot and the *maquis* were committing the Calamity Jane murders?" Monks said. "That that's what they were doing with the names and addresses you provided?"

Glenn shook his head emphatically.

"No way, man. He told me we were putting together information on enemies of the people. I never dreamed anybody was getting killed."

Monks kept his face emotionless, but his fear took a sickening jump. Before Glenn had spoken, his eyes had flickered away just a tiny bit—the look of the same boy that Monks had raised, a very smart, accomplished liar, who was undoubtedly aware that the issue was going to be crucial in his sentencing.

Monks steeled himself for the next, almost worse, question. "Were you the one who attacked me and cut off my hair, that night in the camp?"

"That was Shrinkwrap. She wanted to get back at you for pissing her off." This time, Glenn seemed disinterested, as if the issue wasn't at all important. That had the ring of truth.

"Do you think she was in on setting you up?" Monks said, perhaps cruelly.

"I don't know." Glenn's head rolled to the side, facing away.

"All right, I'll let you rest." Monks stood. "We're there for you, your mom and me. You know that, son."

"Thanks, Dad."

Glenn's voice was laced with unmistakable sarcasm. But at least he hadn't brutalized and humiliated his father, and there was some relief in knowing that.

In the hospital's lobby, Monks stopped at a pay-phone kiosk and called Glenn's mother. She hadn't yet been allowed to visit him, and Monks had promised to check in.

"I just talked to him," Monks said. "He's doing fine."

"Fine?" Gail said shrilly. "He's going to prison, isn't he?"

Monks exhaled. "That's going to depend on a lot of factors."

Pietowski had assured Monks that if Glenn was what he seemed—a dope-ridden pawn under the brainwashing influence of Freeboot and Shrinkwrap and who hadn't been part of any violent acts—a plea bargain with a minimum sentence could be reached.

But if it was proved that Glenn had known about the killings, that would be a very different order of business.

"He should have a lawyer with him every second," Gail fumed.

"He needs to tell the FBI everything he knows, as fast as he can," Monks said, trying to stay patient. "If they have to put up with a lawyer interfering, you can *bet* he's going to prison. We're talking killers out there."

"I think you're handling this horribly!"

"Why am I not surprised," Monks said and hung up.

He walked on outside to the parking lot. The afternoon was clear and sunny. Queen of the Valley was a long, low modern building surrounded by greenery and trees, without the forbidding aspect of older, urban hospitals. But all hospitals had plenty of grief and guilt passing through their walls.

Monk was terrified that Glenn was guilty and would be punished—and almost as afraid that he would scheme his way out of it.

When Monks had left Bodega Bay, after hours of helping paramedics evacuate casualties, the town looked like it had been hit by an earthquake. Storefronts were shattered, shops and private homes savaged and looted by the fleeing mob. Police were still dealing with the tangle of abandoned vehicles. Most of the crowd had gotten away, catching rides in the cars that had managed to get out, or melting into the woods and nearby communities. Police eventually questioned hundreds of stragglers and detained dozens, but, owing to the identical T-shirts and caps, it was almost impossible to figure out who had done what.

It was clear that the riot had been carefully orchestrated. Glenn's instructions had been to incite the crowd until the police intervened, then wipe off his blackface makeup and get back to the RV. But no one had said anything to him about shooting.

What happened next seemed to have been a series of double-crosses planned by Freeboot. Hammerhead, dressed as a Highway Patrolman, had inflamed the mob by shooting the speaker who was championing them. A sniper then killed *him*, enraging the cops, who had taken him for one of their own. More snipers kept shooting at police, who returned fire into the crowd, and from there, it was unchecked mayhem. Police and media videos showed armed bikers and gangstas joining the attack. Six law enforcement officers had been killed and eleven wounded. The civilian toll was more than twice that. Many more people had been injured in other ways, some of them local residents—trampled, beaten, cut by flying glass, hit by the cars trying to escape. Three women had reported being raped, and there were probably more who hadn't come forward.

Only one of the escaping dirt-bikers had been caught—Callus, the limper who had given the RV away. He was being held in isolation on twenty-four-hour suicide watch, refusing to say a word. Freeboot might be wounded or even dead, but his status as a daring Robin Hood figure had jumped explosively.

And his message of the ugly violence hovering close at hand had come through loud and clear.

Monks found his car, the same rental that he had driven to Bodega Bay. His Bronco was highly visible, and he wanted to stay underground just now. Besides the threat of Freeboot and his men still at large, Monks had been propelled into another media furor. This time, he had checked into a Napa motel under a phony ID that he sometimes used for investigation work.

He drove across the north edge of Napa, crossing Highway 29, once a charming little road through the grand old California wineries, now a major traffic artery. The motel was a mile or so south on a frontage road—big, modern, and anonymous, just what he wanted.

When he opened the door to his room, he caught the faint scent of perfume. Then he saw another suitcase on the extra bed, open beside his own.

Sara was curled up in an armchair, sipping wine, looking out the window over the expanse of greening vineyards to the west. She turned at the sound of his entry. They hadn't seen each other since the night that Monks had abducted Mandrake. He'd invited her to join him here, and had left instructions at the desk to give her a key, but he hadn't been sure that she would come.

"How did it go?" she said. Her eyes were soft with concern.

"It could have been better. Worse, too."

"He's okay?"

"Physically," Monks said.

She stood and came to him. He put his hands on her waist and kissed her. She started crying. Monks held her, feeling helpless. Now she was the one waiting to find out whether her child was alive. Acting on Glenn's information, police had raided the place where Marguerite had called from, an isolated backwoods shack near the tiny town of Annapolis. But it was deserted by the time they got there, and she hadn't been heard from again.

"He's not going to hurt her, she's carrying his bloodline," Monks said, although the fear that he was wrong was another bitter gnawing in his heart.

"I just want it *over*," Sara said shakily. "Lia back home again, everything like it used to be."

"Soon," Monks said, stroking her hair. "The net's closing on Freeboot."

"I want him dead," she whispered.

Forty-one

Six days later, late in the afternoon, Monks was driving back to his house from Sara's and stopped for gas in Santa Rosa, at one of those big plazas with a dozen pumps and a convenience store. The price of gasoline had gone up ten or fifteen cents per gallon since he'd last filled up, a couple of weeks earlier. He put thirty-four dollars' worth into the Bronco and went inside to pay.

The clerk at the cash register was a woman who had to be at least seventy years old. She was carefully made up and groomed, and her dignified bearing was very much a lady's, in spite of the store employees' clownlike uniform of a pink polka-dotted shirt and a bow tie. It seemed odd that she'd be working at all, let alone in a place like this, probably for minimum wage. Skyrocketing living expenses on a fixed income, Monks thought, or maybe a gutted 401K, and this was the only kind of job she could get.

Feeling vaguely guilty, he walked back outside. His path was intersected by a man coming toward him—skinny, with lank shoulder-length hair, jeans and T-shirt that had been worn for days, and several highly visible tattoos.

"Hey, pardner," he called to Monks. "Me and my friends got a little car trouble. We need a couple bucks for some oil. Could you help us out?" He jerked his head toward a big old sedan pulled up outside the store. Two other men of roughly the same description were leaning against it.

Monks hesitated, then said, "Sure." He was used to being tapped by street people in San Francisco—it could cost several bucks to get across Union Square at night, paying tolls at every street corner—and when he was there, he carried folded one-dollar bills in his pocket. But here he was unprepared. He pulled out his wallet, extracted two singles, and handed them over.

"How about making it twenty?" the skinny man said, eyeing the other bills inside.

Monks blinked, taken aback. "Sorry. That's going to have to do it."

"Come on, man. You got plenty."

"I'm glad to help within reason," Monks said. "But I need money, too." He started to put the wallet back in his pocket.

The man took hold of his wrist with a clawlike grip of surprising strength. He might have been thirty and was certainly not yet forty, but his thin, sallow face was ageless, his eyes burning with dead black fire from another world.

"Are you threatening me?" Monks said in amazement.

"*Threat?* Don't insult me, man. I'm asking very *politely.*" The hand stayed on Monks's wrist. His buddies who had been leaning against the car were walking closer now.

Monks almost laughed at the sheer outrageousness of this.

"You realize I can go back into that store and have police here in two minutes?" he said.

The skinny man's mouth tightened, and his eyes drilled into Monks's for a few more seconds. Then he let go his grip and went back to his car. The other men gave Monks measuring looks before they turned around, too.

He got into the Bronco and drove away, checking his mirror in case they followed. But they were back to leaning against their vehicle—probably waiting for the next mark, who might be more cooperative.

He realized that he was shaken, more so than he should have been. Partly, it was the brazenness of what had almost amounted to robbery, in a public place, in broad daylight. But something else disturbed him more deeply. He had to think for a minute to grasp it, but then it came—the way the skinny man's mouth had tightened, and that final searing gaze. That was not just anger. It was a look that said, *Okay, asshole, if you want to play hardball, that's how it's going to be.*

The Bronco's radio was tuned to a Golden Oldies station. Monks usually preferred quiet while he drove, but these past days he'd been keeping up with the news constantly, hoping for the welcome word that Freeboot had been captured.

After a few minutes, he caught an update.

"One of the largest manhunts in California history continues, for a charismatic ex-convict named James Reese, known to his followers as Freeboot," the news announcer said. "Law-enforcement officials believe that Reese is the mastermind behind the Calamity Jane killings, as well as last week's riot at Bodega Bay, which left twenty-one dead, including six police officers, with many more injured, and a damage toll in the millions of dollars.

"A San Francisco police car was attacked with gunfire earlier today, while making a drug-related arrest. The shots apparently came from a nearby building, but police were unable to locate a suspect. No one was injured."

Monks turned the radio off. What the announcer hadn't mentioned was that there had been two similar incidents during the past days, one in Philadelphia and one in Miami, where police cars had been fired on. The one in Miami had had the aspect of an ambush, with cops lured in on a phony call. An officer was killed and another wounded. There had also been a spate of random shootings in several cities—cars driving around at night, firing into parked vehicles, store windows, even private homes. No one yet had been hurt during those, but if they continued, it was only a matter of time.

In general, there was a sense that whatever mysterious societal force held chaos in check—not just law enforcement, but the awareness that there were lines that couldn't be crossed—was eroding, fast.

He had been keeping in touch with Pietowski, and so he knew that FBI informants in the fringe world were aware of a sort of verbal underground newspaper that was developing, a word-of-mouth communication that spread through the country with amazing speed. It was urging the stockpiling of weapons and ammunition, attacks on law-enforcement officers, and random violence, especially against the affluent. It also threatened more incidents like Bodega Bay. Authorities admitted that they'd been caught napping, and vowed that nothing like it would happen again. But if thousands of people just started showing up someplace, what could be done? Call out the National Guard? Haul them all off to jail?

What if they started shooting?

Pietowski had hinted that behind the scenes in the political world the alarm was even more acute. The president himself had made a veiled allusion to Bodega Bay at a press conference, repeating his insistence that the United States government would not tolerate terrorism.

But these weren't terrorists. These were citizens.

Monks turned off Highway 101 at Petaluma, relieved as always to get off the freeway onto two-lane country roads. Traffic thinned as he drove farther west, with the thick canopy of oaks, laurels, redwoods, and eucalyptus groves bringing an early dusk. It started to sink into him how exhausted he was. With all the troubles that still hammered at him, he felt a kind of numb joy at getting back to his own home. The world might be going crazy—crazi*er*—but here, all was serene.

When he stepped inside his house, he was immediately hit by an ugly, fetid smell. It wasn't one he encountered often, but he never forgot it.

Rotting flesh.

"Just like old times, huh?" Freeboot said from the darkened living room.

Monks had been cautious about his own security at first, but as the days passed, he had decided that the risk of Freeboot's coming after him were nil, and the FBI had a lot more important people to protect. His gaze swung toward the telephone. It was dead, its lights out.

Taxman stepped into sight, holding a submachine gun at the ready.

Monks felt a dizzying lurch inside his head, and feared that he was having a stroke, that he was going to seize up like a burnt-out engine and collapse to the floor.

Then, just as swiftly, the same euphoria that had come to him after his showdown with Freeboot touched him again—the sudden certainty that nothing more could happen that was worse than what already had.

"If you're going to shoot me, go ahead and get it over with," he said. He walked across the kitchen and got a bottle of Finlandia out of the liquor cabinet.

Freeboot made a hoarse hacking sound that seemed to contain amusement.

"Let's get down to it," he said. "I ran out of junk. You keep Demerol here, your kid told me."

"The kid you tried to have killed?" Monks said, dropping ice cubes into a glass. He felt detached, disembodied, almost like he was floating. He noticed that his hands were remarkably steady.

"That was nothing personal, just business."

"Whose ear was it?"

"Nobody you know. I need a shot—now. So quit fucking around and get it."

Monks set the ice tray on the counter and said, "All right. Where's the wound, by the way?"

"How'd you know about that?" Freeboot said suspiciously.

"Are you kidding? I smelled it as soon as I walked in the door."

"Get the shot."

Monks walked down the hall to his office, with Taxman following. The phone in there was dead, too. He knelt on the floor and opened the safe where he kept an emergency supply of narcotics, his .357 Magnum, and several thousand dollars in cash.

"All the drugs, and the money," Taxman said. He pulled the plastic liner bag out of a wastebasket, emptied it on the floor, and tossed it to Monks.

Monks stuffed the bundles of bills inside it, along with an unopened twenty-milliliter vial of hundred-milligram-strength Demerol, a packet of syringes, and a bottle each of Percocets and Vicodin. He waited, expecting Taxman to demand the pistol, too, but he said, "Okay," and jerked his head back toward the living room. Apparently they had plenty of guns.

When they got there, a light had been turned on. Freeboot was sprawled on the couch, with one leg extended over the coffee table.

At the couch's other end, huddled into herself, was Marguerite. She looked bewildered, dully frightened, but unhurt.

Another wave of relief washed over Monks.

"Say *your* little bitch ratted you off," Freeboot said, pointing a thumb at her. "What would you do with her?"

"She's carrying your child," Monk said quickly. "Genetically pure this time."

"Ain't that a fucker?" Freeboot said, annoyed. "Confuses the whole issue."

He took the plastic bag from Taxman. His left arm was already tied up with his belt, popping blood vessels thick as nightcrawlers in his forearm. He held the bottle to the light, examining the label, then unwrapped a syringe and inserted the needle through the vial's seal. Monks watched him draw out just over one milliliter.

"For a guy who distrusts medicine, you know your dosage," Monks said.

"This ain't medicine, man. This is dope."

Freeboot slid the needle into a vein, and a few seconds later, relaxed and laid his head back with a grunt. The lines of pain eased visibly out of his surgically thickened face.

Now Monks could see the wound—a hand-sized patch of crusted, blackened blood and scab toward the right side of his groin. The bullet must have missed the femoral artery, and the entry point was beneath most of the abdominal organs. But it almost certainly had penetrated the intestines—besides the gangrene, there would be infection, maybe peritonitis—and it might have ricocheted off bone, causing more organ damage.

"If that gets treated immediately," Monks said, "you might make it. I'm talking hours."

Freeboot smiled faintly. "The same argument we started with. Kind of like our song. It makes me go all gooey, thinking about it."

"Let's try another old song," Monks said. "'I hate to say it, but I told you so.' Remember that one? It was one of those sixties Brit groups."

He walked back into the kitchen and filled his glass with vodka.

"How about 'Revolution No. 9'?" Freeboot said.

"A theme song for murder and havoc?"

"The motherfuckers are paying attention, you got to admit."

Monks took a long sip, savoring what he figured was going to be his last drink.

"It looks to me like a giant step back toward barbarianism," he said.

"You kick a dog long enough, that dog's finally gonna bite you. This isn't over, Rasp. It's just getting started."

Freeboot grimaced suddenly, his face contorting in a spasm. The Demerol would provide a little relief, but the agony had to be nearly unendurable. Only unconsciousness was going to keep it at bay now.

Freeboot reached for the bottle again and inserted the needle through the seal. Monks watched with surprise, then alarm, as he drew three milliliters, then five.

"That's getting up toward lethal," Monks said.

Freeboot ignored him and filled the syringe to the ten-milliliter mark.

Monks glanced quickly at Taxman and his weapon. Both looked ready.

"Remember one thing, Freeboot," Monks said. "I had you in my sights and I let you walk away."

Freeboot looked up at him—not with the stare that Monks was used to, but with weariness, and maybe pity.

"There's no fucking truth," Freeboot said. "Everybody's full of shit, including me. I done what I could, man."

This time, Monks got the sense that *man* was intended to include all of humankind.

Freeboot slid the needle into his arm. His thumb pushed the plunger all the way home. Almost immediately, he sagged, forward this time—chin falling onto his chest, right hand dropping to the couch, palm up, fingers slightly curled. The syringe still hung from his left forearm. Marguerite made a whimpering sound, turning her face away and curling more tightly into herself.

Taxman moved without hesitation, stepping forward to pick up the plastic bag of money and drugs.

Monks edged in front of Marguerite. "There's no reason to hurt her," he said.

Taxman looked at him curiously, as if Monks was a puzzle he couldn't get a handle on.

"I watched you playing with the kid that night, making him laugh," Taxman said. "I never could have done that."

He flipped the weapon into the air, catching it by the breech in a quick, practiced motion. Then he strode across the room and out into the dusk, breaking into a lope, footsteps crunching lightly on the gravel drive until the sound faded.

Monks leaned down to Marguerite and carefully unclenched her hands with his own, then helped her to her feet.

"Come on," he said. "Let's get to a phone and call your mom."

Arm around her shoulders, he guided her out the door where he had first seen her standing on that night when all this had started, a million years ago.